Praise for the Baby Boomer Mysteries

"Susan Santangelo's **Mistletoe Can Be Murder** is the perfect blend of family drama, humor, and murder. The author's gentle ribbing of husbands will make you laugh out loud while her well-placed clues and list of suspects will keep you guessing until the end."
—Ang Pompano, Agatha Nominated Author

"In **Politics Can Be Murder**, Santangelo serves up a humorous story with a serious underpinning and an appealing main character—you have to love a woman who always tells you what she would have said but didn't."
—Leslie Wheeler, Author of the *Berkshire Hilltown Mystery* Series

"**In-Laws Can Be Murder** is the eighth in Susan Santangelo's *Baby Boomer Mystery* series, and as hilarious as all the rest!"
—Carol J. Perry, Author of the *Witch City* Mystery series

"If you're a fan of Susan Santangelo's humorous *Baby Boomer Mystery* series, **Dieting Can Be Murder**, the seventh book in the series, won't disappoint. Carol Andrews needs to lose the weight she gained on her recent second honeymoon. But where Carol goes, dead bodies follow, and such is the case when another dieter in her weight loss group is murdered. Of course, Carol can't help but start nosing around to find the killer. After all, the woman collapsed and died on top of her."
—Lois Winston, *USA Today* Bestselling Author of the Critically Acclaimed *Anastasia Pollack Crafting* Mystery Series

"Susan Santangelo's latest *Baby Boomer Mystery*, **Second Honeymoons Can Be Murder**, keeps a smile on your lips and the pages turning one right after the other. What's not to like? An engaging mystery and laugh-out loud characters right to the very last page."
—Susan Kiernan-Lewis, Award-winning Author of the *Maggie Newberry* Mystery Series

Masquerades *Can Be* Murder

Every Wife Has a Story

A Carol and Jim Andrews Baby Boomer Mystery

Eleventh in the Series

Susan Santangelo

SUSPENSE PUBLISHING

MASQUERADES CAN BE MURDER
by
Susan Santangelo

DIGITAL EDITION
* * * * *
PUBLISHED BY:
Suspense Publishing

COPYRIGHT
2024 Susan Santangelo

PUBLISHING HISTORY:
Suspense Publishing, Paperback and Digital Copy, June 2024

ISBN: 979-8-218-44546-1

Cover and Book Design: Shannon Raab
Cover Artist: Elizabeth Moisan

All rights reserved. Without limiting the rights under copyright reserved above, no part of this publication may be reproduced, stored in or introduced into a retrieval system, or transmitted, in any form, or by any means (electronic, mechanical, photocopying, recording, or otherwise) without the prior written permission of both the copyright owner and the above publisher of this book.

This book is a work of fiction. Names, characters, businesses, organizations, places, events, incidents are the product of the author's imagination or are used fictitiously. Any resemblance to actual events, locales, or persons, living or dead, is coincidental.

Publisher's Note: The recipes in this book are to be followed exactly as written. The publisher and the author are not responsible for a reader's specific health or allergy needs which may require medical supervision. The publisher and the author are not responsible for any adverse reactions to the recipes contained in this book.

Acknowledgements

Thank you to my wonderful family—David, Mark, Sandy, Jacob and Becca. And especially to my husband Joe. Your support and love mean everything to me.

A big thank you to the First Readers Club for this book—Leanne Wasikowski, George Eastman, Marti and Bob Baker, Judy O'Brien, Mark Santangelo, and Carole Goldberg—for their helpful comments and suggestions.

Thanks to Elizabeth Moisan for once again providing such beautiful front cover artwork.

To all my long-time New England friends, my pals from the West Dennis MA Library, and the members of the Clearwater FL Welcome Newcomer Club and St. Brendan's CCW, I appreciate you all very much.

Thank you to all my friends and cyber friends from Sisters in Crime, the Cape Cod Writers Center, and the International Thriller Writers, for sharing your expertise with me.

Boomer and Lilly send special doggy love to Lynn Pray and Courtney Lynn Ross, Pineridge English Cockers, Rehoboth MA.

To Shannon and John Raab, Abbey Peralta, and everyone at Suspense Publishing, who help me in so many ways, you're the best! I'm so proud to be a member of the Suspense family.

To all the bloggers who love mysteries as much as I do and support the mystery genre in so many ways, especially Dru Ann Love, Lori Boness Caswell, Jerri Cachero, Heather Doyle Harrisson and Shawn Stevens, a huge thank you!

And to everyone who's enjoyed this series—the readers I've met in person or via Zoom book events; those who have e-mailed me; those who've posted online reviews for the books; and followed me on Facebook, Twitter, and BookBub—thanks so much! Hope you enjoy this one, too. And keep those chapter headings coming!

Lilly wants to add huge thanks to Dr. Snell and the surgical team at VCA South Weymouth MA. You are all amazing!

This book is dedicated to Sandy Pendergast, my dear friend and "agent," for her unwavering support from the very beginning of this series.

Masquerade: To assume the appearance of something one is not.

"And, after all, what is a lie? 'Tis but the truth in a masquerade."
—Alexander Pope

Masquerades *Can Be* Murder

Every Wife Has a Story

A Carol and Jim Andrews Baby Boomer Mystery

Eleventh in the Series

Susan Santangelo

Chapter 1

It's the start of a brand-new year, and I'm off like a herd of turtles.

"What are you doing on July 7?" My husband, Jim, bounded into the kitchen, his face ruddy from the cold, and enveloped me in a huge hug.

Due to our recent furnace fiasco, which forced us to move to a hotel until after Christmas, I'll probably still be sitting at the kitchen table, addressing holiday cards to people I don't even know but you insist we keep on the list, just like I'm doing now. I hope to finish by Labor Day.

"Carol, I asked you a question. What are you doing on July 7? Or, better yet, what do you think *I'm* doing on July 7? Go ahead, guess. You'll never figure it out."

I swear, I hadn't seen my husband this excited since he'd discovered that CVS was having a special midnight blowout sale offering double coupons to preferred customers.

"You may be shocked to hear this," I replied, marking the point in our Christmas card list where I'd left off addressing envelopes so I could begin again later, "but as of now, I have no plans. What exactly do you have in mind?" I squinted at the list. "And who the heck are Lydia and Joe White? I never heard of them."

"I have no idea," Jim said. "They must be your friends. Take them off the list. Heck, take everybody off the list. Or don't send out any cards at all." He frowned. "The cost of postage is going up, you know. We need to watch our expenses."

Oh, joy! *Hallelujah*! It didn't matter what Jim was doing on July 7 if it meant no more handwritten holiday cards. I just hoped he never found out about ecards. Then, I'd have to start a whole new list.

I wriggled my right hand to get the circulation going and gave my husband my complete attention. "July 7," I repeated. "Let me think. Are you going to the beach to work on your tan? Mowing the lawn? Painting the shutters on our house?"

Reality dawned. I jumped up and gave my husband a big smooch. "Oh, honey, you finally bought that boat you've been talking about for so long. What a great present for both of us! When the weather finally warms up, we'll have a champagne christening party for the boat and invite all our friends to come. It needs a name, though. What should we call it?"

Jim looked at me like I had taken complete leave of my senses—a familiar facial expression. "I haven't bought a boat, Carol. What I'm doing on July 7 is even better." He grinned, then announced, "The Fairport Business Association is organizing the first-ever reenactment of the British attack on Fairport on July 7, 1779. I'm on the steering committee and will be one of the militiamen defending our town. I'll even get to wear a uniform and carry a musket. And you, my dear wife," he said, kissing me on the forehead, "will be getting all spiffed up to go to a fancy masquerade ball at the Porter Mansion that evening as part of the commemoration. What do you think about *that*?"

Jim grabbed an apple from the fruit bowl on the kitchen table without waiting for a response. "I didn't have lunch at the meeting, so I'm hungry. Here's more information about the event. We're calling it Celebrate Fairport." He dropped a folder on the kitchen table, causing my carefully arranged pile of Christmas cards to topple to the floor in a heap, and headed toward the bedroom to change clothes. Honestly, that Jim.

I've often wondered how long it takes before a married couple becomes completely in sync with each other. Whatever that magic number is, my husband of almost forty years and I still have a long way to go.

My name is Carol Andrews, and I've lived in the beautiful Connecticut town of Fairport all my life. Fairport is one of the Nutmeg State's best-kept secrets. Not quite as tony as Greenwich, Darien, or some of the other Gold Coast towns, it's a convenient and fast train ride (assuming Metro-North is running on time) into Manhattan, making it an ideal location for commuters.

Fairport is also a very historic town, one of the oldest in Connecticut, and was originally called Uncoway. It was founded in 1639 by Puritans and Congregationalists from the Massachusetts Bay Colony, who purchased a large tract of land from the Pequonnock Indians. Truth to tell, the only reason I know all this stuff is because our son, Mike, had to write a paper on the history of Fairport in junior high school, and I made it my business to be sure he did a good job.

I also knew that on July 7, 1779, during the American Revolution, British troops attacked Fairport and burned down the vast majority of its structures. To this day, there are houses in our historic district whose floors still have burn marks from that savage attack. One of the houses the British totally destroyed was the Porter Mansion, home of the wealthy John and Elizabeth Porter, who were known for giving lavish parties there. The attack took place during a masquerade ball at the mansion. Legend has it that our town was re-named Fairport to honor Elizabeth, reputed to be "fair of hair and fair of face." John was particularly outspoken about his anti-Tory views and was killed by the British during the attack. The mansion was eventually rebuilt and still stands to this day.

As horrible as the Burning of Fairport must have been, I was surprised that the Fairport Business Association had suddenly decided to make such a big deal about it. But if Jim was getting involved in something that would keep him busy and out of my hair for the next several months, I was all for it.

I, however, would not allow myself to be roped into helping organize it in any way. Period. And I had the perfect excuse. Our daughter, Jenny, an American literature instructor at Fairport College, and her husband, Fairport Police Detective Mark Anderson, had recently presented us with our first grandchild, Carlton James, nicknamed CJ. I became the official Babysitter-In-Chief when the parents returned to their demanding jobs. Yay!

I sent up a silent prayer of thanks to the Good Lord for the unexpected gift of a busy husband involved in a new project in the new year, leaving me free to lunch and shop with my retail support posse as often as I wanted.

The Good Lord, as it turned out, had other plans for me.

Chapter 2

At my age, I am good at multitasking. I can listen, ignore, and forget all at once.

"I thought seven was supposed to be a lucky number," Claire said as she folded and stuffed a "Save The Date" flyer into an envelope and sealed it. "We've been at this for hours. This wasn't how I'd planned to start the new year, Carol."

"I don't know what you're complaining about," I said, glaring at my sometimes friend (and sometimes not, depending on how critical she's being). I folded another flyer and carefully placed it in an envelope. "Stuffing envelopes is mindless and stress-free. I think it's fun. I'm enjoying myself, even if you're not, Claire."

"What exactly is your problem?" asked my very best friend, Nancy Green, making herself comfortable at my dining room table. "Hand me some flyers, and I'll start folding them. Someone else can stuff them into envelopes. I don't want to risk ruining my manicure."

"That's because you've arrived an hour late," Claire shot back. "We've been at this for a while. Trust me, the fun fades fast. And, knowing you, you also can't stay long because you have to meet an important real estate client soon."

Even for Claire, that was harsh. I was about to speak up and defend Nancy, but she saved me the trouble. "Seven *is* a lucky number. Celebrate Fairport is on July seven, which is the seventh day of the seventh month. I'm really looking forward to it, especially the masquerade ball, when we get to put on fancy clothes for a change. That's a whole lot of luck if you ask me."

"I don't agree," Claire said, not willing to back down. Barely taking a breath, she continued, "And as to your question, Nancy, my problem is that once again, Carol's allowed herself to be coerced into volunteering for another local project because she just can't say no. Which has resulted in her coercing the rest of us to get involved, too."

I was itching to take a quick slug at Claire but restrained myself because I abhor violence. Besides, much as I hated to admit it, there was some truth in what she was saying.

"When Jim initially sprang this whole Celebrate Fairport event on me, I wasn't excited about it. I was even less enthused when he told me that Ray Thompson, the new President of the Business Association, was behind the whole event. You know what a terrible person he is."

"I know *you* think he's a terrible person," Nancy said. "But I was never clear on why you disliked him so much. He's owned Fairport Toys for years, and people love going there, whether they have little ones to shop for or not."

I wasn't ready to tell my best friends that when my son, Mike, was ten years old, Ray had accused him of shoplifting. Mike was innocent, but Ray didn't believe him. He threatened to call the police and have him arrested. The poor kid was terrified. It was just good luck that I arrived at the toy store to pick Mike up and heard the whole thing. After a heated argument with Ray, I spotted the supposedly stolen toy on the floor and slammed it on the counter. Ray didn't even apologize to Mike or to me for his unfounded accusation. I've boycotted the store ever since.

We were getting off track, which was not my fault. "It's a long story, and I'm not getting into it now." *Or ever.*

"Anyway, I realized that the more Jim got involved in planning the reenactment, the less time he'd be home bugging me. I have a positive attitude now and hope to keep it. New year, new me. I've made it clear to Jim that stuffing flyers is all I'm doing for the reenactment, so I don't have to deal with Ray Thompson. And this was a good way for us to all get together and catch up before you desert us and head to Florida until spring, Claire."

"Ever since grammar school, we've always been there for each other," Mary Alice, always the peacemaker in our group, chimed in, giving my hand a quick squeeze of solidarity. "You know you can count on us for help whenever you need it." My eyes misted over for a quick second, especially when Nancy and then Claire nodded in agreement.

"I'm proud of you for saying no to Jim," Claire said. "I confess I'll miss hearing about Jim's latest transgression while Larry and I are away. They're always good for a laugh."

I zipped my lips. "No more complaining about Jim from me." I paused. "There is one thing that's driving me nuts, though."

"I knew it," Nancy yelled. "I knew this so-called *new you* wouldn't last long." She moved a pile of empty envelopes in front of her. "I'll even stuff these myself and risk my manicure just to hear it. Talk."

I jammed another "Save The Date" flyer into an envelope. "Let's just say that Jim is getting carried away with his role in the event."

"I don't see what's wrong with that," Mary Alice said. "Everyone in town is excited about it, including me." She gave me an apologetic look for disagreeing with me.

"Celebrate Fairport is a terrific way to bring new people to town," Nancy added. "When they see how wonderful Fairport is, naturally, they'll want to live here, too. Property values will soar."

"And so will your real estate business," I said, giving her a dirty look. "Admit it. You don't really care about the town's history at all."

"That's not true," Nancy protested, her cheeks flushed. I continued to stare at her, and she finally said, "Maybe it's partly true. But I do care about the town's history. That was a low blow."

Claire clapped her hands and bellowed, "Quiet. You're all giving me a headache."

For a few minutes, we all worked in silence. Then, all that quiet began to get on my nerves.

"You have no idea what's been going on around here," I finally said. "And it'll only get worse as we get closer to July seven.

"None of you would believe how many committees and subcommittees a small local event like this has. And nobody seems to agree with anybody else, so Jim ends up playing peacemaker all the time. Then he comes home and bores me with all the details. Not stimulating dinner conversation, for sure."

I held up my hand as Claire started to interrupt me. "I'm not finished talking." *So be quiet for once in your life.*

I thought I heard someone mutter, "You never are." But I could have been wrong.

"The worst part is that Jim insists the militia volunteers have all their practices here. Can you imagine a bunch of old men marching in formation around my house for hours? Believe me, it's not pleasant."

"They're not using real guns, I hope," Mary Alice said, looking worried. I wasn't surprised that she'd asked that question. As a nurse here in town, it was a sure bet she'd taken care of victims of gun violence at our local hospital over her long career.

"Not so far, thank goodness. Everyone brings a yardstick and pretends it's a musket. But they're hoping to use actual muskets for the reenactment." I rolled my eyes. "Although where they'll find those is anybody's guess. I don't think Amazon carries them."

"Are they marching inside the house?" Nancy asked, trying hard not to laugh.

"They're outside, thank goodness. Unless it snows. If the weather's bad, Jim wanted to drill inside the house, but I put a stop to that idea right away. If you come over around three this afternoon, you can check them out yourself. And that's not even the worst part of it." I was getting warmed up now, and there was no stopping me.

"Jim's growing a beard, and he's not getting a haircut before the reenactment. He wants his hair to be long enough to tie in a ponytail by July. I can't imagine how horrible he's going to look. I'm going to die of embarrassment when he shows himself in public looking like that." I slammed my hand on a pile of flyers. "After these are mailed, I want nothing more to do with Celebrate Fairport. You can all celebrate without me."

"I'm sure you're exaggerating just a teeny bit," Claire said. "It can't be *that* bad."

"You're behaving now the same way you did about our fortieth high school reunion, Carol," Nancy added. "You didn't want anything to do with that, either. We finally talked you into it, and look at the great time we all had."

"Finding the dead body of a classmate in my bed the night before the reunion isn't my idea of a great time, Nancy," I shot back. "In case you've forgotten about that part."

"You do seem to have a knack for stumbling over dead

bodies with increasing frequency," Claire said.

"That's totally Jim's fault," I said with a straight face. "When he retired, I had to find a new hobby."

Chapter 3

People who say they can't complain should just try harder.

Sleep wouldn't come. Maybe it was Jim snoring next to me that was keeping me awake. Or perhaps it was our dogs' insistence on spreading out on my side of the bed so much that I was practically on the floor. I checked my cell phone for the time. Rats. It was almost midnight. I'd been tossing and turning for over an hour.

Get up, check your email, or read a good book for a while. When you stop thinking about sleep, it's guaranteed to come.

I took my own good advice and eased myself off the bed as quietly as possible. Our two English cocker spaniels, Lucy and Ethel, stirred a bit, then spread themselves out even more, completely taking over my spot in the bed. I decided I'd deal with that problem later.

In a jiffy, I was at my computer, checking and deleting my newest emails. The whole process took less than ten minutes, and I was still wide awake.

It suddenly occurred to me that I'd been given a perfect opportunity to check out more of our town's history on my own. I entered "Fairport, Connecticut" into the search engine and prepared to saturate my brain with local knowledge.

I first learned was that some houses in town are designated as "BB"—"Before Battle"— referring to the ones in our historic district that were built before 1779. "BB" houses are considered more valuable, especially if the structures have burn marks from the battle on their floors. I wondered if Nancy knew that.

We live in an antique home, so I decided to research the history of our own house. A preliminary search only told me that it was built in 1795 and was an "AB" or "After Battle" structure. Oh, well. I still loved it. My curiosity was really piqued now. I decided to do some digging and find out more.

I was overwhelmed by the amount of additional websites I could choose from and had no idea where to begin. I yawned and decided I'd done enough research for one night. It was time to get some shut-eye.

Suddenly, a drawing of my house popped up on the screen. As I studied the image, I sensed someone watching me.

I turned around to apologize to Jim for waking him up. But no one was there.

Chapter 4

I miss the good old days when white bread was good for you and nobody knew what kale was.

I woke from a restless sleep, reluctant to face the day. No matter how much I tried, I couldn't forget my feeling that someone had been with me last night. I wanted to tell Jim, even though I could predict his reaction in advance—that my late-night visitor was merely my overactive imagination working overtime. In fact, I was counting on him to convince me that he was right.

I made my way to the kitchen, anticipating the first cup of Jim's delicious coffee—one of the few pluses of having a retired husband in the house. Jim rustled the newspaper and mumbled a greeting as I sank onto a chair opposite him.

There's an unwritten rule in our house that if one person is reading a book, newspaper, or magazine, the other person is not allowed to interrupt them except for a real emergency. Recalling how freaked out my late-night experience had made me feel, I was sure the "emergency" criteria had been met.

"Jim, I have to talk to you. It's important. Someone was in our house last night."

"You must have been dreaming, Carol. I didn't hear a thing."

Big surprise. Your selective hearing probably works even when you're asleep.

"I wasn't sleeping," I insisted. "I was wide awake. And I wasn't in bed. I was in the office on the computer."

"It's obvious that you were only dreaming you were using the computer, so you only dreamed you heard someone. You know what a vivid imagination you have."

A teeny part of me insisted that someone had been there, but I forced myself to ignore it. After all, Jim was saying exactly what I wanted him to say. In the light of day, the idea of an invisible guest seemed ludicrous. "I guess you're right, dear. I must have been dreaming." I took a fortifying drink of coffee and immediately felt better.

"Attagirl," Jim said, handing me the newspaper. "Maybe this will cheer you up. There's a story about the reenactment on the front page. We aim to recreate every single detail of the march from the beach into town and the attack on the Porter Mansion."

"Every single detail? You're not actually going to burn the mansion down, are you?"

"Of course not, Carol. What a silly thing to say. We're thinking of simulating the burning with a fireworks display at the mansion." He made a note on his phone. "I'm off to another planning meeting. I'll be gone most of the day." He grabbed his briefcase with all the event files and was out the door before I could say goodbye.

You just got lucky, Carol. You have the whole day to search for information about your house without interruption. Then you can give Jim a local history lesson for a change.

Chapter 5

When you ask me what I'm doing today, and I say, "nothing," it doesn't mean that I'm free. It means I'm doing nothing.

After a quick shower and a satisfactory visit to my bedroom closet—meaning I found a pair of pressed khaki pants that actually fit me and a matching blouse—I was ready to spend some time at my computer. Lucy and Ethel, always eager to expand their knowledge base, trotted after me into the office and settled themselves under the desk.

My computer sprang to life, and I immediately saw that my desktop wallpaper had been changed from a picture of our grandson to one of our house. Darn that Jim. He must have done it early this morning without asking me first. I had no idea how to fix it, so I'd have to wait until he got home.

Muttering a few curse words so the dogs wouldn't hear me (they're very sensitive), I ordered the search engine to wake up. Another drawing of our house appeared, but this time, a giant red X was scrawled across a widow's walk on the roof.

"We don't have a widow's walk on our roof," I informed Lucy and Ethel. Lucy gave me one of her famous looks, pointing out how stupid I was. I hate it when one of my dogs is smarter than I am, but I realized she was right. The house must have had a widow's walk years ago that was torn down long before we bought it.

"I get it, Lucy. But who marked the drawing with the red X?" Even more puzzling was why the red was so bright when the rest of the drawing was a faded black and white.

Deciding this was one puzzle I didn't need to deal with right now, I put our address in the search engine again and began to read. In no time at all, I was lost in its fascinating history.

"This house was built sixteen years after the burning of Fairport," I informed the dogs. Knowing what a stickler for details Lucy always was, I clarified. "That's when the first owner, Elizabeth Porter, moved into the house, not when construction started."

Receiving no rebuke from Her Majesty on my historical accuracy, I returned to my reading, then stopped, realizing what I'd just discovered. The first occupant of our house was Elizabeth Porter. I'd assumed that Elizabeth went back to live in the Porter Mansion after it was rebuilt, and that's where she died. But I was wrong. I had no idea she'd ever lived in our house.

I was interrupted from my musings by a text from my daughter, reminding me of today's babysitting gig and wondering where I was. Yikes! It was time to reset my priorities. There was no way I'd be late for a date with my favorite grandson.

I made it to Jenny and Mark's condo in only fifteen minutes, thanks to years of carpooling duty that had forced me to learn every back road in town. "I hope you're not mad at me," I said, giving Jenny a big hug. "I got here as quickly as I could. I set my phone alarm for eleven-fifteen, but it never rang. When I checked my phone a little while ago, I swear it was only nine-thirty." I glanced at my phone, which now read 11:45. I checked the alarm setting, which showed it had rung at the correct time. Why didn't I hear it?

You're not losing your mind, Carol. Maybe you didn't have your glasses on before. Or you had the phone setting on mute.

But I'd heard a ping when Jenny texted me. When I considered the scary feeling I'd had last night, the drawing of my house that popped up on the computer, and now losing track of time, maybe something was wrong with me.

"It's okay, Mom," Jenny said, misinterpreting my worried look. "I'm glad I gave you a gentle reminder, though. I just fed CJ and put him down for a nap. With any luck, he'll probably sleep for a few hours. You can peek in and say hello, as long as you don't wake him up. Go ahead and do that, then let's talk for a few minutes."

Focus, Carol. And for heaven's sake, stay calm. Don't anticipate the worst. CJ doesn't have a life-threatening illness, Jenny and Mark aren't getting a divorce, and you're absolutely fine.

Rather than speed walk down the hallway to gaze at the most perfect grandchild ever born, I parked my posterior onto the nearest chair. "CJ is sound asleep, and I'm not really late. What's going on?"

"Mark asked me to talk to you." Jenny fidgeted in her chair. "It's about Celebrate Fairport."

I laughed. "Aren't you talking to the wrong parent? Your father is the one who's involved in that event. I'm trying my best to stay out of it."

"I know it's Dad's project, not yours. But Mark was hoping you could get Dad to see reason about some of the plans before things get completely out of control."

"Out of control? I don't understand."

"Here's what Mark told me, and this is 'off the record,' okay?"

"Whatever you say," I said, relieved that I'd have something else to think about rather than my possible lost grip on reality.

"Fairport's population always soars in the summer with all the tourists who come to enjoy the beach. The reenactment celebration on July seven is bound to attract even more people and make traffic a nightmare. The department will have to hire extra police, and there's no money in the budget for that. Does the steering committee have money allocated to pay them?"

"I have no idea."

"The police chief also heard a rumor that the committee wants to add a fireworks display at the Porter Mansion to the reenactment, which could be a major safety hazard."

"It seems to me that the police chief should talk to the First Selectwoman or the Fairport Business Association directly about these concerns. And wouldn't the committee need a permit for the fireworks?"

"The chief wants to stop the fireworks plan before it gets to the permit phase, but he's reluctant to bring up anything that might damage the department's relationship with our new First Selectwoman. Carla Grimaldi is the first female ever elected to that position, and unofficially, he's heard that she's all for it. He passed the buck to Mark, and Mark passed it on to me. And now, to you. So, will you help? Please?"

"I think Mark's boss is being a little ridiculous."

"I agree with you. But the chief's contract comes up for renewal in a few months, and he's being extra sensitive. He wants to keep his job. Will you talk to Dad?"

"Okay. But I can't guarantee how your father will respond."

"Thanks so much, Mom. I knew I could count on you, and Mark's not expecting a miracle. At least he can tell his boss that he tried." Jenny picked up her backpack and slung it over her shoulder. "I'm proud of you for not getting sucked into this Celebrate Fairport event. Things are getting a little nuts."

"I'm getting more interested in Fairport's history than I

expected," I confessed. "I just found out that Elizabeth Porter was the first owner of our house. I wonder what she looked like."

"I bet you already know," my smarty pants daughter said. "There are portraits of Elizabeth and her husband on display at Town Hall. Stop by and say hello after you leave here. I'll be back by three." She gave me a quick kiss and was on her way.

For the next few delightful hours, I put all thoughts about Celebrate Fairport out of my head. Spending time with an adorable baby, even if that time is mainly spent sitting beside his crib and watching him sleep, is a foolproof way to bring joy to any grandmother's heart. Jenny arrived home much too soon for me, but she is his mother, so I surrendered my little love back to her and reluctantly headed back home.

On impulse, since I had to pass by there anyway, I suddenly turned into the Town Hall lot, earning a loud horn blast from the driver behind me. I gave him a quick wave of apology (using my whole hand, in case you were wondering) and zipped into a convenient parking space right in front of the building. "Ready or not, here I come, Elizabeth," I said as I walked up the front steps of the white colonial building. "I hope you're easy to find because I have to get home and start dinner."

Once inside, I immediately saw a pair of large oil portraits flanking the front door of the First Selectwoman's office. The brass plaques identified the couple as Elizabeth and John Porter. How stupid I was. Despite passing by them hundreds of times on my way to renew dog licenses or pay our property taxes, I'd never noticed them before.

As I moved closer to get a better look, I heard a woman say, "I never liked that picture." I turned to see if the speaker was someone I knew. But there was no one there.

Chapter 6

Don't bother walking a mile in my shoes. Spend 30 seconds in my head. That'll freak you right out.

"I'm sure the odd things that keep happening have a reasonable explanation," I told myself, running water over our dirty dinner dishes before I loaded them into the dishwasher. (And Jim re-loaded them. It's one of his many post-retirement hobbies that drives me up the wall.) "For instance, someone could have passed by me today at Town Hall, commented on the portrait of Elizabeth Porter, then quickly disappeared into an office. That's why I didn't see her."

Yeah, sure, Carol. And pigs fly, too.

I hate it when I argue with myself. I never know whose side I'm on.

I looked down at Lucy and Ethel, who were reminding me with gentle nudges that their dinner service was running late tonight. "You don't think I'm going crazy, do you?" I asked them as I poured kibble into their bowls. It suddenly dawned on me that I was talking to two dogs. Not only that, I expected them to answer me. And I'd been doing it for years.

I had a brief moment of panic, picturing the moment

when my family finally figured out my declining mental state. Jenny and Mark wouldn't trust me to take care of CJ, Jim would quietly divorce me, and our son Mike would confess that the real reason he'd moved to Florida was to put as much distance between himself and his loony mother as possible.

There was only one thing I could do. I turned off the kitchen lights, trusting Jim to take out the dogs for one last walk. As an FYI, I sent Jim a quick text outlining Mark's concerns about the upcoming reenactment and suggesting he deal with his son-in-law directly, leaving me out of it.

Then I went to bed.

Chapter 7

I came, I saw, I forgot what I was doing. Retraced my steps, and now I have no idea what's going on.

The sunshine streaming through the bedroom window made last night's dark thoughts seem laughable. But just to be sure, after I sent Jim off to still another marching practice—this one retracing the actual 1779 route, so it would take a lot longer—I decided to give my sanity a little test.

I often walk into a room and don't remember why I'm there. Or I put something down, and later, when I try to find it, I can't remember where the darn thing is. As a test, I walked around my house and carefully placed three everyday objects in three rooms: my cell phone, reading glasses, and wallet. I was playing my own version of Hide and Seek. Next, I forced myself to take an extra-long shower, followed by a romp outside with Lucy and Ethel.

Satisfied that enough time had passed, I sent a silent prayer to St. Anthony, the patron saint of lost objects (just in case I needed a little extra help), and set off on my quest. Every object was where I remembered. *What a relief.* Maybe there was hope for me after all.

I decided to reward myself with some retail therapy. I had to find something suitably fancy to wear to the masquerade ball at the Porter Mansion that was capping off Celebrate Fairport. After all, my husband was an important planning committee member, and as his wife, I had to look my best. Although the event was months away, I *never* left important decisions like what I should wear until the last minute. And if more than one retail opportunity was necessary to find the perfect dress, that was just fine with me.

I had my hand on my cell phone, all set to invite Nancy to come with me when I realized I had to devise a clever strategy to justify the expensive purchase of a dress I'd probably only wear once. I'd saved a few of the cocktail dresses I wore during those long-ago New York City party days when Jim and I were invited to black tie events on a regular basis. If one of those worked, I could impress Jim with my thriftiness, which could be useful if he ever found my hidden stash of brand-new purchases.

I remembered one basic black number that I still had in my bedroom closet. It was perfect for any occasion—simple enough to wear for a solemn event (i.e., a funeral) but easily jazzed up with sparkly accessories for a night on the town. In the interest of keeping peace in the family, I resolved to try that one on first. If it fit, I promised myself I'd wear it for the masquerade ball. And for once, my dear husband wouldn't have anything to complain about.

"I know just where that dress is," I said to the dogs as I sifted through the hangers in my closet. "It's way in the back, next to the navy-blue suit I also never wear." I realized I was talking to Lucy and Ethel like they were people instead of dogs and clapped my hand over my mouth. "I've got to stop doing that."

I found the navy suit without any problem, but not the black dress. I was sure I'd hung the dress in my closet after I'd worn it the last time. All of a sudden, I was right back where I'd started this morning, before my successful game of Hide and Seek.

I closed my eyes and ordered myself to think rationally for a change instead of flipping out like I did yesterday. I searched my mental filing cabinet, and—wonder of wonders—a memory popped up, clear as day. I'd taken that black dress to the attic and stored it in the same garment bag I used for my other fancy duds. Phew.

I usually reserve daytime trips to the attic for when Jim is home. My attic is spooky, which isn't unusual for a house as old as ours. Being up there creeps me out, and if you were ever up there with me, you'd feel the same way. Knowing Jim was within screaming distance gave me much-needed peace of mind (assuming he heard me). But that scenario wasn't going to work today.

Be a brave girl, Carol. Go upstairs, grab the garment bag, and scurry back to safety. You can do it.

No matter how many times I lied to myself, climbing those steep, creaky stairs to the only spot in our antique home that scared the daylights out of me was daunting. But I had no choice. There was a fancy party on my calendar, and I had nothing to wear.

"You're an adult woman, and you're not going to panic," I told myself. "You'll be back downstairs in a jiffy. Easy peasy."

I walked slowly up the staircase to our second floor and marched toward the attic door, followed by two curious pups. "Stay put," I ordered them. "I'll be right back."

Taking a deep breath, I wrenched open the door and switched on the dim light. Since Jim's retirement several years ago, he's insisted on many cost-cutting measures. Replacing a dim flickering light bulb in the attic with one that would actually spread light is one of them.

"Stay," I ordered them. "I'll only be a few minutes. And

if you're good, I'll give you a biscuit when we go to the kitchen." I saw their stubby tails wag when they heard the word "biscuit," so I figured they understood.

I made my way carefully up the attic stairs and was relieved to see the garment bag hanging exactly where it should be. Thank goodness. I lugged the bag downstairs into our bedroom and dropped it on the bed. It seemed heavier than I remembered, but I was a lot younger and stronger when I'd taken it upstairs.

I was excited to have a chance to dress up again. Maybe I'd have fun at the masquerade ball, assuming Jim put away his musket before we started dancing.

After giving Lucy and Ethel the promised dog biscuits, I unzipped the garment bag and took out one dress at a time, pausing to check each one out before placing it on the bed. They were all black, in sizes I hadn't had on my body and successfully zipped up in years. *Depressing*! But where was the simple black dress I'd been counting on? I prayed that I hadn't remembered wrong. Maybe it had fallen off its hanger and was at the bottom of the bag.

I reached in, felt around, and pulled out one more dress. But not the one I was expecting. This one looked very old, and although its blue color had faded, I could tell it must have been beautiful in its day. Was it possible that the dress had been lying at the bottom of the garment bag for years, and I'd never noticed it?

I picked it up carefully and wondered if it would fit me. That's when I noticed stains on the skirt. They looked like dried blood. Yuck.

"I've never seen this dress before in my life," I said to the dogs. "I don't know how it got here, but I'm getting rid of it as soon as I can."

I felt a prickle on my neck, then heard a woman say, "It's my dress, Carol."

Chapter 8

When I was a kid, I wanted to be older. This is not what I expected.

OMG. *Now I was hearing voices.*

"You're not imagining this. Please don't be afraid."

In that split second, I didn't want to know if someone was there or not. Both possibilities were equally terrifying.

Holding my breath and sending up a silent prayer to whichever saint might have a little extra time to protect me right now, I turned around and saw a young blonde woman sitting on my favorite chair. On her lap was the black dress I hadn't been able to find.

"I borrowed this to see how it would look on me and didn't get a chance to put it back. I'm sorry."

I stood as still as a marble statue, but the dogs didn't. Both canines bounded over and sat at the woman's feet, allowing her to stroke their heads like they were old pals.

"I love your dogs, Carol. Thank you for sharing them with me."

This entire conversation was much too strange for me. And believe me, that's saying a lot.

I snapped my fingers to call the dogs, but they both ignored me, content to focus their attention on my "guest."

"I don't understand," I said. "Who are you? How did you get here? And why do my dogs know you?" I reached out my hand, then stopped. "Are you really here, or am I imagining this?"

The woman stood up, and I was surprised to see how petite she was. Not even five feet tall. "You're not imagining anything. I live here. I've always lived here. And because you finally found my blue dress, it was time for us to get to know each other face-to-face." She held out my black dress. "This looks much better on you than it does on me. I shouldn't have taken it."

Our hands touched as I reached out to take the dress. Hers felt like real, honest-to-goodness, flesh-and-blood hands.

"I'm sure this is a shock to you. I've been trying to get your attention before I revealed myself." The woman frowned. "But you didn't react to my little hints as I hoped you would. Fortunately, you've finally found the blue dress. That's the key for me to tell you my secret."

I was speechless—a rare moment Jim would be sorry to have missed.

Jim. What if he walked in right now? What would he think?

As if reading my thoughts, my visitor responded. "Jim won't be back for two hours, so don't worry. We won't be interrupted." She gestured for me to sit on the bed, then made herself comfortable on my chair. *My* chair!

"I know you have many questions. I don't blame you. I'm not allowed to explain everything to you the first time we meet. You've heard me speak before but didn't realize who it was. You were looking at my portrait at Town Hall yesterday, and I told you I never liked it. Remember?"

"Do you mean to tell me that you're Elizabeth Porter? But you can't be here. You've been dead for over two hundred years!"

"I know. I look pretty good for my age, don't you think?"

"I have no idea. I've never seen a person this old before," I blurted out without thinking.

Nice going, big mouth. Now, she'll probably put a curse on you.

"I don't mean to get too personal, but I have another question," I said, emboldened by Elizabeth's apparent friendliness. "Are you a ghost?"

"I'm still working on it. That's where you come in."

"Me? What do I have to do with it? I hope you don't mean I'm going to die soon and join you. I just became a grandmother for the first time."

Elizabeth tsked, sounding very much like Sister Rose, my old high school English teacher. "Don't be so dramatic, Carol. I'll come back tomorrow, and we'll continue our chat. Meanwhile, you must promise not to say a word to anyone about our conversation. Agreed?"

"Sure." That was an easy promise for me to make. If I told anyone I was having friendly, girlish chats with a long-dead woman, nobody would believe it. I wasn't even sure I believed it.

"Excellent, Carol. Thank you. I suggest you get to bed early again tonight. Sweet dreams." Then she disappeared.

Chapter 9

The only reason we all get heavier as we get older is because there's a lot more information in our heads.

I woke up the following morning feeling like I'd never slept at all. I vaguely remembered having terrible dreams, but none of their details. Squinting at the clock on the bedside table, I was shocked to see it was already 9:00. Yikes. I sprinted to the bathroom and then into the kitchen, where a fresh pot of coffee was waiting for me. My two canines barely raised their heads to wish me good morning, so I figured Jim had fed them breakfast before he left for yet another meeting or militia drill.

I'd been completely unresponsive last night at dinner as Jim droned on and on about the ever-changing event schedule. I didn't even react when he announced he was thinking of keeping his beard after the reenactment because he thought it made him look distinguished. Nor did I ask if he'd read my text and talked to Mark about the police department's concerns. I had enough things of my own to worry about.

If I'd seen Jim this morning, I might have been tempted to spill the beans about yesterday's surprise visitor. Maybe even brag a little that I had inside information about Fairport history that I couldn't tell him about. But I couldn't run the risk of making Elizabeth angry.

Knowing in advance that I would have "out of this world" company, I decided to spiff up the house a little after a quick shower. I was dragging the vacuum out of the front hall closet, where it had been sitting unused for several weeks when I heard a discreet cough behind me.

"Please don't feel you have to clean the house because of me," Elizabeth said, startling the heck out of me.

"You surprised me," I said. "I thought you'd be here in the afternoon like yesterday."

"Let's just say I have a flexible schedule," my new pal said with a smile. "This is a conversation I've been waiting to have for over two hundred years. I'm anxious to start if that's all right with you."

"Sure," I said. *Talking to a dead person is tops on my to-do list today, too.*

"Great. It's tops on my to-do list, too."

Realizing I'd better be more careful with my thoughts, I gestured toward the kitchen and reverted to my tried-and-true hostess role. "Let's sit down and have some coffee. Or would you prefer tea?"

"That was in Boston, not Fairport," Elizabeth said. I guess I looked puzzled, so she clarified. "The Boston Tea Party. I was trying to make a joke. I'm a little nervous."

I put two mugs of steaming coffee on the table, sat down, and waited for her to begin.

"How did you sleep last night?" Elizabeth asked.

"I think I slept through the whole night, which is very unusual for me," I said. "But I woke up feeling exhausted like I hadn't slept at all." I yawned for emphasis. "Excuse me."

"You're exhausted because you didn't sleep," she said. "You were wide awake, and you were *really* there."

"There? Where?"

"Before I answer you, can you remember anything about the night? Did you have any dreams?"

"Yes. Horrible ones. I don't want to remember them."

"I want you to concentrate on your dreams," Elizabeth said. "It's important. Tell me what you saw."

I closed my eyes, and everything came back to me. It was like watching a movie inside my head. "There was screaming. People were running for their lives. They were trying to get away from soldiers. There were so many soldiers. They were dressed in red uniforms, killing everyone they caught. It was complete carnage. Buildings were burning. There was so much blood everywhere. It was horrible." I started to cry.

"I know it was horrible," Elizabeth said gently. "You were at the Battle of Fairport. The real one, not the silly one the reenactors are trying to replicate. They have no idea what it was like."

"I was there?" I repeated. "Are you kidding me? How did that happen?"

"I had to take you there to see how it happened. Now I can tell you the rest of my story. Please, close your eyes again. Do you see a woman running into a garden with soldiers chasing her? She's wearing a beautiful blue gown. Tell me what you see."

"I see a woman in a blue gown, crying," I said. "Men are attacking her. It's too much. I don't want to see anymore."

"I know it's hard to watch," Elizabeth said. "That's enough. You can open your eyes now. Take a deep breath and tell me when you're ready for me to continue."

A few minutes must have passed. I have no idea how many. "I'm calmer now. Go on."

"The woman you saw being attacked was me," Elizabeth said.

I exhaled the breath I didn't realize I was holding as she

continued to speak. "And the blue dress you found in the garment bag is the one I was wearing that night."

"How in the name of heaven did you manage to survive?"

"I fought like crazy to save myself," Elizabeth said. "And I was able to save my two girls before our house burned to the ground."

"I admire you so much. You were incredibly brave."

"I have to tell you the rest," Elizabeth said. "This is the hardest part. During the battle, I murdered my husband."

Chapter 10

It's been a rough week. But on a positive note, I didn't need bail money and didn't have to hide any bodies.

I was stunned. Here I was, sitting in my own kitchen, having a cup of coffee with a dead person who'd just confessed to a murder she committed over two hundred years ago. I didn't even bother to search my mental filing cabinet for an appropriate response because I knew I wouldn't find one.

"I can see that you're shocked. I don't blame you. Please, let me explain what happened."

"Are you sure you want to tell me?"

"Yes, very sure." Elizabeth took a minute to compose herself, then continued. "John and I married when I was only seventeen. He was twenty years older and wanted a young wife who would provide him with an heir to his fortune. A male heir. I became pregnant right away, and we had a beautiful daughter, Abigail. I had barely recovered from giving birth when I became pregnant again." She made a face. "Unfortunately for John, I produced another female. That's when things began to deteriorate between us. After a few months, I became pregnant again and finally birthed a son. John was ecstatic and insisted the baby be named after him. Then, our son died. He was only two months old."

"How sad for you both to lose a child. I can't imagine how terrible that must have been."

Elizabeth nodded, her eyes glistening with unshed tears. "I knew I had to give him the single thing he married me for, so I tried again. I became pregnant twice more, both boys who died at birth. I was a complete failure in my husband's eyes. So he punished me."

"Punished you? For something that was completely out of your control? That's unbelievable."

"He locked me in my room and had meals delivered to me. Most of the time, the only person I ever saw was Molly, my maid. She was a godsend."

"What about your children?"

"I wasn't allowed to see them. He hired a governess to live in the house and told my daughters I was dead. It wasn't until the night of the battle that they discovered I was still alive."

I was having trouble taking all of this in. It was horrible to hear of any man treating a woman this badly. I sent up a silent prayer to the Good Lord, thanking Him for sending me Jim.

"John loved to show off his wealth," Elizabeth continued. "At the beginning of our marriage, we hosted many parties at our home. John continued to do that, and that saved my sanity. He insisted I still act as his hostess, so I was allowed to attend every time there was a party. It was the only time I saw people, and I had strict orders on how to behave and what I could say, or I would be punished even more. July seven was our fifth wedding anniversary, and John threw a lavish masquerade ball to commemorate it."

She laughed bitterly. "A masquerade was a perfect metaphor for my life. I'd been pretending to be happily married for years."

For a few minutes, neither of us spoke. Finally, Elizabeth broke the silence. "I need to tell you about the murder."

If I'm reading a mystery and the details get too gory, I skip that part. I dreaded hearing how an actual murder was committed, but I had no choice.

"Don't worry, Carol," Elizabeth said, correctly reading my thoughts again. "It's important that I tell you this part, but I promise I won't share too many graphic details."

"Thank you," I whispered.

"When the soldiers broke into our house, my first thought was to protect my children. I grabbed a carving knife from the buffet table, ran upstairs, and shook them awake. Poor sweethearts, they had no idea who I was. They were so frightened. I kissed them, and then my four-year-old daughter, Abigail, recognized me. She told her younger sister later that she knew it was really me because I smelled like Mama. Thank goodness I'd worn perfume that night."

Elizabeth stopped speaking and lowered her head. Tears spilled from her cheeks. "Please give me a minute. This is very hard."

After a few seconds, she continued. "We tiptoed down the back stairway and out the rear door into the garden. John must have spotted us from a window, and he tried to stop us. Imagine, he was willing to risk the lives of our precious children to prevent me from having them. British soldiers came after him, followed by members of the Fairport militia. There was blood everywhere, and I told the children to run. John tackled me and threw me to the ground, calling me horrible names. I knew he was going to kill me. I stabbed him with the carving knife. When the battle was over and John was dead, everyone assumed that a British soldier had killed him with a bayonet. I never shared the secret of what truly happened. Until now."

My mind was exploding. I had so many questions, but I

only asked one. "Why me, Elizabeth? Why are you telling me?"

"When our original house was finally rebuilt, I decided I couldn't live in it again. I had this house built, and it became my home. At the moment of my death, however, instead of passing over to the other side, I was told that, no matter how justified it was, I had committed murder and had to be punished. I could not be with my loved ones in the afterlife until I confessed my crime. I could only choose one person to tell. If that person refused to hear my story, I would be in limbo forever. I've waited for the right person to tell for over two hundred years. When you and your family moved into this house, I knew you were the one I'd been waiting for."

I guess I'd received a high compliment, in a weird way.

Elizabeth stood, and I knew that she was leaving. I still had so many questions.

"Continue to trust your instincts," she said. "You can often be impetuous and overly emotional, and your method of reasoning is creative, to say the least. But you have a heart capable of great love and compassion." She smiled at me before she continued. "More than most people have. That's why I chose you." She leaned forward and kissed me on the cheek. "Thank you for listening, Carol. And now, I'll be on my way."

"Wait," I cried. "Can I tell anyone about this? Jim? My kids?"

"I'm going to leave that up to you," Elizabeth said. "If you're not sure what to do, ask Lucy and Ethel for advice. Dogs will always tell you the truth; you can trust them with your secrets. They understand everything you say." She reached down and gave each dog a loving pat, and they licked her hand.

"I left you a gift in the bedroom to be sure you don't forget me. I hope you like it." And she disappeared.

I don't remember how long I sat at the kitchen table, thinking about Elizabeth's tragic story. It was unbelievable how the Celebrate Fairport event was the catalyst to connect me with a woman who'd died more than two hundred years ago. Finally, the dogs nudged me, bringing me back from eighteenth-century Fairport to the present day.

"I get it," I said. "You want to go outside. Give me a minute to get your leashes."

Both canines raced to the bedroom door as I stood, then stopped and gave me The Look. I suddenly remembered a gift waiting for me, which shows how preoccupied I must have been with the past.

Hanging on the closet door was Elizabeth's blue gown, along with a handwritten note. "I thought this would be perfect for you to wear to the masquerade ball. The color matches your eyes."

The gown was now in perfect condition. All the bloodstains were gone.

Chapter 11

The best thing about the good old days was that I wasn't good, and I wasn't old.

I sat on my bed, staring at the gown. Truthfully, I was afraid to touch it, much less wear it. I'm not by nature a superstitious person, but maybe that's because I've never had reason to be. Until now.

Don't be ungrateful, Carol. Elizabeth meant this dress to be a special thank-you gift. She waited over two hundred years for the right person and the right moment.

"Thank you," I murmured. "I hope you're now at peace wherever you are." *Because I'm not. I'm a wreck.*

I suddenly realized I could be in big trouble if Elizabeth Porter could read my mind for the rest of my life. I'd have no secrets at all.

That idea made me laugh. Once I started, I couldn't stop. I laughed like a complete nutcase for the next few minutes until Ethel licked my hand.

"I get it. I was going to take you and Lucy outside before I found…this." And I pointed toward the gown.

"Come on, girls, let's go out now. Sorry for the delay."

Ethel shook her head. I swear, that's exactly what she did. I would have thought she disagreed with me if I hadn't known better. Lucy planted herself in front of my walk-in closet and sat there like a doggy statue.

If neither canine responded positively to the magic words, "Let's go out," there was no way I would force them. I just hoped I wouldn't regret my decision later.

Like a bolt of lightning, it suddenly occurred to me that Jim would be home this afternoon. If he saw the blue gown, he was sure to ask me a ton of questions about where I got it and how much it cost—the usual third-degree about any additions to my wardrobe. He might even notice a resemblance to the one Elizabeth Porter wore in the Town Hall portrait.

I wasn't prepared to answer any of his questions. Heck, I wasn't sure if I'd ever be. I carefully picked up the dress, gently shoved Lucy aside, and hid it in the far recesses of my closet. I quickly arranged part of my too-extensive (and too expensive—Jim's opinion) Lilly Pulitzer collection in front of it. I figured Lilly P. and Elizabeth P. might enjoy getting to know each other.

Ethel licked my hand, and I figured I had her approval for my fast thinking. I suddenly realized how exhausted I was. Trust me—a conversation with a visitor from the spirit world can really drain a person's energy.

"I need a nap." I checked the time and realized I had at least one hour of uninterrupted slumber all to myself. As I drifted off to sleep with my two canine confidantes snuggled close beside me, I had a disturbing thought. What if I'd dreamed the whole encounter with Elizabeth Porter? Maybe it never really happened at all.

Chapter 12

Who knew that the hardest part of being an adult would be figuring out what to cook for dinner every single night until you die?

The next thing I knew, someone was shaking me. I awoke, terrified that I was being attacked in my own home, to see my husband looming over me. And he didn't look happy.

I figured he was miffed because he'd caught me "sleeping on the job," so to speak—instead of preparing tonight's dinner. I firmly believe that the best defense is a good offense, so I matched his angry look with one of my own. "You scared me. I took a nap this afternoon because I wasn't feeling well." I coughed for effect. "I may be coming down with something." I grabbed his hand. "Feel my forehead. Do you think I have a fever?"

Jim immediately looked contrite. "I'm sorry I scared you. I called your name when I came into the house, and you didn't answer. I knew you were home because your car's in the driveway. When I found you in bed, I wasn't sure if you were alive or dead. You scared me."

"And you accuse me of jumping to conclusions," I said,

using Jim's hand to help me sit up. "This time, which one of us is guilty of that?"

"I suppose I'd better get dinner started." I gave my husband a plaintive look. "I feel a little better now."

"What if I told you you were off the hook for cooking tonight? Would that hasten your recovery?" Now Jim had a mischievous look on his face. "There's a big surprise waiting for you in the kitchen."

I've already had as many big surprises as I can handle today.

I followed Jim into the kitchen, Lucy and Ethel close behind us. Ignoring the toy musket that had been placed on a chair, I zeroed in on two shopping bags bearing the logo of Don Pietro's, one of Fairport's fanciest (and most expensive) caterers. "What's going on? Did you actually buy this food?"

"You must be kidding. You know me better than that." Jim pulled out a chair (not the one with the musket on it) and gestured for me to sit. "The Celebrate Fairport committee is starting to interview caterers for the ball. Don Pietro's provided samples for us today. There was way too much food left over, so I brought some home to my lovely wife, who slaves in the kitchen making delicious meals every day."

I looked at Jim to see if he was either kidding or being sarcastic. One of my dear husband's frequent complaints is that I don't make a home-cooked meal if I can possibly avoid it. The Queen of Takeout, that's me. But he appeared completely serious.

"Thank you for the compliment, dear, even though we both know it's slightly exaggerated."

"Maybe just a little bit," Jim said, opening the takeout boxes and spreading the feast on the table. "Tonight's menu consists of..." and he rattled off a litany of dishes I'd never even heard of. I wasn't even sure if he was pronouncing them correctly.

"What exactly are these?" I asked. "In English, please."

"I wish I could translate for you," Jim said. "But I can't. I have no idea what they are. All I know is that these two…" he pointed to the ones nearest me, "are some kind of beef. And these round boxes are fish courses. The rest are assorted side dishes, or as Don Pietro called them, 'Piattone.'"

I eyed them with suspicion. "I make it a point never to eat something if I don't know what it is. Maybe I'm allergic to it. I could break out in hives. Or worse. Is there a translation included?"

"Not so far," Jim said. "Don Pietro explained everything in a mixture of Italian and English. We all sat there and nodded like we understood every word. Nobody wanted to admit they had no idea what he was talking about."

"No wonder you had so many leftovers."

"They're all delicious," Jim assured me. "And safe to eat. I had seconds of everything, and I'm still alive."

"You're a brave man, Jim Andrews." I sighed. "Okay. I'll try a little of the beef." It was yummy.

To be sure I really liked it, I had a second helping. I tasted what was in the other boxes, and in no time at all, they were all empty.

"I'm sorry there's no dessert, Carol. I know what a sweet tooth you have. The committee really liked those."

"That's fine with me. I couldn't eat another bite," I said, pushing my chair away from the table. "But what does Italian food have to do with the original Battle of Fairport? Am I missing something? I thought this whole celebration was supposed to reenact an actual historic event. I doubt that the Porters sent out for pizza that night." If I ever saw Elizabeth again, maybe I'd ask her.

"Very funny, Carol," Jim said. "Why am I not laughing?"

"I'm sorry. I didn't mean to be so critical. It's entirely up to the committee to choose the caterer and the menu. I promise to stay out of it and not offer my opinion. Maybe Italian food would be a good choice. Everybody likes it. There's a big problem with serving this food at the ball, though."

I picked up a few takeout boxes. "Do these recycle? I'm not sure if I should rinse them first."

"Never mind that, Carol. I'll clean up. And quit changing the subject. I know you're dying to tell me the problem with serving Italian food, whether I want to hear it or not. Go ahead. Get it over with. I have something else I want to tell you, too."

"There's no better place in Fairfield County for Italian food than Maria's Trattoria. We've been loyal patrons since Maria Lesco opened her restaurant after retiring from teaching so many of Fairport's kids—including ours. You can say goodbye to free meal samples if another Italian restaurant is chosen to cater the ball. Are you willing to risk that?"

Jim's eyes widened as the enormity of that possibility hit him in his two favorite places—his wallet and appetite. "I never thought of that."

"It's a good thing I did." I gave him a smooch on the top of his head. "You'll figure it out. You're the organized one in the family."

"Thanks for the kiss. How about a real one for a change?"

I shook my head. "Not while you're growing that horrible beard. It's scratchy. And besides, you've got a little food in it."

Jim snatched a napkin and rubbed his face. "Sorry. I'll try to be more careful. I promise I'll shave it off after the reenactment is over."

"I'm going to hold you to that. And I hope you'll get your hair cut, too. It looks terrible."

"I'm just trying to look authentic for the reenactment. You could be a little more supportive."

"I just want that handsome man I married back," I said with a smile. "Besides, there must have been some clean-shaven soldiers back in 1779. I bet they didn't all have beards."

"Some of the committee researched the Battle of Fairport at the library a few weeks ago. For such an important town event, there's not much information about the actual battle. And no pictures, either. So, we decided that all committee members should wear beards. We may shave them off at the same time on the day after the reenactment." He made a note on his phone. "That'd make a great photo for the paper."

"I didn't realize the entire committee was male," I said. "Or am I jumping to conclusions again, the way some people who shall remain nameless but are near and dear to my heart say I always do?"

"The Fairport Business Association came up with the Celebrate Fairport idea, and the majority of their members are local business owners who happen to be men," my husband answered, looking a little defensive.

I couldn't let that go. "Maybe the female business owners are too busy running successful businesses to bother getting involved with the business association, dear. It really is an old boys' club."

"It's not an old boys' club. FBA has some women members. They didn't volunteer to serve on the planning committee."

Humph. I'll bet.

"What about the First Selectwoman?" I continued. "I can't believe Carla Grimaldi isn't involved in planning such a huge event for the town."

"Her assistant, Peter Robinson, is at every meeting and reports back to her. She's a de facto committee member, but so far, her busy schedule won't allow her time to attend our meetings in person."

"I've heard rumors that several local powers-that-be, like the police chief, are still trying to figure out how to deal with a female holding the highest political office in town. Forgive me for being skeptical about how warm her welcome would be should she decide to pop in on a meeting sometime."

Jim was silent, and I figured he'd finally gotten my point. Either way, it was clear that we could be headed toward a full-blown "domestic" triggered by my big mouth about something that was none of my business.

Be grateful that Jim's entire life, except for visits to CJ and CVS, now revolves around Celebrate Fairport instead of micromanaging your life. He's having fun. Let it go.

"You're right, Carol. The committee should be more inclusive. I'll send off an email to the group tonight before we go to bed with some additional names for the event. If you have any suggestions, let me know and I'll add them to my email."

I know the perfect addition to the committee, but I don't think she has an email in the other world.

"You always come at things from a different perspective. Thanks, honey."

My radar went up instantly. Yes, including more diversity on the committee was a good idea, even a great idea. But Jim rarely—if ever—credits me with having a good idea about one of his pet projects. I hadn't been married for almost forty years without being able to read him like a book. He had something else to tell me about the upcoming extravaganza, which required softening me up first.

"It's interesting that you suggested adding to the planning committee," Jim said. "I got an email today from someone I haven't heard from for quite a while. You'll never guess who it was. Want to try?"

"Nope. If I'll never guess, why bother? Just tell me."

"My old boss from Gibson Gillespie, Mack Whitman."

Chapter 13

I'm ready for some blessings that aren't in disguise.

Some of you may not be up to speed on the details of my life for the past few years and don't recognize Mack Whitman's name. In the interest of being honest and open, without trying to prejudice any of you (much) against the man in advance, I'll start by saying that my current situation of a retired husband with too much time on his hands who now micromanages my life is directly due to a change in leadership at Jim's former public relations firm, when Mack Whitman, a young "genius" with no professional credentials whatsoever, was brought in as President and CEO.

One by one, the seasoned staff (the ones over forty), including my husband, were encouraged to retire. There was a brief time when Mack brought Jim back to market a television show aimed at senior citizens, but it never made it on the air. The shocking death of the show's producer, an old grammar school friend of mine, plus having my life threatened by a maniac during the show's production, has left me with even more bitter memories.

I hope you understand why I didn't greet the fact that

Mack Whitman's name had just come up in our post-dinner conversation with overwhelming joy. However, in the interest of marital harmony, and because my husband had gone out of his way to present me with the gift of a delicious dinner, I decided to hear Jim out without screaming, "Whatever Mack wants you to do, say no." I hope you're all impressed because it took a heck of a lot of effort.

Instead, I took a deep breath and calmly replied, "My goodness. What a surprise hearing from Mack after all this time." Then, I took a good look at my husband.

A specific facial expression appeared on Mike's or Jenny's faces years ago when I'd caught either of them telling a fib. Most parents have seen that look over the years, and it telegraphs loud and clear that the *looker* has been busted by the *lookee*. And I knew before Jim uttered another word, what my husband was going to admit.

"Tell me more about your email from Mack. What's he been up to these days? How are things at Gibson Gillespie?"

Jim cleared his throat. "Well, as a matter of fact, it turns out that Mack and the agency are diversifying. Going in a completely different direction."

"Oh, really. Such as...."

"Mack's decided to start producing Revolutionary War documentaries like Ken Burns does and add them to the GG portfolio of services. He's starting with the New England states and the Battle of Fairport. Then he's doing Bunker Hill and Lexington/Concord."

"How interesting that Mack's beginning this new documentary project by highlighting a minor skirmish like the Battle of Fairport rather than a more well-known one, like Bunker Hill. I wonder how he got that idea."

"You know that Mack keeps in touch with me regularly," my husband said, his face now a mirror image of Mike's in seventh grade when he swore that he'd finished his math homework and it wasn't his fault if our dog ate it. Since our canine at the time was Skippy, the first of several English cockers who've owned us over the years, and the finickiest dog we've ever had (he only ate one brand of dog food which cost a fortune, and we had to buy through our vet), I knew right away Mike was fibbing, just like Jim was now.

"I didn't realize that," I said with a straight face. "How nice for you."

Jim's face flushed, and he straightened up in his chair. "Yes. Well, every now and then, Mack needs some background history on an agency account or two. Or to ask my advice on a possible new client. I'm always happy to help.

"I realized Celebrate Fairport was a perfect choice for Mack's first historical documentary," Jim continued, shifting a little in his chair. "As I said before, when Mack needs any advice, I'm happy to help."

You're a regular Boy Scout.

"You're always helpful to me around the house, too," I said, smiling sweetly. "As a matter of fact, I'm impressed that you have so much time to spend organizing Celebrate Fairport when you're so busy helping others." I was waiting for Jim to admit that he was the one who reached out to Mack and pitched the historical documentary idea, not the other way around.

I had to give the guy credit for being single-minded and ignoring my not-so-subtle attempts to back him into a corner. Or maybe I was losing my touch.

"Mack's coming to Fairport tomorrow afternoon, and I'm giving him a tour of the reenactment locations. I thought you could join us for dinner before he heads back to the city. We're also supposed to meet a woman who's an expert on historical reenactments, Liz somebody. I can't remember her last name, but she has a company called Reenactments Unlimited. Mack hired her to be the technical advisor for any filming. I hope that makes you happy."

"It's a good start," I admitted.

Especially if she actually knows what she's doing because the rest of you certainly don't.

"What do you say? Maria's Trattoria at 6:00 tomorrow?"

"Sure, that works for me."

No cooking two nights in a row? Count me in.

"This is a win-win for both the agency and the town," Jim said. "It'll put the reenactment in the national spotlight."

That's what I was afraid of.

Chapter 14

You're about to exceed the limits of my medication.

Maria's Trattoria was packed, as usual, and the line waiting for a table stretched all the way out the front door. Jim and Mack had managed to score a prime corner booth at the back of the restaurant, no doubt due to our close friendship with owner Maria Lesco.

I was betting Jim and Mack had skipped the line entirely, earning the many dirty looks headed my way from several other customers. *Just keep walking and pretend you don't notice them, Carol.*

I took a seat beside my husband and studied the man who'd ruined my life several years ago, causing a seismic shift in our husband-wife dynamic that I was still getting used to. Gone was the public relations wunderkind who'd forced my husband into early retirement from a job at Gibson Gillespie Public Relations, which we both loved (for different reasons), with his pristine, designer wardrobe, gold cufflinks, and Gucci loafers (often worn without socks). The person sitting across from me was attired in what I described later to Nancy as Hollywood grunge, including the oh-so-casual longer hair that just brushed the shoulders of his black shirt. He was sporting the obligatory facial stubble made super cool by a long-ago television show, and I couldn't help but notice that his hairline was now receding a tiny bit.

"Carol, you're looking lovelier than ever." Mack grabbed my hand, and I tried not to flinch. He smiled. Jim smiled. So, I smiled. Jim nudged me under the table and tilted his head toward Mack slightly. I realized this was husband-to-wife shorthand, telling me to take the lead in our pre-dinner conversation.

I wanted to say, "I see you've changed your persona from Madison Avenue slick to show business sleaze." Don't worry, I restrained myself.

"I understand Jim gave you a guided tour of Fairport this afternoon. What do you think of our town?"

"Fairport is a great place," Mack said, favoring me with still another smile. "It's so historic. So picturesque. So quaint. I can see why you and Jim have lived here for so long." He punched Jim on the arm playfully. "Although, I remember the commute from here into the city was the main reason you decided to retire. We were so sorry to see you go. The agency just isn't the same without you, buddy."

I almost choked. Or, to be more accurate, I almost choked Mack. What a complete crock. Jim left Gibson Gillespie because Mack made it impossible for him to continue working there.

I felt another nudge under the table, this one a little harder than the first one. I shot a quick glance at my husband. He made a quick "zip" movement across his lips, and I nodded. Why my dear husband wanted to work with Mack again was a mystery to me. But I'd go along with it as long as this collaboration didn't involve any dead bodies (except the fake ones in the reenactment).

"I hope you like Italian food," I said. "I can guarantee it'll be delicious no matter what you order."

Jim patted his stomach. "I can attest to that. Maybe a little too much. But if you're looking for suggestions, I'd recommend the veal saltimbocca. It's delicious." He looked at me for support, and I realized he was as hard-pressed to make small talk as I was.

"Why don't we order appetizers first?" Mack said. "One more person is joining us and…"—he checked his Rolex—"she seems to be running late. I can assure you both, though, that Liz is definitely worth waiting for."

"Liz," I repeated. "Does she work at Gibson Gillespie now?" I was picturing some statuesque blonde in her early twenties with a killer figure and the I.Q. of a limp lettuce leaf.

Mack laughed. "I wish I could hire her full-time, but we're only working together on the Celebrate Fairport project." His face brightened. "There she is now." He stood and waved as a stunning woman of a "certain age" threaded her way through the crowd.

I followed Mack's gaze and almost fainted. It was Elizabeth Porter.

Chapter 15

I'm at that time of life when I think everyone my age looks way older than I do.

"Sorry I kept everyone waiting," Elizabeth said, sliding into the booth next to Mack and giving Jim and me a bright smile. "I was on a conference call for another project, and it went on forever."

"Mack has been singing your praises, Liz. I'm Jim Andrews, and this is my wife, Carol. It's a pleasure to meet you."

Jim gave me another nudge under the table, and I gave him a dirty look. At this rate, I'd be black and blue before we even ordered dinner.

"Yes," I echoed. "It certainly is."

Mack handed Elizabeth a menu. "Carol and Jim say the food here is wonderful. We were waiting for you to order, but take your time."

I had to figure out how to get Elizabeth alone and find out what the heck she was doing here. She took the menu, then said, "I'd love to freshen up a bit first. Carol, would you show me where I can do that?"

"Of course, *Liz*," I said, emphasizing the name a little

more than was necessary. "It would be my pleasure. We won't be long, and meanwhile, why don't you order drinks? I know I'd love a house chardonnay. A large one." *Oh, heck. Bring the whole bottle.*

"I'll have the same," Elizabeth added.

"We'll be back in a jiffy," I said, grabbing her hand and squeezing it just a teensy bit, then giving her one of my best glares. "It's this way." Without even bothering to see if she was following me, I headed to the women's room, passing the kitchen where Maria reigned supreme. I wondered if she would have devised a more "out-of-this-world" menu if she knew a ghost was here.

Fortunately, we were the only people in the women's room. This conversation required complete privacy, although if someone else overheard us, they'd probably think they'd had too much vino.

"Okay, what's going on? I thought you'd left to join your family on the other side. Why are you back here? Didn't it work?"

"You're angry," Elizabeth said, looking a little hurt. "I thought you'd be glad to see me again."

"Let's say I'm surprised to see you again and leave it at that, okay? That's the best I can do until you tell me why you're back in my life."

"First of all, everything worked fine, Carol. Thanks to you, I was able to pass over to the other side without any problem. It was so good to see everyone, especially my two girls. And to meet their children, their children's children, and their children's children's children. You get the idea."

"I get the idea. There were lots of people to meet. Go on."

"Yes, well, here's the thing. Once all the hugs and kisses were out of the way, my new afterlife began. And it was okay, nice. Sweet. But not…exciting. I realized that I missed Fairport, and I especially missed you. And your closet, of course. You have a lovely wardrobe, and I was able to borrow your clothes without you catching on."

I remembered all the times I couldn't find an outfit and worried I was losing my marbles. My clothes led a double life, and probably had more fun than I did.

"Thank you. I think. But you still haven't answered my question. Why are you here?"

"I'm getting to that."

"Could you speed it up a little? The guys are going to wonder what's happened to us." *And I'm dying for a glass of wine.*

Elizabeth grinned. "I'm looking forward to a glass of wine, myself."

Rats. I'd forgotten entirely about her ability to read my thoughts.

"My whole family wanted to hear about what I'd been doing for the last two centuries," she continued. "I told them all about you and your interesting life. Everyone got really excited when I told them about the upcoming reenactment of the Battle of Fairport. They'd heard stories about the Battle, of course. It's an important part of the Porter family history. We received special permission to return to Fairport to participate in the event. Everyone, especially my two daughters, wants to meet you and see the house and the old Porter Mansion. Abigail and Becky were too young to remember the actual battle, thank goodness, but they have fond memories of your house. They were both married there."

Oh, good lord. I hoped neither of the Porter girls wanted to renew their wedding vows during the reenactment. That was all I needed.

"We won't be any trouble while we're here," Elizabeth said. "As a matter of fact, we'll be so quiet you won't even know we're in the house."

"In the house? You mean you're all staying in my house? How many are we talking about?"

Elizabeth thought for a minute. "If everyone comes, about a hundred, give or take."

"A hundred? Are you crazy? Where will they all sleep? Will they expect to be fed, too? How am I supposed to explain a huge food bill to Jim when, as far as he knows, it's just the two of us living in the house? Unless you expect to convince him that I'm pregnant again. I don't think he's going to fall for that." I glared at my ghostly pal, but she was laughing too hard and didn't notice.

"Trust me, we won't take up any room, and we don't eat much. We're from the spirit world, remember?"

I leaned against one of the stall doors, so that I wouldn't faint. Then I saw the mischievous look on Elizabeth's face and realized she was putting me on.

"You are so funny," I said. "Why am I not laughing?"

"I apologize, but I just couldn't resist teasing you a little bit. Relax. I'm the only one who will be staying in Fairport, although the girls may pop in from time to time."

"Are you really going to be involved in filming the reenactment with Mack?"

"Mack and I have agreed that my expertise would be most helpful in supervising the filming of the masquerade ball. I'm hoping the reenactment committee will also allow me some input into the planning process, too. Who better than someone who was actually there?"

At my shocked look, she added, "Don't worry. You're the only person who will know who I really am. As far as everyone else is concerned, I'm a Revolutionary War reenactment expert. Trust me. Everything will be fine."

I disagreed, but I knew there was no point in arguing with a visitor from the other side. I followed Elizabeth back into the dining room without another word.

Chapter 16

Of course, size matters. Nobody wants a small glass of wine.

Because I like you, I'm skipping the details of the next few hours of The-Dinner-I-Thought-Would-Never-End. Consider yourselves lucky. Suffice it to say that I had to sit and listen to Mack, Jim, and Elizabeth discuss the intricate details of Celebrate Fairport without being allowed to make one single comment or contribution myself. Every time I opened my mouth to insert a teeny weensy (brilliant) suggestion, one of them interrupted me and changed the subject.

Please don't bother to remind me that I've already said many times that I wanted nothing to do with such a silly event. The players had changed, and I was now involved, whether I liked it or not.

I looked at Elizabeth at one point, and she winked at me. I had to remember that she was playing a role, and I was the only other person who knew what was actually going on.

How would Jim and Mack feel if they found out they were having dinner with a ghost?

I tried to control myself, but I couldn't help it. Suddenly, the whole scenario struck me as hysterically funny, and I started to giggle. Bad timing because I'd just had a sip of wine, and the giggling led to a coughing fit. My gallant husband slapped me on the back a few times and handed me a napkin. "Sit back in your chair and take some deep breaths, Carol." He immediately picked up the thread of conversation without missing a beat.

I concentrated on finishing my delicious meal and refrained from thinking any more ghostly thoughts. It wasn't easy. Not the eating part. The thinking part.

I almost lost it again when Elizabeth said, "This was an excellent dinner." She pulled a Visa card from her Brahmin purse and handed it to our server, who scurried away to run it through the credit card machine. I couldn't believe Elizabeth had an honest-to-goodness credit card. I just hoped it was the real deal and didn't bounce.

"A gentleman never allows a lady to pay the check," Mack said, reaching for his wallet.

"That's so old-fashioned, Mack," Elizabeth said. "So… eighteenth century. Don't you agree, Carol?"

"I sure do," I said, laughing. "Jim's always thrilled when I pick up the check, aren't you, dear?"

Jim nodded, then added, "Of course, all our credit cards and bank accounts are in both our names, like any married couple, so I'm still paying the bill."

Except for that secret credit card I keep for my personal shopping adventures that I hope you never find out about.

"Don't worry, Mack," Elizabeth reassured him. "I'm keeping a record of all expenses connected to this project. You'll end up paying for the meal eventually."

I was suddenly aware of Maria Lesco walking toward our table, waving what I feared was Elizabeth's credit card. Her facial expression brought back memories of her terrorizing parents, including us, at long-ago parent-teacher conferences.

Rats. It must have been rejected. I glanced around the restaurant and prayed no one I knew was there. This was going to be so embarrassing.

"Carol and Jim Andrews," Maria said, "of all people. I can't believe you two." She placed Elizabeth's Visa card on the table, then continued to scold Jim and me. "Why didn't you tell me you were coming for dinner tonight and bringing guests? The server finally told me you were here. I hope your meal was satisfactory."

Fortunately, Jim jumped right in. "Maria," he said, "you know how loyal we are to you and this restaurant. Where else would we bring friends we wanted to impress?"

"Maria, this is Mack Whitman," I said. "He and Jim were colleagues at Gibson Gillespie many years ago." Maria raised her eyebrows, and I knew she remembered Mack.

Before I could continue with the introductions, Elizabeth interrupted me. "I'm Elizabeth Peterson. Mack and I are here to film the reenactment event. This meal was out of this world. Absolutely delicious."

She smiled at Mack. "I prefer being called Elizabeth, not Liz. I'm not into nicknames. I should have mentioned it before."

I was impressed that Elizabeth corrected Mack's attempt at familiarity. And relieved that I didn't have to remember her nickname.

"It's a pleasure to meet both of you," Maria said. "I hope to see you here often."

"Is there a problem with my credit card?" Elizabeth asked, looking worried.

"This dinner is on the house," Maria said. "That includes Jim's favorite dessert, tiramisu. Unless any of you would prefer another choice."

"You're so generous," I said. "Thank you. Maria is one of our dearest friends," I explained to Elizabeth and Mack.

"Her tiramisu is legendary."

"I'm sure the dessert will be as wonderful as the rest of the meal," Elizabeth said as Maria speed-walked to the kitchen. "This is the best restaurant meal I've ever had."

"That's a high compliment because I'm guessing that, in your line of work, you eat out a lot," Mack said.

"I usually eat at home," Elizabeth said. "I like simple, old-fashioned cooking the best, even though I'm not much of a cook myself.

"We need someone to plan the menu and cook the food for the masquerade ball at Celebrate Fairport, right, Mack? It couldn't be an Italian menu, though. That wouldn't fit with the theme. I wonder if Maria could come up with another menu." Elizabeth looked at me. "You know her well. Should we mention it to her and see what she says?"

Before I had a chance to answer, Jim spoke up. "The event planning committee is already interviewing caterers for the ball, Elizabeth." I could tell by his frosty tone of voice that he was ticked off. How dare this new person take over the entire event. He turned to Mack for clarification. "I was under the impression that Elizabeth had been hired to oversee the reenactment for *filming purposes* only. Perhaps I misunderstood. No offense to your expertise, Elizabeth."

"None taken," she assured him, giving me a "what did I do?" look, which I ignored. No way was I getting in the middle of this power play.

I did feel sorry for Jim. Most of his time had been devoted to organizing Celebrate Fairport for months. I was betting he figured hiring Elizabeth was another underhanded coup d'état by Mack Whitman.

On the other hand, who better to organize Celebrate Fairport—including the menu for the ball—than the person sitting opposite me right now?

I put my hand on Jim's arm and squeezed it gently. "I'm

sure all these details about who does what will be worked out. Everyone wants the reenactment to be a success." *So, calm down before we have to call the paramedics.*

"I got carried away by my enthusiasm for the event," Elizabeth said, looking embarrassed. "I should have known an event this large in scope already had a planning committee in place."

Mack had been quiet during this interchange, which was interesting. He was always the one who put in his two cents, whether it was welcome or not.

"I'm sure we can all work together," he said. "To your point, Jim, let me clarify that Elizabeth's primary responsibility is to oversee the filming, particularly for historical accuracy. But since she has additional special event expertise, perhaps she can be helpful to your committee as well."

"Have you ever planned a masquerade ball?" Jim asked. I bit my lip to keep from laughing.

"I can honestly say I've had years of personal experience with masquerades of all types, including a formal ball," she said straight-faced. "As a matter of fact, several years ago, I was a guest at one very similar to the one being planned." I flashed a warning look at her. She was having a great time baiting the guys, but I didn't want her to go too far. I especially didn't want to face a cross-examination later by my one and only about Ms. Peterson's credentials.

I needn't have worried because the desserts arrived, and Jim brightened up immediately. Saved by the tiramisu.

Chapter 17

How's adulting going, you ask? Well, I turned on the wrong burner on the stove, and I've been cooking nothing for about 20 minutes.

Alas, Jim's good mood had disappeared by the time we arrived home. I tried my usual can't fail activity and suggested we go to bed early (as soon as Lucy and Ethel's needs were properly attended to, naturally), but Jim looked at me like I was crazy.

"It's only eight o'clock, and I'm not sleepy. Plus, we've both eaten a big dinner. Cardiologists say that going to sleep after eating a heavy meal is very bad for the heart. What are you trying to do, kill me?"

My baby blues immediately filled with tears. I know, stupid. But my sprinklers are set on automatic, and there's not a darn thing I can do to change it. Whenever someone (especially You Know Who) criticizes or is mad at me, they overflow like a leaky drainpipe.

"I wasn't suggesting sleeping," I said in a small voice.

Jim either didn't hear me or ignored me. No matter what, he clearly had something more important to do, which surprised the heck out of me. He was always interested in… well, I'm sure you all get the idea without my spelling it out.

"I'm calling an emergency breakfast meeting tomorrow morning to bring the reenactment committee up-to-date on what happened tonight at dinner. And plan a strategy."

"A strategy for what?"

"Weren't you paying attention?" Jim asked. "That woman is trying to take over my event. And she's not going to get away with it."

"But, Jim…."

It was no use. Jim stormed into the office and powered up the computer. "Who does she think she is? Ha. She doesn't know who she's tangling with."

"Neither do you, Jim," I whispered. "Neither do you."

Chapter 18

Becoming an adult is the stupidest thing I've ever done.

I'm embarrassed to admit that I pretended to still be sleeping when Jim rolled out of bed the next morning. After tossing and turning most of the night, I was in no mood to start the day with another conversation about That Woman hijacking Jim's precious event. I was afraid he'd press me for a reasonable explanation as to why I was "taking her side" when I should be supporting his point of view.

Jim probably knew I was faking, but he let me get away with it, thank goodness. He also took care of the dogs' early morning needs and started the coffee before tiptoeing back into the bedroom to grab a jacket. Gotta love a guy like that, despite the fact that he often makes me crazy.

When I finally heard his car engine start, then the crunch of gravel as he drove down our driveway, I sat up in bed and stretched, careful not to strain my temperamental back.

Stumbling into the kitchen, muttering to myself about the fragile egos of the male of the species, I found I had an early morning visitor. Elizabeth had made herself comfortable at the kitchen table, Lucy and Ethel curled up at her feet.

"What a cozy scene," I said, mustering up as much sarcasm as I could. "May I help myself to a cup of coffee, or did you drink it all?"

"I'm sorry," Elizabeth said. "I don't usually drink coffee."

"You're sorry you don't usually drink coffee?" I asked. "Or are you apologizing for something else?"

"You know what I mean, Carol. I'm sorry that I handled things so badly last night. It was much easier before when you couldn't see me."

"Yeah, those were the good old days when I thought I was losing my sanity."

I held up my hand. "Not another word until I have some coffee. I may drink it straight out of the pot. One less mug to wash."

Elizabeth frowned. "I don't think that's a good idea, Carol. You might spill it on yourself."

Good grief. "I was only kidding."

"I was concerned you might get burned," Elizabeth said defensively. "In my day, there wasn't any time for kidding around. I guess I have a lot to learn about living in the twenty-first century."

I know a golden opportunity when I hear one. "Since you brought up the subject, I have a few more questions. Why didn't you let me know in advance that you were coming? How long do you plan on being here? And how come other people can see you now? Before, you were only visible to me. And the dogs, of course."

You can call me a terrible person if you want, but I wasn't pleased that Elizabeth had suddenly decided to pop back into my life. Dealing with Jim and the reenactment was bad enough. Now, I had to deal with a ghost who wanted to run the event, too.

"I think I'll have a cup of coffee after all," Elizabeth said.

"Maybe I'll develop a taste for it."

"Can't you just wiggle your nose a little, and a cup will magically appear?" I asked, only half kidding. "That's what Elizabeth Montgomery used to do in *Bewitched*."

"I'm not a witch; I'm a ghost. Is it all right if I help myself to a cup?"

"Why not? It's your house."

"No, it was my house. Now, it's your house, and I'm just a guest. A guest ghost."

That struck me funny, and I started to giggle. Elizabeth looked at me like I was nuts. "What's so funny? You're laughing again like you did last night at dinner. Are you making fun of me?"

"You made a joke without realizing it. You called yourself a guest ghost, which made me giggle. If you giggled too, you'd be a giggling guest ghost."

"Oh, now I get it." Elizabeth laughed, and I realized what a beautiful smile she had.

"I'm not usually this silly," I said. "Last night at dinner, I wondered how Jim and Mack would react if they knew who you really are. And that struck me funny. I'll try to control myself in the future."

Since we were now getting along so well, I was a good sport and poured a cup of coffee for my guest before topping off my own. "Okay, enough of this levity," I said. "How about some answers to my questions?"

Elizabeth took a sip from the steaming cup and made a face. "It's an acquired taste," I explained. "I'll get you some milk and sugar, but only after you tell me exactly what's going on. Do you and your family actually want to be involved in the reenactment for old times' sake? Why don't I believe that's all there is to it?"

I sat back and waited. It almost killed me to keep quiet, but I've discovered that silence is an excellent way to get questions answered.

Finally, Elizabeth spoke. "If I tell you the truth, I'm sure you won't believe me. It sounds ridiculous."

"Try me."

"I answered a Help Wanted ad in the *Ghost Gazette*."

Chapter 19

Dogs make me happy. You...not so much.

"You've got to be kidding." I was losing patience with my ghostly visitor.

"It's true. That's exactly what happened."

"What, pray tell, is the *Ghost Gazette*? I've never heard of it."

"Of course you haven't heard of it, Carol. You're not a ghost."

"Point taken. Please explain. I promise I won't interrupt you." *Or laugh at you.*

"The *Ghost Gazette* is a daily newsletter that keeps ghosts up to speed on what's happening worldwide. In addition to all the news, there's a Help Wanted section. There was a blind ad asking for a ghost to oversee a local New England event to make sure it ran smoothly. My daughters tell me those ads are very common, and the name and place of the event aren't divulged until a ghost applies and is hired. I applied, just for the heck of it, and got the job. It was only after that I found out I'd been assigned to Celebrate Fairport. I was as surprised as you are."

"Assuming I believe you, what are your specific duties?"

"That's the challenging part." Elizabeth was grinning. "I have to make it up as I go along. There's no job description. I figured you and I could work together on it, just like we used to do before I passed over."

I rubbed my forehead. I could feel a massive headache coming on. "What do you mean, work together the way we used to do?"

"Some of those scathingly brilliant ideas that popped into your head when you were solving a murder came from me, whispering in your ear. You just didn't know it."

"As crazy as all this sounds," I said slowly, "I believe you. Were any of the ideas mine?"

"Many of them were, Carol. You're very intuitive. I already told you that. And the inspiration for me to contact Mack Whitman was totally from you. It was brilliant."

"I did that? Please, tell me more. Nobody ever tells me I'm brilliant, and my ego can always use a boost."

"I've overheard you talking about Mack for years. I figured being hired by him was the perfect way to get involved in the reenactment. It was easy to convince him he needed my expertise."

"What do you want me to do?"

"Jim talks about the reenactment all the time. If he says anything that sounds worrisome, let me know. My job seems to be heading off trouble before it starts, so any information you can share will be helpful. And maybe you could give me a teensy bit of help with the masquerade ball. Jim wouldn't have to know. For instance, I need to find someone to do hair and makeup for the filming. Do you know someone who might be interested?"

"I might," I said.

Elizabeth gave me a dazzling smile. "You're being helpful already. If you come up with someone, give me her contact information later today."

As much as I hated to admit it, Elizabeth's proposition was interesting. And, besides babysitting the most perfect grandchild in the world and being sure Jim had dinner on time, what else did I have going on in my life right now?

Lucy nudged my leg, then jumped in my lap and nuzzled my face. Such blatant displays of affection are rare from Her Majesty. She jumped from my lap to Elizabeth's, nuzzled her face, then turned and gave me a doggy stare, clearly telegraphing that, in her opinion, I had to help Elizabeth.

I sighed. I knew when I was licked, especially when Ethel, always Lucy's faithful follower, started in on me, too.

"I give up. Even my dogs are against me. Okay, I'll help you."

"Perfect," Elizabeth said. "Right now, I have to meet Mack at the Porter Mansion. I can't wait to see what the interior looks like now."

"Not so fast," I said, grabbing her arm while I could still see it. "I have another condition, and this one is non-negotiable. Since you're here in living bodily form and visible to others besides me, you must promise to behave like a normal human being. No more appearing to me unexpectedly, the way you always do."

"How about if I just whisper in your ear and then appear?"

"That'd scare the daylights out of me! No way. Do you promise?"

"Oh, all right. I'll text you first."

"You're kidding."

"Nope. I was given a cell phone as part of the job. I have to return it when the assignment is complete, though. It's the latest iPhone, whatever that means. State of the art."

"My goodness. I'm impressed."

"I'm having some trouble figuring out how to use all the functions, but I know how to text."

You may think it's ridiculous for me to ask a ghost to text

before appearing. On the other hand, if any of you should ever encounter a ghost, let me know how you deal with it.

Chapter 20

Hell hath no fury like a spurned hair stylist.

"I can't believe I've allowed myself to be talked into getting involved in this silly reenactment by a ghost," I muttered as I made a half-hearted stab at cleaning the kitchen. "It sounds like no big deal, but if this turns out to be the stupidest thing I've ever done, I'm blaming you two for talking me into it." Lucy and Ethel, now lounging in a sunbeam which showed off my dirty kitchen windows beautifully, ignored me, turned over, and went back to sleep.

"I'm taking charge of my own life for the rest of the day," I told the dogs. "And tops on today's agenda is solving a deeply personal crisis that does not involve ghosts, reenactments, or husbands."

This is hard to admit, but I'd been unfaithful, and I had to make it right.

Not to Jim. I can tell how many of you are already condemning me. It's true confession time, so here goes.

Since before Christmas, I hadn't made a hair appointment with Deanna, my local stylist and good friend. I'd been seeing another stylist in a posh New York City salon for the last few months.

There. I said it. But it wasn't my fault. Honestly, I was coerced into it (at first) by Jenny's mother-in-law, the always glamorous (and frequently annoying) Margo Anderson. Maybe some of you remember how she arrived unexpectedly for Christmas with her new boyfriend and all the chaos that resulted from that. If your memory is as bad as mine sometimes is, don't sweat it. I'll tell you another time.

Moving on. After the aforementioned chaos had settled down a bit, Margo suggested it would be peachy keen to take Jenny and me for a girls' day out in New York City. We could see the tree at Rockefeller Center, go to lunch, shop, and even go to a fancy hair salon and get spiffed up for New Year's Eve.

I tried to weasel out of it, but Jenny begged me to come, and what could I do? She's my daughter, and I knew a whole day with Margo would be sheer torture for her. One thing led to another, and my personal stylist, Monsieur Paul, and I became fast friends for three hair appointments.

Margo treated us all the first time. The other two times, I paid cash so I wouldn't leave a credit card trail for You Know Who to give me grief about. One positive thing I have to say about Celebrate Fairport is that my dear husband was so busy growing his hair long and practicing with a musket that I was able to slip away to the Big Apple for a few quick trips without him asking me too many questions.

A month had passed since my last dalliance with Monsieur Paul, and I needed a touchup. I did not doubt that Deanna already knew about my hair affair, and she would make me suffer for it, one way or another. I had to devise a fool-proof plan to get back into her good graces pronto.

And just like that, I had a plan. A pretty good plan, if I do say so myself. Elizabeth was looking for someone to do hair and makeup for the filming. I knew Deanna would be perfect. I had to get to her before Elizabeth did and make her an offer she couldn't refuse. And since Elizabeth and Mack were touring the Porter Mansion right now (I couldn't wait to hear how that went!), time was of the essence.

A quick shower gave me the opportunity to wet my hair and then comb it flat against my head. I looked so terrible that I even frightened the dogs.

I'd play the pity card. "Oh, Deanna, you have to help me. Jim cut non-essential items from our budget again and had the nerve to put my hair appointments in that category. Can you believe it? I finally stood up to him this morning and told him I was coming to see you, and if he didn't like it, he could lump it. And here I am, throwing myself on your mercy." If I was able to whip up a few tears, so much the better.

After she forgave me (as I knew she would), I'd ask her about doing the hair and makeup for the reenactment video. I was sure she'd be thrilled about that. Maybe she'd even do my hair for free.

Just to be sure, though, before I left, I practiced my pitch in front of the dogs. Lucy is a severe critic—even worse than Jim if you can believe it—and Ethel usually goes along with her. But after a few Milk Bones to guarantee a positive reception, I was satisfied I'd pull it off without a hitch and arrive home a few hours later with shiny, highlighted locks and a (mostly) clear conscience.

Too bad it didn't exactly work out that way.

Chapter 21

I am what I am. Your approval is not needed.

I knew I was in for trouble before I even opened the door to Crimpers. Once I drove into the salon parking lot and spotted the old silver Ford Taurus station wagon parked snugly beside Deanna's Subaru, I tried to back my car onto the street before anyone saw me—bad move. I almost hit a town recycling truck, which earned me a one-finger salute and a whole new vocabulary that would make even my son, Mike, blush.

Idiot. Do you want to kill yourself? Or somebody else? So, what if Phyllis Stevens is in the salon now? No big deal. Park the car, pull up your big girl undies, and march yourself right inside.

I took my good advice and eased the car into a space as far away from Phyllis's vehicle as possible, then gave myself a few minutes to calm down. I checked my email. I checked my Facebook page. I scrolled through my photos. I checked myself out in the rearview mirror to see how bad my hair really looked. Did I absolutely have to see Deanna today? After all, I didn't have an appointment, so she wasn't even expecting me. Maybe I should just leave.

I bet some of you are thinking I'm overreacting. That's

because you haven't yet had the pleasure of meeting my across-the-street neighbor, Phyllis Stevens, and her long-suffering, largely silent husband, Bill. Please allow me a few minutes to bring you up to speed before I open the salon door. The rest of you who have met her will have to suffer a little, but I promise I'll make it up to you. And, yes, I'm stalling for enough time to come up with another brilliant idea, which I dearly hope will happen soon.

Phyllis is the (unelected) head of the town's historic district, particularly our street, Old Fairport Turnpike. She lives, eats, and breathes for every house and is known to start her day with a slow walk around the neighborhood checking for infractions, like trash cans left outside after garbage pickup, grass that needs cutting, bushes that should be trimmed…you get the idea, right? Many a neighbor has found a note taped to their front door listing their latest transgression and a "suggestion" that the situation be corrected immediately.

When Phyllis is not outside patrolling the neighborhood, she can usually be found at the large picture window in her living room, entertaining herself with the comings and goings on the street. There's a rumor she also has a telescope for night vision, but that has yet to be confirmed. Unfortunately, our house is dead within her sights, so Phyllis frequently knows more about what's happening behind our white picket fence than either Jim or me. She's also a frequent contributor to the "Fairport Patch," our local online news (gossip) blog.

Phyllis also considers herself an expert on Fairport history, so I didn't want to get into a discussion about the reenactment, or she'd be hounding Jim to be on the committee. So far, she hadn't tried to insert herself (and her expertise) into the planning process, but it was just a matter of time before she did.

A few months ago, Bill had a bad fall at home and broke his hip. He spent several weeks at the rehabilitation center, and I did my neighborly best by providing my share of meals when he came home.

One night, Jim commented that a broken hip was a small price to pay for some time away from Phyllis. I banished him to a night sleeping in the recliner instead of our comfy bed as punishment, even though I (silently) agreed with him. And now, I was being punished for all my unkind thoughts. I knew I had to change my strategy, but I couldn't come up with a single thing. As I opened the salon door, I sent a prayer to St. Jude, the go-to saint for hopeless causes, hoping he'd come through for me one more time.

Phyllis was totally focused on correcting Deanna's efforts to style her hair, so I was able to slink inside unnoticed. "I always wear my hair parted on the right side. You have it parted on the left. I thought I made myself clear. Please change it."

Just as Deanna began re-styling her hair, Phyllis stopped her. "On second thought, I think I like it better parted on the left side. It makes a nice change."

Deanna gritted her teeth. "Sure, no problem." She noticed me hovering in the doorway, rolled her eyes, and mouthed, "Save me."

Thanks to Phyllis and St. Jude, I'd been handed a sure-fire way to get into Deanna's good graces.

"I know I don't have a hair appointment today but I happened to be driving by and noticed Phyllis's car in your parking lot. I hoped that I could convince her to share her appointment time with me. You know we're across the street neighbors, Deanna. And close friends, too."

I whipped off the bandana I'd used to cover my hair in case, heaven forbid, one of my friends saw me outside in my current unglamorous condition. "You can see that I really need help. I'm desperate and throwing myself on your mercy." I gave a startled Phyllis a quick peck on the cheek. "You don't mind, do you, Phyllis? Your hair looks gorgeous, and there's no other client in the salon."

My neighbor and "close friend" Phyllis pursed her lips in an expression of disapproval, one that I'd been on the receiving end of too many times to count. "Well, I don't know. I'm not sure we're completely finished here."

"I was planning a quick break, but how can I say no to such a good customer?" Deanna gave Phyllis's hair a quick spritz of hairspray and turned her around toward the mirror so she could check herself out. "What do you think?"

"I like your hair parted on the left side, Phyllis," I said. "I think it makes you look younger. And we all need a change every so often."

That did it. Every woman over a certain age loves to be told she looks younger than she truly is.

"Do you really think so?" Phyllis asked, turning from side to side and patting her hair. "I don't know if Bill will approve. He likes me just the way I am."

"Of course he does," I said. "But a little change adds excitement to a marriage. He'll love it. Just wait and see." *And if he doesn't, he won't have the nerve to tell you so.*

"I've always wanted to thank you for being such a good neighbor, but I didn't know how. Your new look is on me. And Jim, of course."

Phyllis actually blushed. "That is so sweet of you, Carol. I don't know what to say."

"There's no need to say anything. Deanna can add it to my bill." I whipped off her cape. "You just scoot home and surprise Bill."

It took her a few minutes to process what I'd said, but finally, she responded. "I'll do just that. Thank you, dear. I guess I never realized how much you thought of me." She winked at me. "I'll let you know how it goes."

Oh, dear heaven, please don't.

Phyllis was out the door after one more spritz of hair spray for the road.

Deanna gave me an appraising look. "Okay, I owe you big time, girlfriend. You obviously need your hair done. But I know you too well. Something else is going on. Let me get you a clean cape to cover your clothes and mix up your color. I'll be right back."

I was planning to give her an (edited) version of the truth when I heard the shop door open. I turned around to see Nancy walking in. And right behind her was Elizabeth.

Chapter 22

The ability to speak several languages is an asset, but the ability to know when to keep your mouth shut is priceless.

"Hi, sweetie." Nancy gave me an air kiss. "I texted to see if you were free for coffee, but you didn't answer. That's not like you, and I got worried, so I cruised around town until I spotted your car. I hope Deanna has time for me today, too." She raised her eyebrows, which in "Nancy Speak" meant, "What are you doing here? I thought you were going to that fancy New York hairstylist."

"I'll tell you later," I hissed, beckoning to Elizabeth, who was standing by the reception desk. "Come and meet my friend Nancy Green. This is Elizabeth Peterson. She's working with Mack Whitman to film the reenactment."

"Mack Whitman? You must be kidding. How did he get involved? Does Jim know?"

"Elizabeth is an expert on historic reenactments," I said, ignoring Nancy's questions.

"Lovely to meet you," Elizabeth said, shaking Nancy's hand. "I'm particularly excited to be part of this event because my firm specializes in the American Revolution. I promise you that Celebrate Fairport will be something the whole town will remember."

"It's going to be so exciting," Nancy squealed. "And I'm sure the reenactment will inspire even more people to move to town. I can hardly wait."

"Nancy is a local real estate agent," I said. "She's always interested in anything that'll drive up housing prices. Don't you have a property to show now? You're always so busy." I motioned toward the door, hoping she'd take the hint and leave." Nancy ignored me, so I concentrated on Elizabeth.

"I'm glad you stopped in. We can talk to Deanna together."

"Talk to me about what?" Deanna asked, her face pink and looking harried. "Whatever it is, I hope it can wait." She tossed me a plastic cape. "Chit-chat time is over. Put this on and sit down."

I'd never seen Deanna like this. Phyllis had done a number on her.

"Yes, ma'am," I said meekly. Goodness. If she was this mad at me already, I knew I'd better tread carefully, or she might shave my head. Accidentally, of course.

"Nancy, you're one of my favorite clients, but I can't do your hair today. I'm already making time for Carol, who didn't call to make an appointment, either. I'm doing her on what was supposed to be my lunch break. After her, I'm booked solid for the rest of the day."

She turned to Elizabeth. "Please accept my apologies. If you're here to make an appointment my next opening isn't until early next week. My other stylist called in sick, and I'm not sure how long she'll be out."

"I'm not here to make a hair appointment," Elizabeth clarified. "My name is Elizabeth Peterson. I've been retained as technical advisor for the filming of the reenactment event for television. The producer, Mack Whitman, is looking for someone to do the hair and makeup for the principal actors, and I've heard you do excellent work. I assure you, you'll be generously compensated. Although you'll have to close your salon temporarily to accommodate the filming schedule."

"There's no way you can do that," Nancy said, looking stricken at the very thought of no access to her favorite hairstylist. "You'll lose all your regular clients."

So far, Deanna hadn't said a single word. She was probably in shock. She took a deep breath, then said, "Elizabeth, this is a fascinating offer, but I'm afraid I have to turn it down. There's no way I could risk losing a single one of my clients just for a brief moment in the spotlight. Several of them, like Carol and Nancy, are very close friends who've been coming to me for years."

She shook her head. "I'm sorry. My answer is no. Thank you. But, no."

I had to give Elizabeth credit. She wasn't the least bit flustered. "I'm sure we can figure out something."

"This is like a real estate negotiation between the seller and the buyer," Nancy said, making herself comfortable in the other styling chair. "I'll stick around for a while, Deanna, in case you need some help closing the deal."

I had difficulty controlling myself at that point. The only reason Nancy was sticking around was to find out as many juicy details as possible about the behind-the-scenes drama now swirling around Celebrate Fairport. Thank heaven, at least Phyllis was gone. She'd probably record the conversation on her phone for the "Fairport Patch."

"There are only three principal actors you'd be responsible for, not the whole cast," Elizabeth continued. "And only for the masquerade ball scene. I should have clarified that." She ticked off the characters' names. "Elizabeth Porter, John Porter, and Molly Walker, Elizabeth's maid. Local Fairport residents will play the non-speaking parts of other guests at the ball. My assistants can provide them with appropriate costumes." She made a note on her phone.

I could tell Deanna wasn't convinced. "I can't close the salon and let my regular customers down. It isn't fair to them, and in the long run, it could ruin my business."

She began combing my hair while commenting on the terrible shape it was now in. "I can tell you've been coloring your hair yourself, Carol. It looks terrible." Big sigh. "But I suppose I can fix it. You know what a miracle worker I am."

I shot Nancy a warning look to keep her big mouth shut about my dalliance with Monsieur Paul. "I'm sorry. I spent too much on Christmas presents, and Jim cut my allowance." Nancy rolled her eyes, and I wished with all my heart that she would leave.

"Let me text Mack and see if he has any suggestions," Elizabeth said. "He has a better idea of how many days filming the ball scenes will take. I'll be right back."

I bit my lip to keep from laughing. Mack was even more clueless than Elizabeth. At least she'd been at the actual event in 1779.

And just like an answer from heaven, the obvious solution to this stalemate popped into my head. It was so simple; I don't know why nobody else had thought of it.

"Deanna, all you have to do is close the salon for a few vacation days. All your clients will be fine with that as long as you tell them in advance."

"Carol, you are brilliant," Deanna said.

"I know," I said, trying to look modest and failing.

"I have an update," Elizabeth said, rejoining the conversation. "Mack estimates filming the ball scenes will only take two days, but he suggested you figure on three days just to be on the safe side. What do you think?"

"Carol has suggested I just close the salon for vacation. All my clients will understand that. I'll do the hair and makeup for the filming, as long as it's only for a few people. I'll need to have the dates as soon as possible so I can let everyone know."

"Deal," said Elizabeth. "You won't regret it."

I hope I won't, either.

Nancy's smartwatch alarm beeped. She leaned over and gave me a quick peck on the cheek. "I can't be late for my meeting with a possible buyer. Keep me posted about… everything. Deanna, I'll text you for an appointment." In a flash, she was gone.

"I thought I moved fast," Elizabeth said, laughing. "That woman is faster than the speed of sound."

"Only when real estate is involved," I said.

"So, if we're all set, Deanna, I have to leave, too," Elizabeth said. "I'll be in touch very soon with specific dates so you can plan your schedule."

For a split second, Elizabeth looked like she would fade from sight as usual. I shook my head, and she caught herself just in time. "I'll be back in touch," she repeated, walking out the door like a normal person.

Chapter 23

It's a scientific fact that if you wait long enough to make dinner, everyone will just eat cereal.

The next few hours flew by, and when Deanna was finished working her magic on me, I felt more relaxed—and guilt-free—than I had in months. "I promise I'll come every four weeks from now on," I said. "In fact, if I could just live here for the rest of my life, that'd be great with me."

Deanna laughed. "You'd get bored very fast." I handed her my credit card (not the secret one), and she zipped it through the machine. "I'm only charging you for Phyllis's appointment," she said. "You saved me from coming to blows with the most challenging client I've dealt with in a long time. That deserves at least one complimentary styling.

"But you have to promise me that if she shows up another time, I can call you, and you'll come right over and save me again. That woman is too much."

"I know. It's unfortunate. Phyllis has no idea how annoying she is." I signed the credit slip and left a very generous cash tip at Deanna's station. We hugged, and I was on my way home in a much better mood than when I'd left. I had the rest of the day with nothing planned, and I would enjoy every single second of it.

I'd barely turned into my driveway when my phone pinged. I squinted at the screen, and my good mood vanished.

Jim: Crisis solved. Checked out Elizabeth's website. Very impressive. Previous events are so realistic, like being at the original event. Lifelike actors, too. Lincoln at Gettysburg was incredible. Unanimous vote to have her organize banquet as long as she keeps us in the loop.

Ping.

Me: Glad to hear it.

Jim: I invited Mack and Elizabeth for dinner tonight. Hope that's okay.

A million snarky responses popped into my brain as I remembered the good old days, BJR (Before Jim's Retirement) when I often had spurts of culinary creativity that would result in an amazing (in a good way) meal cooked entirely from scratch. But now, with Jim often looking over my shoulder and making "suggestions" about my cooking, the fun is gone.

With any luck at all, something was hiding in the dark recesses of my freezer that I could defrost, nuke, and serve on a pretty Spode platter. Candlelight would hide the dust in my antique house and provide the right atmosphere, and we had enough wine. If I really got stuck, I had the best takeout restaurants in Fairport on speed dial.

You got this, girl. It's going to be fine.

My phone, showing no mercy, pinged again before I even reached my kitchen door.

Elizabeth: I'm in the kitchen with a big surprise for you. Hope you like it.

A surprise? From a ghost? I was almost afraid to find out, but curiosity got the better of me.

I opened the kitchen door and stopped dead. (Okay, poor choice of words.) Elizabeth was seated at my kitchen table with Lucy and Ethel snoozing at her feet. I sniffed the air. Something smelled wonderful.

I took a step forward, then stopped dead again. A very tall woman with a dish towel tied around her waist was stirring a large pot on my kitchen stove. Her back was to me, and she was humming to herself. (Off key, not that I'm being critical.)

"And now, we add more wine," she said in a high-pitched voice. "You can never have too much wine in Boeuf Bourguignon. Wine has saved many a novice chef from disaster." And she laughed.

OMG. It was Julia Child.

Chapter 24

I've been watching my weight. It's still there.

Elizabeth had a huge grin on her face. "Do you like your surprise, Carol?"

"Like it? I'm in shock. How did you…?"

"Even though I just crossed over a short time ago, I'm finding out fast that it's easy to make friends in the other world." Elizabeth guided me to a kitchen chair, and I collapsed onto it. "When Jim invited Mack and me to dinner tonight on the spur of the moment, I was very excited," she continued. "Then it dawned on me that he hadn't consulted you first. I know how much you avoid cooking these days, so l thought you could use some help. I put out an SOS, and Julia popped in and saved the day."

"Saved the day? You're not kidding! By the way, what's she making?"

"Boeuf Bourguignon, of course!" Julia trilled from the stove. "I haven't made it for such a long time. I'm having such fun." She beckoned me to the stove with a serving spoon. "Carol, taste this and tell me what you think. Is it to your liking?"

I was at a loss. What was the protocol here? Dare I dab my pinkie onto the spoon to taste the food? Was that considered gauche? Instead of dabbing, I stammered like an idiot. "I'm sure it's delicious, Mrs. Child. I don't need to taste it now."

"Oh, for heaven's sake," Julia said in that high-pitched voice that entertained and educated television viewers for years. "First of all, please call me Julia. I've been very rude, taking over your kitchen without asking your permission. My new friend, Elizabeth, was very persuasive and convinced me you'd be thrilled. But how can I be sure what I'm cooking is good if you won't even *taste* it? Maybe I've lost my touch."

"Just let me wash my hands first."

"You're so fussy," Julia said. "I once told viewers that if you're alone in the kitchen and drop the roast, you can always just pick it up and serve it anyway." She frowned. "I remember getting lots of mail about that comment."

Elizabeth was having trouble keeping a straight face during my exchange with Julia. Two ghosts against one mortal was too much for me. I grabbed the spoon and licked it. "Yummy," I said. "But there's one problem. Jim's never going to believe I cooked this myself. And I certainly can't tell him you stopped in to help me."

"Hmm. That is a problem." Julia furrowed her brow. "Let me think for a minute."

"I could tell Jim that I'm a gourmet cook and that Carol and I made the dish together," Elizabeth said. "Would that work?"

"I've got a better idea," Julia said. "You'll start the dinner by serving my favorite appetizer and cocktail." She laughed at my terrified expression. "Don't worry, Carol. You can do this." She reached into a huge shopping bag that had suddenly appeared on my granite countertop, rummaged around, and then held up a large bag of Pepperidge Farm Goldfish crackers. "Voila!"

"You're joking," I said.

"On the contrary, Carol, I never joke about food. I absolutely adore Goldfish crackers. The nice people at Harvard did a symposium about my life back in 2020 and spilled my secret. I especially adore serving these snacks paired with an upside-down Martini. They're the perfect way to begin every meal."

"We always just serve wine," I countered. "I don't even know what an upside-down martini is."

"I anticipated that, so I'm leaving you the recipe. It's effortless—one part gin to five parts vermouth. Serve on the rocks in an icy glass. I took the liberty of providing both liquors." She rummaged in her shopping bag and produced two bottles. "Do you want to practice making one while I'm still here?"

I felt like I was cramming for one of Sister Rose's final exams that I hadn't studied for. I could never pull this off. Darn that Jim for getting me into such a mess.

"I'll help, Carol," Elizabeth said, correctly reading my panicked facial expression.

"And dessert will be my famous floating islands." Julia opened the refrigerator and pointed. "I already made them. All you have to do is serve them. Don't worry, Carol. It's going to be fine. If you need me, I'll be around." She winked. "I won't be visible, of course. *Bon appetit!*" And she disappeared.

Chapter 25

Tip for a successful marriage: Don't ask your wife what's for dinner when she's mowing the lawn.

"Good morning, Carol." Jim gave me a peck on the cheek, waking me from a delightful dream I'm sure I'll never remember. "Breakfast is ready whenever you feel like getting up."

I sat up in bed and stretched carefully. No way was I taking a chance to start my day with back pain, much less disturbing the two snoring canines on Jim's side of the bed. I finished my morning ablutions as quickly as possible and avoided a glance at the old hag who stared back at me from the bathroom mirror these days.

"What's the occasion?" I asked as I caught sight of the feast Jim had prepared to start the day. Not only had he made blueberry pancakes—which we only have when Mike's around—but also an Egg Beaters veggie omelet as a heart-healthier alternative—and whole wheat toast.

I took a sip of Jim's always-delicious coffee and smiled. Now, I was awake. And suspicious. I know my husband very well. He had an ulterior motive and wanted to get on my good side before he sprang it on me.

"You're up to something, Jim Andrews. I can tell. Let me enjoy my breakfast before you tell me the real reason why you cooked this sumptuous meal for me." I wiggled my fork at him. "Don't try to deny it. I know you too well."

Jim attempted an innocent look, which I didn't buy for a single second.

"Can't a man simply thank his beautiful wife for cooking the most amazing dinner ever last night? Mack texted me early this morning, raving about your culinary skills. I know how much you hate to cook these days. You really went overboard, and I appreciate it."

"To clarify, I don't *hate* to cook. I just have different priorities now than when the kids were around. And as far as last night's dinner is concerned, I couldn't have done it without Elizabeth's help."

In more ways than you'll ever know.

"You two seem to be really hitting it off." Jim helped himself to a third pancake, and I pretended not to notice. "What do you know about her?"

I immediately filled my mouth with food and pointed to it, stalling for time.

Answer him, stupid. It's a natural question, and you're overreacting, as usual.

"I know she's an expert on American history. And she has a wide circle of contacts she can call on."

"What about Elizabeth's personal life?" Jim persisted. "Did you two talk about that while you were cooking together?"

"We were too busy trying to get dinner together to exchange girlish secrets," I snapped. "It was lucky for me that Elizabeth stopped by when she did. She felt bad about my having to deal with two extra people for dinner without any advance warning. Although *she* had absolutely nothing to do with issuing the invitation." I stabbed a piece of omelet for emphasis.

"I have no excuse. I handled the whole thing very badly. But Mack was pressuring me, and I couldn't say no."

"Mack? Why? Don't tell me he had a hankering for my home cooking, because I'll never believe you."

"He has a hankering, all right," Jim said. "But not for home cooking."

I took another swig of coffee. I had a feeling I was going to need it. "You've completely lost me."

"This isn't my area of expertise," Jim said, looking uncomfortable. "Mack told me in confidence that he's very attracted to Elizabeth, and he'd like to date her. He begged me to set up the dinner at our house and to ask you to find out whatever you could about her. He doesn't want to make a fool of himself and ruin their professional relationship if she's not interested."

"I can assure you that Elizabeth has no interest in any kind of personal relationship with Mack or anyone else," I said with a perfectly straight face. "She's here in a professional capacity for the reenactment, and when it's over, she's leaving."

I hope.

"You have to give me something more to tell Mack, so he'll stop acting like a lovesick schoolboy," Jim said. "I'm desperate."

I thought for a minute, and then the extra caffeine jolt kick-started my brain. "Tell Mack that Elizabeth was married years ago when she was very young. The marriage ended in tragedy. Besides, Elizabeth is too old for him. Trust me, she doesn't look her age."

Jim nodded. "That sounds plausible. I'll tell him that."

"So, do you forgive me?"

"Of course, silly. But please stop helping Mack out with his love life ASAP. Meddling in other people's love lives brings nothing but trouble. That's why I never do it."

Jim gave me a skeptical look, which I resented.

"It doesn't count as meddling if you know the person well, and have her best interests at heart. When Mary Alice tells me how lonely she is, my duty as one of her dearest friends is to do everything I can to cheer her up. I can't imagine becoming a widow at such a young age, the way she did, and raising two children on her own. She deserves happiness; if I can help her find it, I will.

"And by the way," I continued, pointing my now empty fork at Jim for emphasis, "if I hadn't encouraged Jenny and Mark's romance, they wouldn't be happily married now, and we wouldn't have the most wonderful grandson in the world.

"The situation with Mack is completely different. You already know what a jerk he can be, and you know nothing at all about Elizabeth. Admit it. I'm right."

"Okay, you win. You're right.

"Sometimes I wish I'd never gotten involved with the reenactment," he added. "It's getting much too complicated."

"I know you don't mean that. You're having fun. Don't let Mack Whitman spoil it for you. And, besides, I'm getting used to your beard. You never tried to grow one before."

"Want to check and see if it still tickles?" Jim asked with a familiar gleam in his eye. His cell phone pinged.

"Timing is everything," I said, handing him his cheater glasses so he didn't have to squint to read the text.

"It's Mack. He's arranged a meeting with Carla Grimaldi today at Town Hall and wants me there too." Jim sighed. "It's smart to involve the First Selectwoman in the filming, but I was hoping we could practice marching up Fairport Beach Road outside today, now that the weather's getting warmer."

"You have to go to the meeting," I insisted. "What if Mack says something stupid and ticks off the First Selectwoman? She could shut down the entire project."

Then you'd be hanging around the house again with a lot of extra time on your hands and driving me crazy. No way would I take a chance on that happening.

I could tell by Jim's expression that he was pouting because his buddies would practice marching without him. He hated being left out.

I had to think of something else fast, and fortunately, my fevered imagination didn't let me down.

"If you leave Mack alone today, what if he falls madly in love with Carla Grimaldi and wants you to act as a matchmaker? Do you still want to wiggle out of the meeting?"

"I never thought about either of those possibilities. I don't know which one is worse." A deep sigh followed. "I have to go to the meeting."

"Yes, you do. And maybe you could schedule a later marching practice today. It doesn't begin to get dark until at least six o'clock because of daylight saving time."

"Great idea. I'll text the guys now. Thanks, Carol."

"You're welcome." I blew Jim a kiss and headed toward the shower.

As the warm water poured down (I had a shower cap on so as not to destroy Deanna's handiwork), I congratulated myself on my clever manipulation of Jim's timetable. The idea of a romance between Elizabeth and Mack was so ridiculous it made me laugh out loud. I was sure my resident ghost had no idea that Mack had a crush on her.

It was odd that she wasn't invited to the meeting with the First Selectwoman. I wondered why she hadn't been included and what she was up to today.

Not your business, Carol. Be grateful you finally have some time to yourself for a change.

It wasn't until I was rummaging through my closet looking for my favorite pair of jeans (they have an elasticized waistband) that I realized that to get to Carla Grimaldi's office, both Jim and Mack would have to walk right by the portraits of the Porters. Jim went into Town Hall on a regular basis and had probably never noticed Elizabeth's portrait. But Mack just might. She was very young in the portrait, but still, the likeness was striking.

Suddenly, I was desperate to be invited to the meeting in case I had to do damage control. My usual roster of sneaky tricks came up empty. I scurried around the house, looking for one of Jim's event files. Maybe I could use the file as an excuse to crash the meeting. It was pretty lame, but no other brainstorms popped into my head, and time was ticking away. It would have to do.

Then, good fortune smiled on me via an incoming text from my dear husband.

Jim: Phyllis Stevens followed me to Town Hall, and I can't get her to leave. Help!

Me: Hang tight. I'll be there as soon as I can.

Jim: Thumbs up emoji.

Chapter 26

Oops! Did I roll my eyes out loud?

After giving the dogs a quick run in our yard and checking myself out in the bathroom mirror to be sure I looked presentable (thank goodness I'd had my hair done yesterday), I sprinted to Town Hall as fast as possible.

The places where the portraits of John and Elizabeth Porter usually hung were empty. Or maybe my eyes were playing tricks on me. I've heard it's possible to look at an object and have the brain not register what the eyes see. Something else for me to worry about.

Before I saved Jim from Phyllis, I had to save my own sanity. Where was Elizabeth when I needed her?

My phone buzzed with a text.

Elizabeth: The portraits are being cleaned. All is well.

Me: Phew.

Elizabeth: Yes.

I could hear the unmistakable voice of Phyllis coming from Meeting Room A. "Fairport has not had an official Historical Commission for over ten years. That's disgraceful for a town with so much history. Furthermore…."

I took a deep breath and tapped on the door. Four people were in the room: Jim, Phyllis, Mack, and a young man I didn't recognize. The young man looked terrified. Mack looked amused. Jim was looking down at his cell phone, probably wishing he was anywhere else but here.

Phyllis was sitting at the head of the conference room table. Her furious face was scary to behold.

I cleared my throat, and she stopped in mid-rant. "Carol, what are you doing here?"

Jim immediately jumped to his feet and held out the chair beside him. "This is my wife, Carol," he said to the young man who had been the object of Phyllis's rage. "Carol, this is Peter Robinson. He's an assistant to the First Selectwoman and is her liaison to the reenactment committee."

Peter Robinson didn't look old enough to hold a paying job, much less be an assistant to the First Selectwoman. His sandy hair and brown eyes reminded me so much of a teenage Mike that I wanted to hug him, but I didn't.

"It's a pleasure, Mrs. Andrews," he said, shaking my hand so vigorously I thought he'd break my fingers. "I understand from your husband that you're very involved behind the scenes in Celebrate Fairport. Thank you for your community spirit."

Behind the scenes is one way to put it.

Phyllis looked like she would explode, and I didn't want to be responsible for that happening.

"Thank you for saying that, Peter. But I assure you my love of Fairport pales in contrast to Phyllis Stevens and her husband, Bill. Phyllis and Bill have family roots in this town that go back decades. Maybe even centuries. Didn't you mention once, Phyllis," I asked, turning my innocent baby blues on her, "that one of Bill's ancestors actually was a signer of the Declaration of Independence?"

That was a bold-faced lie, of course. But what the heck?

"That's one of the family rumors," Phyllis said, going

along with my charade like I knew she would. "But we were never able to prove anything."

"Anyway," I said, turning back to Peter, "Phyllis and Bill's devotion to our town has inspired Jim, me, and our children ever since we moved to Fairport over thirty years ago. Without her knowledge and guidance, I don't know what the historic district would do."

Okay, Carol. That's laying it on a little too thick.

Mack finally spoke up. "That is most impressive."

"And another thing," I said. "Phyllis is too modest to tell you this, but she spearheaded the fundraising campaign to restore the Porter Mansion when it fell into disrepair recently from years of neglect." She did it by browbeating most of the population into contributing just to get rid of her, but I wasn't going to share that part.

"I was glad to do it," Phyllis said, looking modest.

Sadly, the goodwill I had tried to spread with a trowel didn't last as she thought of still another grievance. "When the reenactment was at the beginning of its planning, I emailed the First Selectwoman offering my help and expertise. All I got in reply was a form letter thanking me for my interest and saying her office would be in touch. That was two months ago.

"I still haven't heard anything, and today I read in the *Fairport News* all about this high-powered reenactment expert, Elizabeth Peterson, who's been hired as a technical advisor and reenactment expert." She leaned forward and wagged her finger in Peter's face. "You can tell Carla Grimaldi that no one alive knows more about the Battle of Fairport than I do." Phyllis glared at Peter, who inched back in his chair.

"If you want to film an authentic reenactment, Carol knows where to find me." She stood and marched toward the door.

I felt torn. On the one hand, Phyllis's know-it-all, high-handed attitude was enough to drive any normal person batty. On the other hand, I couldn't help but feel sorry for her. Knowing her as well as I did, she was expecting someone to speak up and stop her—namely me. And if I did that, Jim would never forgive me.

Oh, lord, how do I get myself into these messes?

I opened my mouth, preparing to risk my marriage for a good cause and sure Jim would forgive me later, when the door flew open, startling Phyllis and revealing First Selectwoman Carla Grimaldi. Standing right beside her was Elizabeth.

Chapter 27

I couldn't afford an Ancestry DNA kit to find out about my family. Instead, I posted on the Internet that I'd won the lottery.

Phyllis turned and looked at me, her hand still on the doorknob. I didn't get it at first, but then the lightbulb went off. Now that the First Selectwoman had arrived, Phyllis desperately wanted to remain at the meeting and hadn't a clue how to do it after her childish temper tantrum. Neither did I.

"I'm so sorry to be late," Carla Grimaldi said. "Peter has been keeping me informed, of course. I can't promise to make every meeting, but I'll try."

I doubted that anyone but me noticed that Peter was clearly surprised that his boss had shown up. Years of being a mom and reading my kids' body language hadn't been a waste of time. Peter tried to look professional, but the constant clicking of his ballpoint pen betrayed his nervousness.

This was the first time I'd seen Carla Grimaldi up close. She was much taller than I expected and had jet-black hair and piercing blue eyes. Dressed impeccably in a charcoal gray blazer, crisp white blouse, and black slacks, she was a woman who clearly commanded respect. I could see why she'd been such a successful Manhattan financial consultant before she turned to politics. I doubted we'd ever be close girlfriends, but I was glad to see our town government was in such capable hands.

"I'm Mack Whitman, the producer of the reenactment filming. I'm looking forward to getting your input on the project," Mack said, springing from his chair and shaking her hand. "I've heard impressive things about your accomplishments as Fairport's *first* First Selectwoman."

"Really, Mr. Whitman? I've only been in office a few months."

I bit back a smile. Carla Grimaldi was someone who didn't suffer fools gladly. Mack pretended not to notice a pro had just put him down.

"Please, call me Mack," he said. "And may I call you Carla?"

"That's fine," Carla said. "Believe me, that's better than what some people call me, especially the ones who aren't happy there's a First Select*woman* instead of a Select*man* in Fairport."

Carla beamed a hundred-watt smile in our direction. "It's nice to see you again, Jim. And you must be Carol. You have quite a reputation for crime-solving around here."

"Don't believe everything you've heard about me," I stammered like an idiot. "I'm just an ordinary wife and mother. And grandmother."

Jim laughed, and I resisted giving him a dirty look. Points for me, right?

Carla noticed Phyllis, still hovering near the door, and pointed to a vacant chair. "Please, come and sit down, Mrs. Stevens. I look forward to hearing everyone's thoughts on the reenactment, especially yours. I couldn't help but overhear that you're an expert on the history of Fairport. I know your family's roots in town go back generations."

Phyllis raised her head high and marched to the indicated chair, ignoring Elizabeth, who followed a few steps behind and sat beside her. We made quick eye contact, and she winked. Then she turned to Phyllis.

"Mrs. Stevens, I'm Elizabeth Peterson. It's a pleasure to meet you finally."

Phyllis immediately stiffened, and I held my breath, praying that she wouldn't start her tirade all over again. I saw Peter eyeing the door, probably figuring out how fast he'd have to run to make a break for it.

"I've heard wonderful things about you from Carol and Jim," Elizabeth continued. "I'm looking forward to your input about the Battle of Fairport. In fact…" she looked at Mack, "it just occurred to me that we should use Phyllis in the film. What do you think? Perhaps she could portray Molly, the woman who saved Mrs. Porter and the children from the British soldiers."

"I think using one of our local residents in the film is a brilliant idea," Carla Grimaldi said, smiling broadly.

"Oh, my goodness," Phyllis said, her face flushed. "I never thought…I never dreamed…I don't know what to say…."

"It's quite an honor," I added. "Although I'd be terrified to be in front of a camera if I thought millions of people would eventually see me. I'm more comfortable behind the scenes. But I bet you can handle it, Phyllis. You're a natural."

"I love the idea, too," Mack said. "Using a resident in such a prominent role will be an extra boost to the film's marketing."

"I'm not sure if I should do this," Phyllis said. "Although it might be fun."

Jim finally spoke up. "Before you decide, you should talk it over with Bill. If Carol had an opportunity like this, I'd expect her to ask my opinion before she made a decision."

I patted his hand. "Of course I would, dear. The secrets to a successful marriage are communication and honesty."

Phyllis stood up again. "You're right, Jim. I'll go home and talk to Bill right away. And if he says I shouldn't do it, I won't."

"I'll wait to hear from you," Elizabeth said. "I hope he says yes."

"Thank you, Elizabeth. I'll be back in touch with you soon." Phyllis scurried out of the room, a big smile on her face.

Chapter 28

My wife says I only have two faults. I don't listen and something else....

"What happened after I left the meeting?" I asked as I served my husband a generous portion of leftover Boeuf Bourguignon.

"You mean after you ran out of the meeting?"

"There was no reason for me to stay once Phyllis left," I said. "I did what you asked me to, and I'm not an official member of the planning committee."

Jim grunted and concentrated on his dinner. "This is even more delicious the second time around," he said when he finally took a break and put his fork down. "Why don't we eat like this every night?"

"Because Julia Child doesn't live here," I said with a sweet smile.

"Julia, *who*? I thought you and Elizabeth cooked this dinner together."

I realized, too late, what I'd just said—time for some quick damage control.

"Julia Child was a famous chef. She passed away several

years ago. Elizabeth and I used her recipe."

Good comeback, Carol. Phew.

Jim nodded, although I'm pretty sure he hadn't heard anything I said. It didn't really matter to him who cooked dinner as long as it tasted good and there was plenty of it.

"Why don't you and Elizabeth replicate this meal for the masquerade ball?"

I felt a slight movement behind me, followed by the sound of a pot lid crashing, which I knew was meant for my ears alone. Oh, boy. Julia wasn't thrilled about that idea. Or maybe it was Elizabeth. Either way, that menu was so not happening.

"I appreciate the compliment, dear, but neither Elizabeth nor I are professional chefs, much less licensed caterers. I don't think Carla Grimaldi and the Fairport Board of Health would approve."

"It was just an idea."

"It was a lovely idea. Thank you."

Jim waggled his eyebrows. "I can think of another way to thank me." He pulled me to my feet. "Leave the dishes for a while. I have an idea for a special dessert."

And that's all I'm going to tell you about that.

Chapter 29

Behind every angry wife is a husband who has no idea what he did wrong.

"Want a snack?" Jim whispered in my ear just as I was starting to doze off.

"You're such a romantic," I said, turning over and snuggling as close to my husband as Lucy and Ethel would allow. "No, thank you. I'm half asleep already, and I know I'll have sweet dreams tonight."

Jim sat up in bed, disturbing Lucy, who gave him a dirty look. The bedroom was dark, so how was I so sure she gave him a dirty look? Several years of being the recipient of Her Majesty's displeasure has made me an expert.

"You're welcome. But I didn't mean you. I'm hungry, and I want a snack."

I pulled a pillow over my head and pretended I didn't hear him.

"Come on, Carol, let's raid the refrigerator together," he whispered. "It'll be the perfect end to the day."

"My day already ended," I said. "And it's too early to start another one."

Bang, Bang, Bang.

"What's that noise?" Jim asked. "It sounds like someone knocking at our side door."

"Honestly, Jim, you are the limit," I said, my good mood gone. I figured it couldn't be my resident ghost because she's as quiet as…a ghost. But I couldn't deny somebody was knocking.

The dogs started to growl and then jumped off the bed to investigate. Jim followed after them. I grabbed the dust mop I always leave out to fool people into thinking I was cleaning the house and ran after them. It was the only thing I could find that could be a weapon. Ridiculous, I know. Don't say it.

The kitchen lights were all on, and I realized we'd neglected to turn them off when we decided to "retire" early. Lesson learned.

I skidded to a stop when I heard a man's voice. "I hope I didn't wake you. It looked like you were still up from across the street. Maybe I should come back in the morning. Phyllis doesn't know I left. Or maybe she knows and doesn't care."

Good lord. It was Bill Stevens. I couldn't remember any time Bill had shown up at our house without Phyllis. And in the middle of the night? Something was definitely up, and whatever it was, I wanted absolutely no part of it. Even though I was dying of curiosity, I was happy to let Jim provide the emotional support in the Andrews family for once in his life.

I was tiptoeing back to our bedroom when our front doorbell rang. Only one person would have the nerve to ring the front doorbell at this hour without giving it a second thought, and, right now, her husband was sitting at my kitchen table pouring out his heart to my husband.

I froze. Maybe if I flattened my body against the wall, Phyllis wouldn't see me, give up and go home.

Yeah, and pigs fly, too.

"Carol, I know you're there. I can see you. I have to talk

to someone, and you're the only person I could think of who wouldn't mind my coming at this hour of the night. Let me in."

I waited a beat, remembering all the times my late mother always chastised me when I asked her for something. "What's the magic word, Carol?" And I'd say, "Please."

The thought of standing in the dark in my pajamas, waiting for Phyllis to say the magic word, made me giggle.

"Carol." Phyllis's voice broke when she said my name. Was she crying?

"I wasn't sure who it was," I lied as I pulled our creaky front door open to admit our second uninvited visitor.

Phyllis sniffed her disapproval, and I knew she didn't believe me. She marched into the living room like she owned the place, expecting me to follow her. I noted how her voice was no longer shaking. She'd regained her composure in a remarkably short time, which made me angry.

"What's going on, Phyllis? Do you know what time it is? Jim and I were already in bed."

Phyllis sniffed again. "It's only nine-thirty, Carol. I assumed you'd still be awake."

I blushed.

Don't let her get the best of you, Carol. What time you go to bed in your own house is your business, and nobody else's.

"Is he here?"

"He? He who?"

"Don't play games with me. You know I mean Bill. He slammed out of the house in the middle of a conversation. His car is still in our driveway. It was logical that he'd come over here. So here I am." Phyllis sat on my sofa and gave me an angry look.

"Logical? To whom?" My head was starting to hurt.

"To Bill, of course. Although I think you're both to blame."

"Blame," I repeated. "Both of us." My head was now

ready to explode.

I sank onto my favorite wing chair and took deep breaths to calm myself.

"Carol, for heaven's sake, stop repeating everything I say. You sound like a parrot."

I clamped my lips together and sat on my hands to control my temper. I abhor violence, but there are exceptions, and I think the Good Lord might allow me a little leeway under the present circumstances.

The only light in the living room was from a streetlamp near our house. I turned on one of my Waterford crystal table lamps, ignoring the dust that emanated from the shade. In an antique house like ours, any accumulated dust is a part of history, and I never disturb it. That's my story, and I'm sticking to it.

Phyllis winced at the sudden glare, or maybe some dust got in her eye. "That's awfully bright."

"I know. That's the point. I want to see your face while you're explaining exactly what in the world you're blaming us for." I sat back and waited.

"If you and Jim hadn't started this ridiculous reenactment event, Bill and I wouldn't be on the verge of a divorce after almost sixty years of marriage. I hope you're happy now!"

Phyllis went on and on in the same vein for several minutes while I struggled to remain calm. I knew Phyllis was upset, but I never thought she'd become delusional.

Finally, I'd had enough. I got to my feet very slowly and stood over her. "I want you to leave. Now. You are no longer welcome in our home. Ever. Get out now, or I'll throw you out. I'm going to close my eyes and count to ten. When I open them, you'd better be gone."

I stopped and caught my breath. I hadn't ever been this angry, not even when Ray Thompson called Mike a thief.

"One. Two…."

"What's all the noise about? I was sound asleep." Elizabeth walked in wearing my favorite pair of pajamas. "Oh, hello, Phyllis. I'm surprised you're here at this late hour. I had a few things I wanted to follow up on with you after our meeting, if that's all right with you, Carol. I don't mean to take advantage of your hospitality."

Elizabeth's surprise appearance didn't bother me one bit. I was now breathing normally, and I was grateful she'd shown up (without texting first) before I had a heart attack or a stroke. I was confident my favorite ghost would diffuse the situation perfectly, and she didn't let me down.

"I saw your husband in the kitchen with Jim, Phyllis," Elizabeth said. "What a charming man. A little old-fashioned, perhaps. But most men are overly protective of their wives.

"Now, let's talk about today's meeting. I believe you mentioned...."

"Did Bill...did you hear anything he said? About me?" Phyllis asked.

"I wasn't deliberately eavesdropping on your private lives," Elizabeth said. "I overheard Bill say that he loves you very much and is sorry about the argument. I believe he's already left and is waiting for you at home."

"Thank you for saying that." Phyllis's eyes filled with tears. "I've been acting like a darn fool. Carol, please accept my apologies for everything I've said. I'm going home to my husband."

I grabbed Phyllis's hands, pulled her up, and spun her toward the front door before she could change her mind. "Good night, Phyllis." She nodded and left without another word.

I collapsed on the sofa, drained from two high-voltage encounters with Phyllis in less than twelve hours.

"I hope you're not angry with me for appearing out of nowhere the way I did just now. I thought you needed some help."

"Angry with you? Are you kidding? You were a lifesaver, Elizabeth. Saying what you did about Bill was exactly the right thing to calm Phyllis down. I don't know what would have happened if you hadn't shown up. I can't remember ever being so out of control before. I didn't know I had that much anger inside me."

"Even when Jim catches you smuggling one of your retail purchases into the house?" Elizabeth asked with a smile.

"He hasn't caught me yet unless you know something I don't."

Another issue bubbled up from my subconscious. "How long have you been here?"

"You already know that, Carol. Over two hundred years."

I shook my tired head. "I don't mean that. Do you hang around here most of the time?" *Spying on Jim and me.*

"No matter where I am, I can always sense when there's a change in the atmosphere around you. But I'm careful never to invade your privacy. Is that what you're asking?"

I nodded.

"Think of me as your older sister, keeping an eye on you."

"My very *old* older sister," I said.

Elizabeth laughed. "I envy your friendships. I never had a best friend, not even a dog. My maid, Molly, was the closest thing I had. She did her best to take care of me." Her face darkened. "And you already know what my marriage was like. You're a lucky woman."

"I know I am. I never had a sister, either."

Elizabeth kissed me on the cheek. "You do now. Good night, Carol."

Chapter 30

Day 12 without chocolate. Lost hearing in my left eye.

Jim was up, dressed, and out of the house the next morning before I had a chance to grill him about what Bill was so upset about. I wondered if he actually saw Elizabeth in our house last night. I'm learning that she can be visible when it suits her purpose and invisible at other times. This ghost business was very confusing.

I was on my second cup of coffee when there was a knock on the kitchen door. I peeked out and saw Bill Stevens with a black duffel bag.

I panicked. What if Bill and Phyllis were still arguing? Was he running away from home and moving in with us?

No wonder my darling husband left the house so early this morning. I was sure that Jim had offered Bill temporary housing if he and Phyllis still had problems today, the dirty rat.

The dogs saw Bill and barked hello. They love company. So do I, but not today.

I took another fortifying swig of coffee and opened the door a little. "This is a bad time, Bill. I'm on my way to Jenny's to babysit for CJ, and I don't want to be late."

Bill eyed my attire, and I remembered I was still wearing a bathrobe. Oh, well.

"Good morning, Carol. I'm sorry to come so early, but I wanted to apologize for barging in on you and Jim last night. Phyllis was too embarrassed to face you, but please know she feels just as bad as I do about our behavior last night."

Lucy and Ethel were whining now. They saw Bill and wanted to say hello. Traitors.

"May I come in? I won't stay long."

What the heck. I am, by nature, a forgiving person who never carries a grudge. I just prayed that Elizabeth was on duty to rescue me if I needed her. I opened the door, and Bill carried the bag inside and set it on the floor. Lucy and Ethel greeted him like an old friend, which surprised me.

"You look like you're running away from home," I said. "That would be a real shame after being married so long."

Don't think you'll be bunking here, buster, no matter what Jim promised you last night.

Bill burst out laughing. "Is that what you thought? I never realized what a vivid imagination you have." He reached down and gave each dog a chew bone hidden in his pocket. "I hope you don't mind, Carol. Whenever I notice your dogs running around the yard, I sneak over and give them each a treat. Phyllis thought having a dog was too much work, so we never had one."

The poor guy. Yes, I know I'd done a complete turnaround from my original, less welcoming behavior. But any friend of Lucy's and Ethel's is always a friend of mine. And, you know me. My curiosity is easily aroused—my imagination, too, which usually gets me into trouble.

"You're welcome to come and see them anytime you want," I said, sitting at the kitchen table. I waited until Bill was seated opposite me, then blurted out, "What's in the duffel bag?"

"Some family documents I thought Jim would find interesting. When I was a young boy, my grandmother used to tell my sister and me that we were descended from someone who fought in the American Revolution. She also mentioned a legend about a lost treasure but was a little hazy on all the specifics. Neither of us really believed her, but we loved hearing the story."

"A lost treasure," Bill repeated. "That's something we could use right now. The argument Phyllis and I had last night was about money. We have to tighten our belts for a while if you know what I mean."

Bill's here to ask for a loan. Change the subject right away!

"I never knew you had a sister," I blurted out. Probably tacky to be so intrusive, but it was the first thing that came to mind.

Bill's face clouded over. "Mary was a few years younger than me. Our grandmother raised us after our parents died. As we got older, Mary and Grandma argued constantly. Mary finally ran away from home, and we never heard from her again. She was only sixteen."

I grabbed Bill's hand and held it tight. "That's one of the saddest things I've ever heard."

"It was tough for a while. I missed her a lot. But the years passed, I met Phyllis, and she swept me off my feet." Bill laughed at his own joke, as did I.

"With the town doing the reenactment event, I decided to see what I could find out about my ancestor. I guess, in the back of my mind, I thought I might be able to find out something about Mary, too. A few weeks ago, when Phyllis wasn't home, I ordered a DNA test online. I was afraid if she found out what I'd done, she'd lecture me on how I shouldn't be spending money on such foolishness. I've learned over the years that keeping certain things private is the best policy for marriage, at least for mine. I bet you've never done that. Kept something from Jim, I mean. Not from Phyllis."

Who knew that Bill and I were such kindred spirits? Not that I'd ever admit that.

"Anyway, when I got the preliminary results back, they were so interesting that I decided to do more research. I found out that my grandmother wasn't telling a tall tale. One of my ancestors emigrated from England in the early eighteenth century and fought in the American Revolution. For the Americans, not the British."

"Are you kidding?" I squealed. "That's amazing. That's absolutely incredible. What was his name?"

"Edward Stevens."

"Edward Stevens," I repeated. "That's a nice, strong name."

"But what about your sister?"

"I realized that if she was still alive and wanted to find me, she could have done that easily. I'm right here, where our family's been for generations. I had to let that go."

Bill paused to gather his thoughts. "There's more," he continued, "if you have the time. I remember you said you were in a hurry to leave."

For a second, I'd forgotten what I'd told Bill. That's the trouble with fibbing. Sometimes, if you're not careful, you can trip yourself up. Then, the lightbulb in my brain went off. "Jenny will understand if I'm a little late. I'll text her and explain."

Especially since she wasn't expecting me in the first place.

I leaned forward in my chair. "Frankly, Bill, what you're telling me now made me totally forget today's schedule. I'd love to hear more. Please, go ahead. Would you like some coffee?"

"No, thank you. I have to get home before Phyllis returns from grocery shopping, so I'll speed my story along. It turns out that Edward Stevens fought in the original Battle of

Fairport. What do you think about that?"

"What do I think? My goodness, Bill, that's amazing. Phyllis must have freaked when you told her."

"I haven't told her."

"But why keep it a secret? She'll be thrilled to be married to someone who has an actual family connection to such a historic local event."

Bill looked uncomfortable. "That's exactly why I didn't tell her. You know how she carries on about her family's long-standing roots in Fairport. Her family, the Kimballs, emigrated here from England in the late eighteen hundreds. She's very proud of that and tells everyone who listens all about her lineage. I didn't want to take that away from her. She's built her life on it. Plus, it turns out that Edward was kind of a scalawag. When I checked him out more, I found out he was born in England, got in some trouble in his teens, and his parents disowned him. He traveled to America to start a new life."

"Maybe that's true. But that doesn't take away from the fact that he was a patriot. That's something you should be proud of."

I gestured toward the duffel bag again. "Is this your research?"

"Yes. I thought Jim might like to look at it for reenactment background information."

"I know he'll be thrilled," I said. "But I'm sure he'll want to share your research with members of the planning committee, including the First Selectwoman. Have you thought about that? The personal repercussions when the information becomes public?"

"You mean…Phyllis will find out? I'm a stupid old fool. I never thought that far ahead."

"You're lucky she hasn't discovered the bag already."

"I know. I hid it under an old tarp in the tool shed. It's my regular secret hiding place because she never goes in there."

"So far."

Bill nodded.

Then, I had one of my truly brilliant ideas. "Did you tell Jim anything about this last night?"

"No. Why?"

"It just occurred to me that—"

"That I can leave the bag here with you for safekeeping until I get up the nerve to talk to Phyllis? Carol, that's brilliant. Thank you."

"I'll keep your secret and your documents. I won't tell Jim anything until you give me the go-ahead." I put out my hand. "Do we have a deal?"

"Deal."

"Don't take too long to come clean with Phyllis," I warned as Bill began to cross back to his side of the street. "The longer you wait, the harder it'll be."

My new co-conspirator waved and disappeared into his house.

Chapter 31

The adult version of "head, shoulders, knees and toes" is wallet, glasses, keys, and phone.

"I hope I don't regret this," I told the dogs. "I don't like keeping secrets from Jim. And this one is a dilly."

Lucy gave me a withering stare. "Okay, okay. But you have to cut me a little slack. This situation isn't like hiding my newest pair of shoes or a dress way back in the closet. I'm doing a favor for a neighbor. In fact," I continued, "I'm doing a good deed by helping out Bill. Once he gives me the go-ahead, I'm handing over all his research to Jim. You and Ethel told me you like Bill. So, I'm helping one of your friends, too. You should thank me instead of criticizing me."

Lucy yawned and curled up with Ethel under the kitchen table to take her next nap. I assumed that meant I'd gotten her approval.

"I just hope Elizabeth has a chance to go through Bill's research before I give them to Jim."

My phone pinged, then pinged again.

Elizabeth: Can I come now?

I stared at my phone and muttered, "I don't know why

we're bothering with this texting business. You hear all my conversations, whether I allow you to or not."

Elizabeth appeared at the kitchen table before I could text a reply. "I'm your big sister. I'm responsible for you. Your business is my business."

"Correction: My business is your business until the reenactment is over. Then I get my privacy back. Agreed?"

Elizabeth nodded. I hoped she didn't have her fingers crossed behind her back. With ghosts, it's hard to tell.

"Did you overhear my conversation with Bill Stevens?"

"Yes. I couldn't help myself."

"I bet you didn't try very hard."

Elizabeth looked miffed at my sarcastic tone, and I realized getting on the wrong side of a ghost was a very bad thing to do. "I'm sorry. Sometimes, my mouth operates independently without any input from my brain. Just ask Jim. He'll tell you that's one of my only faults."

Elizabeth burst out laughing. "I can't stay mad at you for long."

I breathed a sigh of relief. "Neither can Jim, fortunately."

I handed the duffel bag to her. "Go through all the documents by yourself. I don't need to know what's in them. Let me know when you're done, and I'll figure out where to hide the bag until I can give it to Jim. Or back to Bill."

I hope you're all giving me credit for being so selfless. I was consumed by curiosity, but I knew it was in my best interest to claim ignorance of the bag's contents in case Jim accidentally stumbled across it. I had yet to come up with a satisfactory story to convince my husband that I had no idea how the bag got into our house, should that become necessary. But I was confident I'd come up with something. After all, I'd had years of practice.

"I have a special reason for wanting to look at these documents," Elizabeth said. "I'm hoping to find out what happened to the love of my life."

I opened my mouth, then immediately closed it. I didn't want to make the same mistake twice within a few minutes.

"I can tell by your face that you're bursting with questions. Go ahead, ask me."

"You're not talking about your husband, are you? I know love can turn to hate under certain circumstances, and I wouldn't blame you after everything he put you through. It would be so sad if you loved each other in the beginning, and then, when you couldn't give him a male heir, he punished you so severely that...."

"That I murdered him? Go ahead and say it, Carol. You know it's true." Elizabeth's eyes filled up. "No, I'm not talking about John. I never loved him. My father forced me to marry him because he was wealthy. Our family were farmers and barely made enough money from the crops we sold to support the family. I was the only daughter, and I guess you could say my father sold me, too."

"That's horrible. Despicable. How could a parent do that?"

"Please don't judge him too harshly. The time I lived in was very different from today. From a young age, the boys were taught how to plant and nurture the crops so they could take over from the father one day. Girls tended to the livestock when they were old enough, but their real job was to find a husband so the family wouldn't have to take care of them. My brothers and I were taught to read and write, but just the basics. Anything above fifth grade was considered a waste of time in my house. Except for the Bible. We read that every night after supper."

"I don't think I would have survived such a hard life. How did you do it?"

"It was all I knew."

We were both lost in our own thoughts for a few minutes

and then I heard a car on our gravel driveway. Being me, I immediately figured that Phyllis was back to start another argument. I always assume the worst possible scenario and am happy when it doesn't happen. It's like a little gift to myself that I don't have to hide from Jim. Don't bother trying to figure out the way my mind works. Even I don't understand it.

Instead of an angry Phyllis (or even a nervous Bill), it was Jenny and CJ.

I knew it would take Jenny some time to unbuckle the baby from his car seat. I had to get rid of Elizabeth before they came inside.

"My daughter and grandson are here. Jenny will surely see the resemblance between you and the portrait in Town Hall. She'll start asking questions that neither one of us can answer. You have to disappear."

My in-house ghost was gone in a single blink of my baby blues. Phew.

"This is a happy surprise," I said as Jenny carried a sleeping CJ into the house. "Was I supposed to watch CJ today and forgot?" *Or was the Good Lord having a little fun with me for fibbing about a babysitting commitment when I was trying to get rid of Bill?*

Jenny gently transferred CJ into my waiting arms. "I got called in to teach a class at the college this morning for another professor who's sick. I just took a quick shower, threw on some clothes, packed up the baby, and here I am. I didn't call first. Thank goodness you were home."

She looked around the kitchen. "What happened to your guest?"

"Guest?" Rats. Now, I had to lie to my own daughter.

"I was sure I saw someone at the kitchen table when I drove in." She gestured to the duffel bag, which I'd neglected to hide. "What's this? Are you hiding another new retail purchase from Dad?"

"Very funny. That's something *for* Dad, and your eyes must

be playing tricks on you." I raised my right hand. "I swear there was not another living human being in the kitchen with me when you and CJ got here."

Jenny gave me a suspicious look, similar to the ones I gave her when she begged to go out after dinner for a study date with a few friends; she wouldn't be out late because she knew she had school the next day, and it was only this one time, and I didn't want her to fail her test, did I? In those days, by the time Jenny finished talking and took a breath, I couldn't even remember what she wanted permission to do, which was precisely what she wanted.

Before I could protest my innocence one more time, CJ began to wiggle in my arms and then started to wail. "He's tired and hungry," Jenny said. "I'm sorry to leave him with you when he's cranky, but I'm sure that once he's fed, he'll go down for another nap. I'll be back in about three hours to pick him up. I left the food and the diaper bag on the back steps. Thank you so much. Love you." She gave me a peck on the cheek and dashed out the door.

"Don't rush," I called after her. "We'll be fine. Won't we, my most precious boy?"

I swear, when CJ heard my voice, he stopped crying, opened his big blue eyes, and winked at me.

"You little faker," I said, laughing and giving him a hug. After feeding him and changing him into a onesie that read, "I love Grandma," I settled my little angel down in the porta-crib for an afternoon snooze.

"I'm leaving the bedroom door open a tiny bit in case CJ cries, but don't take that as an invitation to make yourselves at home on the bed," I warned the dogs. Lucy gave me an innocent look, which I didn't believe for a single second.

I was tempted to stay in the bedroom and take a quick nap myself, but I knew I'd never sleep tonight if I did. Besides, I didn't want to take the chance of my darling husband coming home and finding me sleeping on the job, so to speak.

I tiptoed into the kitchen and realized the black duffel bag was still there. I sent Elizabeth a quick text to come and pick it up, but she didn't answer. Swell. What the heck was I going to do with it? Darn that Bill Stevens for putting me in this position.

Thank goodness CJ was fast asleep. He'd already proved that he had a knack for sneakiness, and he was just an infant! Maybe it was hereditary. I decided I'd better watch my step when he was around. I didn't want to give him a bad example.

I picked up the bag, and my back immediately protested. The sucker was heavy, and there was no way I was going to risk injury by lugging it around while I searched for a safe place to stash it. (In case any of you were wondering, my closet was already full.)

I walked around the house trying—and failing—to find the perfect place to hide the bag. I was just about to check upstairs when I heard CJ stirring. By the time I got to the bedroom, he was in a full-throttle wail.

"Poor sweetheart," I crooned, picking him up and cuddling him. "Did you have a bad dream? Or is it something else?" I gave him a quick sniff and determined all was clean in diaper-land.

After taking about a thousand walks around the house with my precious bundle (only a slight exaggeration), the baby and I were both exhausted.

"What we both need," I whispered to my precious grandson, "is a quick nap in the recliner." Not hearing any objections, I sat down carefully and snuggled CJ on my chest. And that's where Jenny found both of us, deep in slumber when she arrived two hours later.

Chapter 32

When you're a child, you make funny faces in the mirror. When you get older, the mirror gets even.

"How was your day?" Jim asked as he helped himself to a generous portion of lasagna (thank you, Stouffers) that I'd doctored up with some pasta sauce I'd found in the freezer (thanks to leftovers from a recent meal at Maria's Trattoria). I had become a non-culinary aficionado, but with buddies I hoped I could call on for help when necessary—like my new bestie, Julia Child—I wasn't worried.

I poured my husband a glass of red wine I'd found on sale at the local liquor store and pondered exactly how much of my day I could talk about. To be on the safe side, I wasn't ready to share Bill's morning visit until my friendly ghost had a chance to go through the duffel bag.

I felt the nudge of a doggy nose, followed by Lucy giving me a pointed stare before she looked at the floor. The black bag was now under the kitchen table. Did that mean Elizabeth had already gone through the contents and put it back after? Or had she not even looked at Bill's documents yet?

After years of practice, I was a pro at hiding retail purchases from my husband until he was in an especially good mood. But I had no idea what I was supposed to do now. Partnering with a ghost was tough.

"Jenny dropped CJ off today for a few hours," I said, figuring correctly that talking about our grandson was my safest answer.

"Lucky you," Jim said. "I wish I'd been here to see him."

"Jenny had to get home, or I'm sure she would have stayed longer." I patted Jim's hand. "Don't worry. You'll have plenty of other chances."

"Speaking of visitors, what did you think about Bill and Phyllis showing up here last night? Good grief." He took another sip of wine. "I hope they never do that again. I don't like being drawn into other couple's marital problems."

I bit my tongue. I wanted to tell Jim that I was mad at him for slinking out of the house early this morning, leaving me to deal with another visit from Bill and hear more Stevens family secrets. I pushed the black bag under the table a little more and prayed for ghostly guidance.

"It was much worse for me," I said. "While Bill was pouring his heart out to you in the kitchen, Phyllis was screaming at me in the living room. But fortunately, Elizabeth was able to calm her down."

I swear, as soon as the words were out of my mouth, I realized what I'd said. "Elizabeth texted me while Phyllis was here," I stammered, worried that Jim would wonder why she paid me an in-person visit late last night. Yes, I was getting paranoid. Please don't judge me too harshly! Keeping multiple secrets was overwhelming me.

"I suppose that freaked you out."

"Freaked me out? Why?"

Jim gave me a suspicious look. "You hate getting late-night texts, Carol. You always think somebody's had an accident or worse."

"True. But I was desperate for anything to stop Phyllis's rampage." My eyes filled with tears, which I hoped was great timing to get a little sympathy from Jim. "She said terrible things to me. You have no idea."

"I'm sorry you had to go through that."

"I blame the reenactment." *And you.* "I never wanted to get involved with the event, but now it seems to be dominating my life."

"About that," Jim said, looking uncomfortable. "I was going to tell you this later, but now's as good a time as any. Ray Thompson finally came to a planning meeting today."

"Ray Thompson? Why?"

Jim sighed. "You always tell me that I never listen to what you say. Sometimes, you don't listen to what I say, either. Ray Thompson is now the president of the Fairport Business Association. I already told you that."

I nodded, guilt all over my face.

"He's been having problems at the toy store, which is why he hasn't made any of our planning meetings, although we keep him up to date with our planning progress by text and email.

"Confidentially, I've heard business isn't so great, and he's looking for a buyer." Jim glared at me. "Not to be repeated."

"I know what confidentially means, dear. I won't say a word." *None of my friends would even care.*

Satisfied that my lips were zipped, Jim continued updating me on Ray. "The bottom line is, Ray's making time to oversee all the event planning from now on."

"How do you feel about that? I know you got a kick out of being in charge of all those marching practices."

"That's not going to change, Carol. I'm still running those. I'm looking forward to working closely with Ray."

"Better you than me."

"It was an interesting meeting," Jim continued, ignoring

my snide comment. "Ray made a very good point. He believes we need more local businesspeople involved in the reenactment than we currently do. He's right. We got too carried away with the filming and lost sight of the original historical focus of the reenactment."

Because I am a supportive wife, I didn't point out that the original idea of filming the reenactment came from the man I said "I Do" to many years ago.

"Is the filming off?"

"No, it will still happen. But Mack and Elizabeth aren't going to be involved in planning the reenactment from now on, including the masquerade ball. Ray insisted someone from the local business community should organize the ball."

"That may not be such a bad idea," I said, trying to be a team player for once. Although my resident ghost probably wouldn't agree. I wondered if she already knew the change in plans or if I had to give her the bad news later.

"I hope you feel that way when I tell you who the businessperson is."

"Don't keep me in suspense. Who is it?"

"Nancy."

Chapter 33

Some days, my supply of curse words is insufficient to meet my needs.

I carefully placed my fork on my plate, then left the table and walked toward the kitchen sink, carrying my dirty dish and cutlery without saying a single word. I turned on the water and began scrubbing the plate so hard it almost cracked in half.

"Carol." Jim's voice floated toward me from the other side of the room. "Did you hear what I said? Are you okay? I hope you're not upset about Nancy taking the lead role in the masquerade ball. She is one of the top real estate agents in town and is committed to doing everything in her power to promote it."

Yeah, and she's making herself rich at the same time.

I mentally slapped myself for my evil thoughts about my best friend.

"I was hoping you'd be happy about this," my clueless husband continued. "You've complained about the reenactment from the very beginning. I shouldn't have implied you were an unofficial committee member to Carla Grimaldi.

Now, you're off the hook."

I threw the sponge into the sink and said, in a very even, controlled tone of voice, "You're right, Jim. I have complained a lot about the reenactment. But Elizabeth Peterson is an expert on these kinds of historical events. Her insight is invaluable. I think it's a big mistake not to involve her."

"Well, as of now, she's out. Maybe the situation will change."

"You just don't get it. I'm on the hook more than ever. When Nancy needs help planning the masquerade ball, she'll reach out to me the way she always does. I'll be involved in the reenactment more than ever, something I did not want to do."

I know. Elizabeth and I had a deal about the masquerade ball. But that was totally under the radar, so to speak. Nobody else would know. Please don't criticize me for being more willing to help a ghost than my best friend. If you'd been around when Nancy and I were "co-chairing" our high school senior prom, perhaps you'd understand why. Let's just say that one of us picked out the color scheme for the decorations, and the other did everything else. I'll leave it up to you to figure out who did what.

Then, I went to bed before I said or did anything I'd regret in the morning.

For those of you who know me well, I suppose you're expecting that (A) sleep eluded me until I gave up trying, snuck into the office, and trolled on my computer for a while, or (B) fell asleep and had a doozy of a nightmare where Phyllis and Bill were in the middle of a boxing ring and I was the referee, while Nancy jeered at me from the audience and criticized me until I cried.

Ha! You're all wrong. I fell asleep instantly (rare, I know) and slept so soundly that I didn't even stir when Jim and the dogs finally joined me.

Chapter 34

I talk to myself because sometimes I need expert advice.

The next morning was a different story. I woke up with a start with the sun streaming in our bedroom windows (note to self: time to Windex them). I heard Jim calling out that he was leaving and something else I didn't quite catch.

OMG. What if he had found the black duffel bag, opened it, and wondered what the heck something that belonged to Bill Stevens was doing under our kitchen table? Or, even worse, what if he took it to the committee meeting to share before Bill finally found the courage to talk to Phyllis?

I jumped out of bed and raced into the kitchen. The bag was gone.

My phone pinged, announcing a text from my resident ghost.

Elizabeth: Bill has his duffel bag. Right now, he's telling Phyllis about his DNA history. It's all going to work out fine.

Me: Not if Jim found the bag and gave it back to Bill. He'll have questions I can't answer, starting with why it was under our kitchen table.

I felt a headache coming on, and I'd barely been up ten minutes. This was promising to be a humdinger of a day.

Elizabeth appeared, and I tried not to notice she was wearing my favorite navy-blue power suit. (My *only* navy-blue power suit, to be completely honest.)

"Relax, Carol. Jim didn't find the bag. Early this morning, I left it on the Stevens' front steps with a note for Bill suggesting he let Phyllis be the person who delivers the DNA information to the event committee. That way, she'll get the attention, making her happy. I signed it with your initials."

"Why did you do that? When she sees it, Phyllis will be over here again screaming at me for interfering."

"Please stop worrying, Carol. I know for a fact that Bill destroyed the note before she got out of bed. And Phyllis didn't see me this morning, either, if that's your next question."

"Speaking of that, Phyllis saw you here in *my* pajamas the other night." I paused to let the implication sink in, but Elizabeth didn't react.

"Phyllis saw you here in the middle of the night when she was having a meltdown. How am I going to handle her when she grills me about why you were here?"

"In her memory, we communicated by text, not in person, just like you told Jim. That was brilliant, by the way."

"Thanks, I think. But how…? I don't understand."

Elizabeth laughed. "There are many things I still don't understand about this new gig, as you would call it. I'm new to this ghost business, so I'm learning on the job."

"And another thing," I said, fortified by a few sips of coffee, which had cleared some of the nighttime cobwebs from my brain and staved off a possible headache, "I'm not thrilled that Nancy is in charge of organizing the ball, and you're not. How could you let that happen?"

"Why, Carol, I believe you're jealous of your best friend."

"That's ridiculous," I sputtered. "It's just that I know

Nancy has no event-organizing skills. Don't get me wrong, she's an excellent real estate agent, though. We all have our strengths and weaknesses.

"I just want Celebrate Fairport, especially the masquerade ball, to go smoothly, without any hitches."

"So do I." Elizabeth checked her phone. "I have to go. I'll check in with you later."

"I still have questions about our deal now that you're not supposed to be involved!"

"I'll answer them later," Elizabeth said, fading from sight.

"How you appear and disappear that way is one of them," I yelled after her.

Chapter 35

I just posted a selfie on Facebook, and friends told me to get well soon.

"Let's go over today's to-do list," I told Lucy and Ethel as I finished my low-fat, tasteless breakfast smoothie. "I'm trying to lose five pounds, and this time, I'm determined to stick to my resolve until they're gone for good."

Lucy gave me a skeptical look, telling me loud and clear that she'd heard all that before, and unless attending to doggy needs was at the top of my to-do list, she wasn't interested.

"People who think a dog is man's best friend have obviously never met you."

Lucy yawned and headed to a sunny spot in the bedroom for a nap. Sweet Ethel licked my hand in sympathy, then joined her.

"Fine. I'll plan my own day without any input from either of you. Fingers crossed that it will be less stressful than yesterday."

After a hot shower to get the kinks out of my aging body, I felt so chipper that I laced up my sneakers for the first time in who-knows-when, determined to walk ten thousand steps, starting today. I'd lose those annoying extra pounds in a week. Yes!

Humming the music from *Rocky* to myself (when Sylvester Stallone finally conquers running up the steps of the Philadelphia Museum of Art), I opened the side door. I almost tripped over the newly appointed chairwoman of the Celebrate Fairport masquerade ball, sitting on the steps.

"Nancy," I said with as much sarcasm as I could muster on the spur of the moment, "what are you doing here? You must have *sooo* much to do these days. I'm surprised you have any spare time for me." I stepped around her. "I'm off to do my ten thousand steps, and you're in my way."

Nancy burst into tears. "Oh, Carol, I'm in such trouble. You have to help me. You're the only one I can turn to. I didn't want this job. I'm not good at organizing events!"

I nodded. "True. As I recall, you even needed major help with your own wedding."

I waited a beat. "So, why are you doing it?"

With some difficulty (not that I'm criticizing her), Nancy stood up and threw her arms around me. "I swear, this is not my fault. My boss forced me into it to promote Dream Homes Realty. I couldn't say no. I was afraid he'd fire me."

Her voice was getting louder. Then, she started to hiccup. "May I have a glass of water?" *Hiccup.* "Please, Carol." *Hiccup.* "I need water!"

"Oh, all right. Come on in. But you can't stay long. I have to do my ten thousand steps."

Nancy drained the glass I handed her and immediately hiccupped again. Then she started to cry. "I'm doomed," she said. *Hiccup. Sob.* "Doomed." *Hiccup. Sob.* "And you're mad at me. I can tell. I can't stand it when you're mad at me."

We sat at the kitchen table for a minute or two while Nancy tried to get herself under control.

"For Pete's sake, you're not doomed."

"I'm not?"

"No. You're not hiccupping anymore."

"I'm cured, thanks to you. You're always there to save me when I need you." Nancy stuck out her lower lip. "But I can tell you're still mad at me."

By this time, Lucy and Ethel, curious about what was happening in the kitchen on the off chance that it involved food for them, had strolled in from the bedroom. They immediately ran to Nancy's side and nuzzled her for some affection. She's one of their favorite humans. Lucy gave me a reproachful look, clearly indicating whose side she was on. Humph.

I gave in. "If my dogs still love you, I guess I do, too. You know I can never stay mad at you for very long."

Nancy threw her arms around me. "So, you'll help me? Please say yes. I'm in a terrible bind, and we can pull this event off together without a hitch."

"Together? I didn't say that. I said I forgive you for taking over the ball because you were forced into it."

I suddenly realized I had the perfect excuse for refusing Nancy's pleas. "But I can't help you. Jim told me that Ray Thompson only wants people from the business community involved, which leaves me out. Besides, you know there's no love lost between Ray and me. He'd hit the ceiling if he caught just a whisper of me helping out."

"That's ridiculous. Ray would be glad that you're helping out. You're just exaggerating, the way you always do."

"That's your opinion. I have no intention of testing the limits of Ray's temper.

"And speaking of Ray's likes and dislikes," I continued, "I understand he doesn't want Elizabeth Peterson involved in the planning anymore. In my humble opinion, he's making a huge mistake. She knows more about the original event than anybody else."

Oops. Too Much Information, Carol.

"She does? Why?"

I thought fast.

"Because she's a professional reenactment specialist, Nancy," I said. "I'm sure she's organized tons of formal events for other clients."

"Including a masquerade ball?"

I was losing patience. "Why don't you ask her yourself?"

"Good plan." Nancy whipped out her phone. "Do you have her cell number? I'll text her right away. Ray's already talked the committee into hiring Billy Baxter to cater the ball. I hope he's the right choice."

"Billy Baxter? Who's he?"

"The new chef at the Fairport Inn and Suites. He's very creative, according to Ray. A real culinary genius. I'd like to bring Elizabeth with me to discuss the menu, but I don't have her number." Nancy handed me my phone. "Please."

I pretended to go through my contact list. "Sorry. I don't have it." Which was absolutely true. There was no record on my phone of a single text from Elizabeth. I'd love to know how she pulled that off, but she probably wouldn't tell me.

"How can you not have it? Isn't Elizabeth your new buddy? Would Jim have it? I'm desperate."

"Nope. Sorry."

Nancy gave me a dirty look. "Oh, I get it. You don't want to share her contact information. And I thought we were best friends forever."

Good grief.

"That's not it. I don't have Elizabeth's number because she never gave it to me. She just stops in if she's driving by and sees my car in the driveway. I never know when she's coming."

"Isn't that a little rude?"

"I told her she could because she doesn't know many people in town. I wanted her to feel welcome. She's leaving Fairport right after the filming is over."

Fingers crossed.

I held my breath. Nancy's one of the few people who can usually tell when I'm "altering the truth," but it looked like this time, she believed me.

"That's very sweet of you, Carol. If you see her today, please ask her to text me."

"Only if you run her name by Ray Thompson first. He objected to her involvement because she's not from the Fairport business community."

"Not a problem," Nancy said, looking a lot better now than the hysterical woman with the uncontrollable hiccups she was a few minutes ago. "If Ray and my boss want the Celebrate Fairport masquerade ball to be a success, I'll tell them in no uncertain terms that I need Elizabeth's help. If she's not involved, I won't be, either."

"I thought you were afraid of losing your job."

"Not anymore. Thanks to talking to you, I've realized they need me a lot more than I need them. And I need Elizabeth Peterson. If they give me any grief, I'll quit Dream Homes Realty and start my own real estate firm."

Nancy's thought process often amazes me. I also had my doubts about her ability to run her own business, but I kept them to myself. I hope I get friendship points for that.

Her phone pinged with a text. She glanced at it and muttered a few words I'd never heard her use before.

"I gotta go. Ray's demanding I set up a food tasting for all committee members within the next two days at the hotel to finalize the menu for the ball."

Her phone pinged again. She read the text and rolled her eyes. "Good grief. Now Ray wants a champagne fountain."

"At the food tasting?"

"Don't be silly. He wants it at the ball."

I started to giggle. "I don't think they had a champagne fountain at the original event."

"No kidding." Nancy grabbed her phone, purse, and keys. "Ray is a total jerk, and this whole project is a nightmare. His constant texts and condescending attitude are driving me nuts. I am *not* his personal flunky. He's called another committee meeting in half an hour when I'm scheduled to show a house to a prospective buyer. How am I supposed to be in two places at the same time?

"Right now, I'm so mad at Ray, I could kill him."

Nancy slammed the kitchen door so hard on her way out that she scared Lucy and Ethel, who both started barking.

"It's okay," I said, squatting down to reassure them with some head scratches. "Nancy was very angry, but not at you. She loves you. And you know how dramatic she can be sometimes. She didn't mean what she said."

As I struggled to get to my feet, Lucy stared at me in a way she never had before. Don't tell anybody else, but that look scared the you-know-what out of me.

Chapter 36

Life is too short to waste time matching socks.

I was folding laundry when Elizabeth appeared unannounced.

"I hope you came to help me, even though you didn't text first." I handed her a bottom sheet with those annoying elastic corners that I could never get right. "Try folding this. I bet you won't be able to do it." I turned to get the matching top sheet out of the dryer.

"All done," she said, handing me the perfectly folded sheet. "That wasn't hard at all."

I grabbed the sheet and put it on top of the laundry pile. "I'm not even going to ask how you did that. But the longer you stick around here and prove how good you are at being a domestic diva, the more housework I'm going to give you, so be warned."

Elizabeth laughed. "Let's just say I used some skills you haven't acquired and leave it at that." Her face turned serious. "I was eavesdropping on the conversation you and Nancy just had. I'm worried."

"Worried? About what?"

"About Nancy. She was so angry."

I dismissed her concerns with a wave of my hand. "That's just Nancy. She's always had a flare for the dramatic, even when we were kids. She'll have gotten over her snit about Ray in an hour, and all will be well."

Elizabeth looked unconvinced.

"Instead of worrying about what Nancy said, why not figure out how to work with her to make the masquerade ball a success? Wouldn't that be more productive?"

"That's a lot tougher than folding a fitted sheet," Elizabeth said. "Ray sees me as a threat to his authority."

"Typical insecure male," I said. "I'm sure you'll figure out a way to pull it off. Maybe you could just whisper suggestions in Ray's ear without him knowing who's doing it like you used to with me."

"Very funny, Carol. I hope it doesn't come to that."

"You're taking the ball reenactment too literally. There won't be a real battle with people dying to ruin it this time. All the guests at the ball, including you, will have a great time. I don't know about ghosts, but I can assure you that not many humans get a second chance for a happy ending."

Elizabeth looked shocked that I was being so critical, and I hoped I hadn't gone too far. Finally, she said, "You're right. I'm allowing myself to get caught up in reliving that original, horrible night instead of concentrating on the fact that this whole thing is just make-believe."

"That's it exactly."

My phone pinged with a text. "Give Nancy this number and ask her to text me. We'll handle Ray together."

I nodded. Before I even started texting Nancy, Elizabeth had disappeared.

"Your pal Elizabeth will keep an eye on Nancy," I told the dogs when they woke up from another nap. "We don't have to worry about her anymore."

They both responded by racing to the side door. Worried that Phyllis or Bill might be paying another surprise neighborly visit, I peeked out to see if I needed to make myself scarce.

Not the neighbors, but my husband. He was home a lot earlier than usual, and he looked miserable.

Chapter 37

My husband told me I should embrace my mistakes. So, I hugged him.

I knew that expression well. I hadn't seen it since Jim retired several years ago.

Resisting the urge to flee and let the dogs handle the situation, I quickly prayed for help from St. Jude. He's not the patron saint of retirement (there isn't one, which is surprising), but he's always there when I need him. I sure needed him now.

Don't stand at the door and wait for him, stupid. That's the worst thing you can do. Leave him alone for a while. You know how he hates it when you fuss over him.

Taking my own good advice and the clean laundry, I beat a silent retreat to our bedroom. I took my time replacing the used towels in our bathroom with fresh ones, hung up clothes (both Jim's and mine), matched up socks (shocking, I know), then crept toward the kitchen and snuck a peek.

Jim was sitting at the table, staring at a large glass of red wine. I held my breath. Finally, he raised it to his lips with shaking hands and took a tentative sip.

That did it. Jim never drinks before dinner. Whatever

happened was an emergency, so I decided to take my chances and interrupt him. I squared my shoulders and walked into the kitchen, a phony smile plastered on my face.

"My goodness, that's a full glass of wine you've got there. There's enough for both of us. Although it's a little early in the day for me."

"It's five o'clock somewhere, isn't it?" He pushed the glass in my direction. "Here. I don't really want it. I thought it would help, but I was wrong."

"I don't want it either, Jim. What I *do* want is for you to tell me what's wrong. Clearly, you're upset about something."

"Upset. Angry. Disgusted. Pick one. Or all of them. It doesn't matter."

"I'm happy to do that, but it would be helpful for me to know what's going on first."

"It's this darn reenactment. It started as a fun project. Believe me, it's not fun anymore."

I pulled out a chair, sat down, and waited for more details. Jim spoke after what seemed like hours but was probably only five minutes (I am not a patient person).

"The whole project changed when Mack got involved. And he brought in Elizabeth Peterson."

I clamped my lips shut in case I was tempted to remind my dear husband how Mack got involved in the project. There was no use rubbing salt in his wounded ego. Or something like that.

"Where is Mack? You haven't mentioned him in days."

"Once he scouted filming locations and was booted off the planning committee by Ray, he went back to New York. But Elizabeth's still here." Jim ran his fingers through what was left of his hair. "That's part of the problem."

You're not kidding. She's always been here. We just didn't know it.

"When Ray took over the committee, he and Elizabeth clashed immediately."

"She's a reenactment specialist," I pointed out. "Ray should be grateful for her help."

"Agreed. Especially since Elizabeth wasn't charging the town for her time and expertise, but Ray wanted her out. Instead, he recruited Nancy to run the masquerade ball. She insists on bringing Elizabeth back, or she won't do it." He gave me a knowing look. "I bet you already knew about that."

My husband had obviously forgotten that we had discussed this already, and when I reiterated how Nancy could really use Elizabeth's help, Jim agreed. And not only that, he encouraged me to suggest that to Nancy. Forget about selective hearing. Jim had selective memory, too.

"This afternoon's meeting was a nightmare with Nancy and Ray arguing about who was doing what, who had the power to make decisions about the ball, and on and on. I thought they'd come to blows."

Jim grabbed the wine glass. "To better days," he said. He took a healthy swig and made a face. "Ugh. This stuff is awful. Where'd you buy it?"

"Fairport Liquors," I said. "The owner recommended it."

"He probably wanted to get rid of it and foisted it off on you."

Let it go, Carol. Just smile sweetly.

"If the arguments between Nancy and Ray weren't bad enough," Jim continued, "guess who else was there to add to the chaos?"

I started to respond, but Jim interrupted me.

"Phyllis and Bill, that's who. It turns out that Bill discovered through DNA testing that he has an ancestor who fought in the Battle of Fairport. Carla Grimaldi immediately invited him to serve on the committee, and naturally, Phyllis came along with him. As the 'local historical expert,' Phyllis had a few opinions to share about the project, especially the ball, which made everything even worse.

"I'm quitting the committee. I want nothing to do with it anymore."

"Jim Andrews, you are certainly not quitting the committee! It sounds like you're one of its few rational members. We just have to think of a way to defuse the situation between Nancy and Ray. Nancy knows she needs Elizabeth's help to pull off the actual ball, or it won't happen. Why not a compromise? The committee can organize the soldiers' march from the beach and the battle at the Porter Mansion and leave the party planning to Nancy and Elizabeth. All Ray has to do is keep his mouth shut and let them do their job. Then he can take all the credit."

"Sometimes, Carol, you're an absolute genius."

"Only sometimes? You need to pay closer attention."

"You're absolutely correct. Starting right now."

Jim pulled me to my feet. "I know just how to do it."

And that's all I'm going to tell you about that.

Chapter 38

I'm glad you're learning to laugh at yourself. It was getting kind of awkward for the rest of us.

I'm happy to report that Jim and I faced the following morning with an unusually positive attitude. Chalk up one for marital bliss. How long our good moods would last remained a mystery, but I was grateful for what few seconds I could grab. Jim even let me sleep in a little more while he walked and fed the dogs, and made the coffee. And I actually went back to sleep—the first time I'd done that since I can't remember when.

Lucy and Ethel, however, were having none of my lollygagging around. Even though I knew Jim had provided both of them with enough kibble to see them through the entire day, they both paced in front of the bed and then starting whining like they were starving to death. Humph.

I reminded myself that all good things must come to an end, then stumbled out of bed to splash cold water on my face and get ready to meet the day.

Mumbling to myself about how spoiled our two canines were—*and whose fault was that?*—I shuffled into the kitchen, hoping for a ghost-free, drama-free start to the day.

I threw a handful of kibble into each dog bowl, then announced, "That's all you're getting until supper. I mean it."

Lucy gave me her usual stink eye and Ethel her plaintive look. Ha! "I'm not falling for that today. But good try."

I sipped a cup of Jim's delicious coffee and debated about turning on my phone, which had been having a nice nap in its charger since last night. Was I ready to have the outside world intrude into my good mood?

No.

Was it possible for me to spend an entire day without glancing at text messages, even once?

Doubtful, but I could give it a try.

What if Jenny needs you? Or Mike texts from Florida? Are you willing to cut yourself off from your own children?

No way could I take that chance, assuming I could find my glasses, which were hiding under yesterday's mail.

As I admired the screen saver of my darling grandson, I scrolled through my messages, most of which I immediately deleted or would answer later.

Ping.

Rats. Just when I thought I was safe.

Praying the text wasn't from Nancy—please don't ever tell her that—I squinted at the screen and felt (almost) as happy as I did last night.

Claire: We're home from Florida, and I'm starved for news. Got time for a catch-up lunch today?

Ping.

Me: Sure. Great! Where?

Ping.

Claire: Maria's at noon?

Ping.

Me: How about 1:00 at the Fairport Diner instead? I'm craving a cheeseburger.

Ping.

Claire: Works for me. Might not for Mary Alice, though. You know she's all about eating healthy.

Ping.

Me: She can have a veggie burger!

Ping.

Claire: Great idea. I texted Nancy. She's not responding. Is she okay?

Ping.

Me: Long story. See you at the diner at one.

Ping.

I felt like a huge burden I hadn't realized I was carrying had been lifted from my shoulders. Claire was our group's no-nonsense voice of reason, and Mary Alice was the kind one. They loved Nancy as much as I did. I was confident that together, the three of us would figure out a plan to help Nancy with her current problem.

The "old me" would have been upset that I was obviously the last one Claire invited to lunch. But the "new me" shrugged it off. I just thought I'd mention it in case any of you were concerned my feelings were hurt.

Chapter 39

I'm sorry. I didn't mean to push all your buttons. I was looking for "mute."

The smell of hamburgers sizzling on the grill assaulted my senses the minute I opened the door to the Fairport Diner. Some people might find that odor offensive. Not me. No siree. My mouth began to water in anticipation of that first delicious bite. I stopped at the door, closed my eyes, and inhaled deeply, causing a collision with the patron behind me.

Mortified, I turned to apologize and saw that it was Claire.

"Hey, lady, you need to signal when you come to an unexpected stop," she said, looking stern. "You could hurt an innocent person, who'd then hire a lawyer to sue you for pain and suffering."

"That would be especially easy if that innocent person happens to be married to a lawyer like you are," I said, laughing.

Claire threw her arms around me and gave me a big hug. "I forgive you. You always were a little klutzy, even when we were kids."

Humph.

Realizing our reunion was holding up a line of impatient patrons, Claire signaled to a harried server passing by with a full tray of food, who pointed us to a nearby booth. "I'll be with you as soon as I can," she said.

"Let's get out of the way and sit down before we cause any more trouble," I whispered. "People are giving us dirty looks."

"You're imagining things, Carol. You always were too sensitive for your own good. Nobody's looking at us."

Good old Claire. We'd been together less than five minutes, and she was already on my case. Sometimes, she carried her "voice of reason' a bit too far to suit me.

Take the high road, Carol. Act like a grown-up for once in your life.

"Where's Mary Alice? Isn't she coming?"

"She should be here in about ten more minutes." Claire scanned the menu, then snapped it shut. "I already know what I want, so let's catch up. What's going on? Is Nancy all right?" She searched my face. "Are you?"

"I'm okay," I said. "No, I'm not. It's this darn Celebrate Fairport event. What a nightmare. You have no idea how horrible...."

"Stop right there, Carol. If you're going to complain again about the reenactment, I heard it all from you before Larry and I left for Florida. I knew you couldn't resist getting involved, even though you swore you wouldn't."

"That is so unfair. You have no idea...."

"I know. I have no idea how much you're suffering. For Pete's sake, Carol, tell Jim, not me, if you have problems with the reenactment. I just got home, remember?"

"Before you jump down my throat, Claire, I think it's only fair that you listen to what I have to tell you. For once in your life, stop criticizing me!"

By then, I'm embarrassed to admit that my voice was just a few decibels louder than my normal ladylike tone. I sensed that every single patron in the diner was staring at me. Why did Claire always have this effect on me? Well, no more.

I leaned across the table and hissed, "We're not doing this again. Or ever. I'm done."

"Done? What do you mean?"

"I mean that we will no longer behave like we're in third grade. This pattern has been going on since we were little kids, and it's about time it ended. First, you'll let me talk without interrupting instead of immediately jumping down my throat like you always do. And I'm going to make an effort to behave like a reasonable adult for a change instead of an emotional crybaby."

I stuck out my hand. "Deal? Or don't you think you can handle your end of the bargain?"

"Deal," Claire said. "I hate to admit it, but you're right. Why is it I only act like this with you? I've been really unfair to you for years. I'm sorry."

"I'm sorry, too. I'll try to act like a grown-up, if you will."

"It'll be hard, but I'll try."

"You try first," I said, laughing. "I'll follow your lead."

By this time, we were both laughing hysterically.

Claire wiped her eyes with a napkin. "I have to admit that no one can make me laugh as much as you do."

"Thank you. I want this to work, but it won't be easy. As Sister Rose would say, 'Old habits die hard.'"

That made both of us laugh even more.

Then, I had one of my frequent brilliant ideas. "How about we set up a check-in system, like Jim and I used to have." (Note to self: need to get this going again on the home front.)

Claire eyed me with suspicion. "Explain, please."

"We'll create a *Honey Don't List* of the things we each do that drive the other person up the wall. We'll promise to refrain from our bad behavior for a week. We'll be together a lot since you're back, so keeping tabs on each other will be easy. The first person who reverts to that behavior has to clean the other's house the following week. Including the bathrooms. What do you say?"

I grabbed another napkin and scribbled, "Claire must not criticize or correct Carol for one week. No matter what." I pushed it toward her. "Agreed?"

"Fine, as long as Carol…."

We were interrupted by Mary Alice, sliding into the booth beside Claire. "Are you two finally finished arguing? I was getting tired of waiting. I've been listening to you two squabble nonstop since grammar school."

"We've just agreed on a temporary cease-fire," Claire said.

"The cease-fire was my idea," I said, wanting to be sure Mary Alice gave me credit for taking the high road first.

"I don't want to know the details," Mary Alice said. "We have more important things to talk about right now.

"Nancy texted me this morning, begging for help planning the masquerade ball. She was desperate, so I agreed for all of us. I had no choice."

"I'm confused," Claire said. "How did Nancy…?"

"You've been away too long baking in the sun and enjoying yourself," I said. "Now it's time for you to start suffering like the rest of us. Welcome home."

Ignoring both of us, Mary Alice picked up the conversation right where she'd been interrupted. "As a start, the three of us are going to lunch at the hotel the day the committee does a food tasting for the ball. She insists she needs us there for moral support. I don't understand why, but I didn't want to question her. It's this Friday at noon at the Fairport Inn and Suites, so put it on your calendar. I'll pick you both up to ensure neither of you cancel at the last minute."

Mary Alice signaled a server that we were ready to order. "I hope you're both hungry. I've already decided on the veggie burger."

And that, as the saying goes, was that.

It wasn't until later that night that I realized Claire hadn't told me what she wanted me to do, or not do, as part of our new, grown-up friendship pact.

I certainly wasn't going to ask her.

Chapter 40

I'd appreciate technology more if I could download food.

Elizabeth hadn't appeared for the last few days, and I missed her.

You were in this house with her for over thirty-five years, and you didn't know it. So why are you missing her now?

I thought about this question while Lucy and Ethel took care of necessary business in the backyard. I hoped with all my heart that Nancy had been able to smooth the way with Ray so Elizabeth was able to help plan the masquerade ball. And that Elizabeth wasn't planning any surprises at the tasting. I'm learning that, with a ghost, you never can tell.

The blast of a car horn interrupted my woolgathering. Yikes. Claire and Mary Alice were already here, and I was nowhere near ready to be seen in public. Thank goodness I'd already taken a quick shower.

I threw on my chosen outfit for the day (all colors had been coordinated the night before), grabbed my makeup bag (which was getting heavier all the time), and dashed out the door.

"Sorry," I gasped, plopping my posterior in the back seat

of Mary Alice's car. "I didn't realize it was so late."

"It's fine," Mary Alice said as she turned onto Fairport Turnpike in the direction of the hotel. "We have plenty of time."

I steeled myself for one of Claire's zingers, pointing out how often my friends have had to wait for me, but none was forthcoming. Instead, she winked at me in the rearview mirror. I realized our truce was working, so I relaxed and began the arduous procedure of applying makeup in a moving car.

A few minutes later, I looked up and realized we'd barely gone one block. I hoped Nancy wasn't freaking out waiting for her posse to arrive because it was a sure bet we were going to be late.

"Can't you go any faster?"

Claire caught my eye, gave me a dirty look (just like old times), and made a zipping motion across her lips.

I sighed and returned to the impossible task of applying enough makeup to hide the bags under my eyes. I didn't know which of my friends was the worst driver. Mary Alice drove at the speed of a dazed snail, while Nancy approached stop signs and yellow traffic lights at the speed of a NASCAR racing driver. Claire was a mixture of both but didn't come close to my superior driving skills.

I looked up again, and Claire was still staring at me, scowling. I refused to match her gaze, and then, like a bolt of lightning, I understood what she was telling me. Mary Alice's late husband, Brian, died in a traffic accident many years ago. No wonder she was an extra careful driver.

Carol Andrews, you should be ashamed of yourself. Either shut up or change the subject.

The driver in the car behind us leaned on his horn to show his disapproval, then attempted to pass us illegally. As he inched by us, he gave us the middle finger salute, and I realized it was Ray Thompson. What a jerk.

Mary Alice, the sweetheart that she is, ignored him. Or maybe she didn't see him. But I did, and I wasn't going to let him get away with it.

I was about to reply similarly when Claire, correctly anticipating my movements, stopped me. "Don't do it, Carol. You'll just make things worse. Ray Thompson is one person in town never to cross."

"You know I can't stand him. But I'm not afraid of him if that's what you meant."

Claire turned in her seat to face me. "Larry recently told me some things about him in confidence. I can't repeat them, so don't ask me any more questions."

"I didn't realize wives of attorneys were bound by client confidentiality laws, too," I said, laughing.

"This is no laughing matter, believe me." She turned and faced forward, effectively ending the discussion and giving me oodles of things to ponder.

Chapter 41

Just because you're a drama queen doesn't mean I'm going to treat you like royalty.

It had been several months since I'd last been inside the Fairport Inn and Suites. Jim and I, the dogs, and several others were forced to spend the Christmas holidays there due to a major snowstorm and various other calamities. Perhaps a few of you remember that.

The hotel lobby was bustling with guests either checking in or checking out, including one petite, white-haired woman wearing the most gorgeous, tailored pantsuit I'd ever seen. The fabric was a gray tweed, and the fit was impeccable. Since I'm also on the short side, I knew immediately the suit had to be custom-made. Whoever the woman was, she had great taste and appeared to have a bank account to match—definitely someone who should get the V.I.P. treatment.

The desk clerk spotted the woman and beckoned her forward with a smile, earning angry looks from others who'd been waiting longer. "Welcome home. Do you know how long you'll be staying? I see you arrived last night. I'm sorry I wasn't here to greet you personally."

"My plans are flexible. I hope to relax and rest while I'm here," the guest said.

"I'll see that you're not disturbed."

"I would like all my meals delivered to the penthouse this time. I hope that's not a problem."

"Not at all. I'll send up a luncheon menu right away."

I patted myself on the back (metaphorically). The woman had to be wealthy if she was staying in the penthouse. I wanted to hang around a little longer to see if I could figure out who the woman was but was interrupted by Claire, who marched over, grabbed my arm, and hissed in my ear, "Come on, Carol. Mary Alice and I are waiting for you."

Ah, well, not all curiosity is meant to be satisfied.

"This must be the darkest corner in the entire dining room," I muttered as we were shown to our table. "If we were any farther back, we'd be sitting outside."

"Sorry, ma'am," the maître d' said. "But as you may have observed when you walked in, a very important private event is happening in the front of the restaurant. I've been instructed to only seat *other* luncheon patrons in this section. I promise you'll receive our usual impeccable service." And he disappeared.

"Nancy acknowledged us when we came in," Mary Alice reassured us. "She knows we're nearby."

"If you consider sitting in another zip code nearby," I shot back.

"It won't seem so dark when your eyes get adjusted properly, Carol," Mary Alice said. "I can see just fine now."

"Our cell phones have flashlights," Claire added. "You can use yours if you're having a problem. Or maybe you should be checked for cataracts. We are at that time of life."

"Hush, both of you," Mary Alice said as a waitress arrived and placed menus on our table. "Welcome to the Fairport Inn and Suites," the girl said. "I'm Abbey, and I'll be taking care of you ladies today." She leaned down and said confidentially, "This is my first day working here. I'm very nervous. I have to serve that private party, too. They're a bunch of important people. I hope I can handle it."

Claire gave her a look, and the girl, realizing her mistake, hastened to clarify what she'd just said. "I don't mean you're not important. You are. I promise I won't neglect you."

"Thank you," Claire said, looking slightly mollified.

I squinted at the server. "You look familiar. Have we met before?"

"I don't think so. I guess I have that kind of face. Can I start you off with something from the bar?"

Abbey's pager beeped. "Oops, I'm being summoned to the front. I'll be back as soon as I can." She scurried away before any of us could respond.

"I hate it when I think I recognize someone, and it turns out I'm wrong," I said, giving the menu a quick perusal. "Makes me think I'm losing my grip on reality."

"No comment," Claire said.

"There are a few surprise guests at the tasting," Mary Alice said, changing the subject in her usual diplomatic way. "Did you know Jim was going to be here, Carol?"

"Yes. He's on the committee. Although he's not as important as he used to be since Ray Thompson took over."

"To his credit, all Jim did was raise an eyebrow when we walked by," Claire said.

"That's because I texted him that I was having lunch with you two but didn't tell him where."

"Aren't you the clever one?" Mary Alice said.

"Years of practice."

"Who is the attractive blonde sitting next to Jim?" Claire asked. "If she were on a committee with my husband, I might be jealous."

"Her name is Elizabeth Peterson, and she's a reenactment

specialist. We've become good friends since she came to town. Believe it or not, she's a lot older than she looks." Points for her for getting invited to the tasting. I couldn't wait to find out how she'd pulled that off.

"She's certainly well preserved," Claire commented.

You have no idea how right you are.

"Why are Bill and Phyllis Stevens included? That really surprises me," Claire continued.

"It turns out that one of Bill's ancestors was a patriot who fought in the original Battle of Fairport," I explained. "So, he's become an honorary committee member, and where Bill goes...."

"Phyllis goes too," Mary Alice said, rolling her eyes.

"Peter Robinson from Carla Grimaldi's office is having a fit trying to get people to sit where their place cards are. I'm afraid he's going to have a complete meltdown," I said.

"So that's who that young man is," Claire said. "I feel sorry for him."

"The biggest surprise is seeing Sister Rose," Mary Alice added. "I wonder why she's here."

"Nancy probably invited her to be sure everyone stayed on their best behavior," Claire said.

I couldn't resist adding, "Including Nancy herself. Did you notice she's sitting right next to Ray Thompson?"

At that moment, Abbey returned with three glasses of water and a basket of fresh, warm rolls. "Enjoy these while you look at the menu. I'll be back to take your orders as soon as I can."

She vanished again, and I grabbed for the first roll. I know, bad manners, but I was hungry. I was just passing the basket to Mary Alice when we heard an odd noise from the front of the dining room. There was a loud thud, followed by screaming.

"He's choking!" someone yelled.

"Somebody call nine-one-one."

Mary Alice was immediately up and running to help, with Claire and me right behind her. "I'm a nurse," she yelled. "Let me through." She dropped to her knees and immediately began the Heimlich maneuver. After several agonizing minutes, she shook her head, stood, and crossed herself. "I did the best I could, but it was too late. He's gone."

Nancy started sobbing uncontrollably. "This is awful! I can't believe it!"

I couldn't believe it, either. The man lying dead on the floor was Ray Thompson.

Chapter 42

Duct tape can't fix stupid, but it can muffle the sound.

I was rooted to the floor, torn between comforting Nancy and making a beeline for the safety of our darkened corner table. Yes, I am a coward. Don't judge me too harshly until you've discovered a dead body as often as I have.

Claire and Mary Alice rushed to calm Nancy, and I felt strong arms hugging me tight. I stiffened, then realized it was Jim. In all the chaos, I'd totally forgotten he was here.

I turned into my husband's comforting embrace. "Oh, Jim, I can't believe it. How did it happen?"

"Ray started to cough like he had something stuck in his throat. Probably one of the rolls since we hadn't gotten to the actual meal tasting yet."

"It was an accident," I said, relieved.

"Of course it was an accident," Jim said in a low voice. "Don't let that imagination of yours start working overtime."

The hotel manager and the restaurant maître d' were doing their best to calm the guests, but nobody was paying the slightest attention to them. I caught sight of Abbey, our server, standing at the edge of the group, looking shell-shocked. Poor girl. Her first day on the job and this had to happen.

The loud sound of approaching sirens interrupted my thought process. Carla Grimaldi clapped her hands and shouted, "Will everyone please take a seat and be calm? Let the professionals do their job.

"Peter, don't just stand there. Seat everybody again. It doesn't matter where. Any empty chair is all right as long as everyone gets out of the way."

Poor Peter was trying his best, but most people were ignoring him. I wouldn't have blamed him if he was so desperate to do his boss's bidding that he started grabbing people at random and shoving them into any handy chair.

Finally, everyone began to move.

"You should go to Nancy," Jim said. "She needs you now. I just wanted to be sure you were okay."

"You're right." I pulled myself away from my husband's arms.

The room was suddenly filled with more emergency squad personnel and police than I'd ever seen in one place. Including one police detective I'd hoped to avoid for the rest of my life, the odious and always annoying Paul Wheeler. When Paul is with Mark Anderson, his detective partner, our son-in-law, and the father of our adored grandson, he's on his best, professional behavior. But when he was on his own, like he was now, he became an obnoxious bully, as I knew from personal experience. I hoped Mark would be here soon.

By the way, years ago, Nancy had once told Paul he was a perfect example of Short Stature Syndrome—a vertically challenged person who overcompensated for his lack of height by bullying other people whenever possible. I prayed that Paul would never remember she said that. Shaking off a feeling of impending doom I couldn't explain, I did my best to ignore the sight of Ray Thompson's lifeless body being checked out by the emergency team and headed in Nancy's direction.

Nancy grabbed my hand like she was drowning, and I had the only life preserver. "Carol, what am I going to do?"

"You don't have to do anything. We'll all be able to leave soon, once...Ray leaves. There's nothing for you to worry about."

"Carol's right, Nancy. That's what we've been trying to tell you," Mary Alice said, moving to block Nancy's view of the body being wheeled out on a stretcher.

"Then why are the police here? I freaked out when I saw Paul Wheeler enter the restaurant." Nancy started to weep again.

"I'm sure Carla Grimaldi made the call to report the emergency," Claire said calmly, which didn't fool me for a split second. She was scared, and so was I. "And this kind of sudden death also requires a police presence. We're lucky the fire department didn't come, too."

"That makes good sense," Mary Alice agreed.

"You're right, Claire. That's standard procedure," I chimed in. We were making all this up as we went along, but Nancy seemed to accept it without question, and right now, calming her down was all that mattered to us.

"I think it would be a good idea for you to go back and sit in your assigned seat, Nancy," Mary Alice said. "The place card next to Ray's has your name on it, so Paul's going to zero in on the fact that you're not there."

"You don't want it to look like you snuck out early because you have something to hide," I added. "That's the worst thing you can do."

"Turn around, stand up straight, and walk back to the table like the wonderful, honest person you are," Claire advised. "Look scared."

"No problem," Nancy said. "To tell the truth, I'm scared I'll be accused of bumping off Ray." She touched her face, and

I suddenly realized she was bleeding. "I'm the one who gave Ray the water to stop him choking. He fought me so hard. Why did he do that? I was just trying to help him.

"And then he collapsed and died right in front of me."

Chapter 43

Some people won't admit their faults. I would, if I had any.

"Let's leave now and find a restaurant that's still serving lunch. I don't know about you two, but I'm starving," Claire said. "We didn't see anything because we were seated so far away, so the police won't bother questioning us."

"You can't be serious," I said, shooting Claire an incredulous look. "Did you hear what Nancy just said? No wonder she's scared."

"We can't desert her now," Mary Alice said. "We're her best friends. We're staying."

Claire sighed. "You're right. I'm not thinking clearly. Being hungry is scrambling my brain."

"Let's sit for a while and think good thoughts," I said, trying to look hopeful. "I'm sure we'll be able to leave soon. Meanwhile," I picked up the basket of rolls, "have some bread. It's all we've got for now. Abbey won't forget we're here."

I hope.

Claire grabbed a roll and began picking it apart until only crumbs were left.

"Rolls could be all we're having for lunch," I said, grabbing her hand before she killed off another one. "I'm sure Paul Wheeler ordered the kitchen to close until everything can be checked out and deemed safe to serve."

"Are you suggesting that Ray's death wasn't an accident?"

"There'll be testing to determine the cause of Ray's death, Mary Alice, to rule out any other possibility."

"The police should check everything in the kitchen, plus the water glass he drank from, for possible poison," Claire chimed in. "You never know. It would be so easy for someone sitting close to Ray at the event or working in the kitchen to...."

"Stop right there, Claire." I was so angry, I was ready to scream. "Listen to what you're saying. Nancy was the person sitting closest to Ray. You're saying she could be guilty of murder. Just lock her up in prison for the rest of her life without any evidence whatsoever. What kind of a friend are you, anyway?"

"You know I didn't mean it that way. It's never going to come to that."

"I hope that's true, Claire," said a familiar voice. "But in the meantime, Carol's right. Don't even *whisper* what I just overheard you say. Better yet, don't even think it."

It was Sister Rose, of course. And for once, the object of her ire wasn't me. She was followed by Abbey, who balanced a tray of lunches and snacks for us with some difficulty.

"I'll take that from you, dear," Sister Rose said. "I believe you're needed in the front." Abbey handed off the tray immediately and scampered away.

Sister Rose deftly placed the tray on our table as if she'd been waiting tables for years. Honestly, the woman was amazing.

"I believe this food is all due to the hotel manager's quick thinking," Sister Rose explained. "He must have realized right away that there'd be problems with serving food from the hotel kitchen after what just happened, so he arranged for food to be delivered while we wait for the police to interview us."

If that was indeed the case, I had to give the hotel manager points for his attempt to restore the goodwill of his customers. He had a problem, for sure. But my best friend could have an even bigger one.

"This is a pretty fancy meal," Claire said as she helped herself to the feast before us. "It's better than what I would have ordered from the menu."

"*Bon Appetit*, everyone," Sister Rose urged.

She shook her head and frowned. "I don't know what in the world made me say that."

"I wonder where the food came from. It's delicious," Mary Alice said. "I'm enjoying every bite."

"I wondered the same thing," Sister Rose said. "I asked the server, but she didn't know."

I had a pretend coughing fit to keep from laughing. It was clear to me who the source of our food was, which was confirmed by the inclusion of Pepperidge Farm Goldfish Crackers, Julia Child's favorite snack, as something extra for us to nibble on. Sadly, she'd skipped adding dirty martinis.

"We were surprised to see you at the tasting, Sister," I said.

"Not as surprised as I was to be invited. It was Nancy's idea, bless her. She wants the masquerade ball to be a fundraiser for Sally's Place. She planned to propose the idea to the committee after the tasting was over and invited me in case there were any questions from the committee about our program."

"What a wonderful idea," Mary Alice said. "Sally's Place does so much in the community."

"Thank you for saying that, dear," Sister Rose said.

"People in our community think the funds we earn from the thrift shop are enough to keep the program going, but that's not true. And the demand for our services keeps growing."

"I'm sure Jim would support Nancy's idea. He appreciates all the good you've been able to accomplish for victims of domestic violence," I said, proud of my husband for being such a caring human being.

"I texted Jim that I'd be at the meeting today and why, and he was all for it, Carol. Nancy also said she'd talked to Carla Grimaldi, who thought it was a wonderful idea."

I was just starting to relax a little when I heard an annoying male voice. "So, this is where you're hiding, Sister Rose. If you're trying to avoid giving the police your statement, it won't work."

I didn't even have to look to know that the person being inexcusably rude to Sister Rose was Paul Wheeler.

He stepped closer and caught sight of me. "I might have known that you'd be here, Carol. Why is it that whenever there's a suspicious death in Fairport these days, you're at the scene? Is this how you get your jollies?"

"You owe Carol an apology for that crack," my son-in-law said, stepping in front of Paul and giving him an incredulous look. "And Sister Rose, too. I know you well enough to realize you were just kidding around, but they don't.

"I didn't realize you all were back here until Jim told me," Mark went on. I could tell he wanted to know what in heck I was doing with two of my best friends and Sister Rose in the back of the hotel dining room, but he wasn't going to ask me in front of Paul.

"Thank you for clarifying your partner's unusual sense of humor," Sister Rose said, rising majestically as only she could. "I'm prepared to give a statement now. Lead the way, Officer Wheeler."

"It's *Detective* Wheeler," Paul said.

"My mistake. After you, Detective Wheeler."

Mark gave us an apologetic look and followed them.

We sat in silence for a while. Finally, Claire stood up. "I

can't stand this waiting. I have to see what's happening."

"Sit down," I hissed. "Someone will see you."

"That's what I'm hoping," Claire said. "What if everyone forgets we're back here and leaves?" She tiptoed toward the front of the restaurant and pressed her body next to the wall.

"Is that any worse than being given the third degree by Paul Wheeler?"

"Be quiet, Carol. What if he hears you? Then, we'll really be in trouble," Mary Alice said.

"This is silly. I'm going to find Jim. I don't see how anybody could object to that."

As if by magic, a text from the Man Himself appeared.

Ping.

Jim: I'm free to leave. Mark says you and your friends are, too. See you at home.

Me: What about Nancy?

Ping.

Jim: I think she's still being questioned.

That's when I really started to worry.

Chapter 44

"I just cleaned out some space in my freezer" sounds so much more productive than "I just polished off another pint of ice cream."

"Today has been one of the worst days of my life," Jim said, helping himself to a spoonful of chocolate chip ice cream I'd found lurking in the freezer. "I can't believe that Ray Thompson choked and died right in front of the entire committee. Poor Ray. It'll take a long time to erase that sight from my mind. Ugh."

Even though I was also depressed, and my dear husband had once again helped himself to one of my favorite snacks without asking permission, I pushed my whole dish in his direction. "Here, you can have it all. I'm too upset to eat."

Jim gave me a skeptical look. "Are you sure? You're not going to wait until the ice cream is almost gone before you change your mind and tell me you were only kidding, are you?"

"No, I'm not. Just eat it. I can't bear looking at food. Not even ice cream. I wonder how Nancy is. I'm sick with worry."

"She's probably already home. Why not text her instead

of making yourself crazy?" my reasonable husband suggested, handing me my phone.

"What if she doesn't answer?"

"You won't know if you don't try." He put his spoon down. "Do it before all the ice cream melts. I'm saving some for you."

I hate it when people are reasonable.

Me: How are you? Where are you?

I was just about to send the text when the two dogs began to yip, raced around the kitchen, and then scratched at the side door. Neither Jim nor I had heard anything, but canine hearing is a lot keener than ours. (Especially Jim's, but don't tell him I told you that.)

"Let us in," Jenny called out. "I forgot my key."

"This is a happy surprise after a horrible day," I said as Jenny handed CJ over to me. "Hello, precious boy." I peered outside. "Is Mark here too?"

"He's bringing in the diaper bag and extra baby food, just in case CJ gets fussy. I can't believe how even a short trip requires bringing along so much stuff when a baby's involved."

Her expression turned serious. "Mark has some questions about what happened today, Mom. He already has Dad's statement. I figured that if CJ and I came along, that might make things a little easier for you."

"But I didn't see anything," I protested. "I was too far away. And it was dark where we were sitting. Mary Alice and Claire will tell him the same thing.

"We didn't see anything," I repeated as Mark joined us in the kitchen. "None of us did."

"I know you didn't actually see anything," Mark said. "This is an unofficial visit, and I'm not here as a police detective. I'm here as your son-in-law. I want you to talk to me as a trusted member of the family, which I hope I am."

"Of course you are, silly," I said. "You have been since you were a kid."

"Jim, you can stay and listen if you want. You might have something to add."

"I'll put CJ down in the bedroom and be right back," Jenny said. "Is it okay if I stay, too? If that's a problem, I won't."

"We're just a family getting together for dessert and a chat," Mark said, eyeing my dish. "I hope there's more of that ice cream left."

"Sorry, no. But we have Oreos." I jumped up and rooted around in a cupboard for my emergency stash, hidden behind an unopened box of dog biscuits.

Mark grabbed a handful and lined them up in front of him, just like he used to do when he was a kid. "I'll save these for later.

"Now, let's get to it. This chat is completely unofficial and off the record. I want you to tell me why you were there today."

Be careful, Carol. Don't say anything that would get Nancy in more trouble.

"It's no big deal, Mark. Claire and Mary Alice wanted to go out for lunch. They'd never been to the Fairport Inn and Suites, so we decided to go there. That's it."

"Nice try. But I don't believe you." Mark leaned forward in his chair. "I could lose my job for talking to you like this. I'm asking you again; you have to be honest with me. Why were you there? The truth. And don't leave anything out. I mean it."

Ohhh. Mark now had a stern Cop Look, not a friendly Family Look, on his face. Not a good sign.

Jenny squeezed her husband's shoulder. "Honey, take it easy. You're even scaring me."

"Sorry," Mark mumbled. "I'm just trying to find some facts that will help clear up this case sooner rather than later. Carla Grimaldi is putting pressure on the police chief to solve this immediately. The chief is leaning on Paul and me to do it. She's hoping Ray Thompson's death was an accident."

"It must have been an accident, Mark," Jim said. "There's

no other possible explanation. Ray choked on a dinner roll and died."

"Here's the problem with that scenario," Mark said, looking more miserable than I'd ever seen him. "Yes, Ray choked. Nancy gave him a glass of water while he was choking. Do we all agree on that?"

Jim nodded. "I saw her do it. We all did. She was just trying to help him."

"When I picked up the glass Ray drank from, I noticed the water inside was a little cloudy, not crystal clear. We're sending it out to the lab to test for possible poison. And...."

"Nancy's the one who gave it to him," I finished.

"And insisted that he drink when he resisted," Jim added. I shot him a dirty look. Sometimes, my husband doesn't know when to shut his big mouth.

"Not only that," Mark added, "but except for Ray's, there are no other fingerprints on the glass. Not even from one of the servers."

The four of us sat in glum silence for some time, each lost in our own thoughts. Finally, Jenny stood and said, "Let's look at this again tomorrow. Maybe the outlook isn't as grim as we think. Come on, honey, let's get CJ and go home."

"Yes," Jim said. "A person is innocent until proven guilty, right, Mark? Not the other way around."

Mark nodded, but he didn't look convinced. I choked back a sob. My very best friend from childhood, who was the maid of honor at our wedding, could be a murder suspect.

After Jenny, Mark, and a still-sleeping CJ (he is the best baby ever) left, Jim and I spent the rest of the night going over what happened at the tasting again and again until we were making each other nuts. "You must have seen something that would help Nancy," I insisted. "You just can't remember it right now."

"If you keep cross-examining me like Perry Mason, I'll

never remember it."

Jim yawned. "Let's take the dogs out and go to bed. Maybe things will look brighter in the morning."

So, that's what we did. Only when I was finally dropping off to sleep did I realize there was one person missing when the police arrived to take statements—Elizabeth. But she must have been the one who reached out to Julia Child for the lunches after Ray died.

My resident ghost had some major explaining to do.

Chapter 45

I made a long to-do list for today. I just can't figure out who's going to do it.

Jim brought me coffee in bed the next morning, which was a lovely way to start the day.

"To what do I owe this kitchen-to-bedroom delivery service? It's not my birthday."

All of a sudden, Ray's agonizing death roared its way into my conscious mind. My hands started to shake so severely that Jim took the cup away and put it on the bedside table.

"I made just regular coffee today. I figured we both needed all the help we could get, and an extra jolt of caffeine once in a while never hurt anyone." He eyed me for a minute. "Maybe that wasn't such a great idea."

"It's fine," I said, taking a tentative sip. "I'll just add a little milk to dilute it. Thank you."

"I'm leaving now for an emergency committee meeting at Carla Grimaldi's office. We were supposed to meet right after the tasting yesterday afternoon, but obviously, that didn't happen. I have no idea how long I'll be. Everyone is pretty shaken up about Ray's death. I'll try to keep you posted."

"Do you think the entire event will be canceled?" *Then, you can finally cut your hair and shave.*

"No idea. But Carla Grimaldi is clearly in charge now. We'll have to wait and see."

"Did Ray have any family? Is there anyone we should reach out to and express our condolences?"

Jim gave me a sweet kiss. "You're a nice person to think of that. I'll see what I can find out. See you when I see you."

"See if you can pick up any information that may help Nancy," I called after him. "I'm sure the local gossip mill is already humming with imaginative theories about how Ray died."

As I splashed water on my face without looking in the mirror (it's not easy), I suddenly realized that the undisputed Queen of the Fairport Gossip Mill lived right across the street. Plus, Phyllis and Bill were at yesterday's tasting. Maybe, if I was very clever, I could "interrogate" her on what she saw. It was worth a try, as long as I could prevent her from veering off from actual facts into her preferred realm of unsubstantiated gossip and speculation.

Pleased that I had a plan of sorts, I downed the entire cup of coffee, scarfed down a glazed donut I had hidden so cleverly that Jim hadn't found it, and made myself look as presentable as possible. After giving the dogs a quick romp in the yard and a little extra breakfast kibble, I squared my shoulders and marched across the street to chat with Phyllis without calling first.

Chapter 46

You know you're getting old when everything dries up, sags, or leaks.

A breathless Phyllis answered the door after I leaned on the doorbell several times. Her wet hair was in curly tendrils, and her cheeks were pink. She actually looked pretty. Clutching a terrycloth robe around her, she gestured for me to follow her out to the screened-in porch. Of course, being me, I immediately started babbling an apology about interrupting her without warning, then stopped short at the porch door when I caught a glimpse of Bill, attired in a similar, casual style, also with wet hair, toweling himself dry.

Note to self: caffeine and sugar together can create a fantastic energy boost, leading to impulsive, regrettable actions.

I was mortified. What in the name of heaven had I interrupted?

No, wait. Please don't tell me.

"Sit wherever you want, Carol," Phyllis said. "Would you like to join Bill and me for…."

Not giving the poor woman a chance to finish her sentence, I answered, "No! I mean, thank you, but no. I can see I've come at a bad time. I apologize. I should leave and come back later."

Maybe sometime in the next year or two.

Bill's eyes twinkled as if reading my thoughts, which embarrassed me even more. "Phyllis and I realized after yesterday's tragedy that we're not getting any younger," he explained.

"That's right," Phyllis said, not giving her husband a chance to continue. That behavior, at least, was normal.

"Sit down, Carol," Phyllis said, patting a nearby chair. "You're making me nervous, standing over me like that."

I had no choice, so I smiled nervously and sat on the edge of the chair so I could make a quick getaway as soon as possible.

"I can't stay long."

"As I was saying," Bill went on, "from now on, we've decided we're living for today. You never know when your number is up. We finally activated the whirlpool feature that came with our bathtub. We didn't know what we'd been missing."

"We've been road-testing it, so to speak," Phyllis said, giving her husband a tender glance.

Yes. Well. Moving on. Concentrate on what you're here for, Carol.

Looking somber and ordering my mind to erase any images of Phyllis and Bill in the bathtub, I got right to the point. "Nancy Green is in big trouble. She's my very best friend, and I want to help her. I'm hoping you do, too."

"I don't understand," Phyllis said. "Why is that lovely girl in trouble?"

"Don't you remember, Phyllis? Nancy's the person who tried to save Ray when he was choking," Bill clarified. "The rest of us just sat there. I guess we were too shocked to do anything."

"That's right," Phyllis agreed. "She did her best to help

by handing Ray that water."

"I'm sure she thought that if poor Ray drank enough water, he could dislodge whatever was caught in his throat. It didn't work, but Nancy tried. She's a hero in my book," Bill said.

I teared up. They weren't getting it. I had to be more straightforward.

"The problem is that the police think the water may have had poison in it. Nancy is the person who handed him the glass. So, she's...." my voice broke.

"That is absolutely outrageous!" Phyllis said. "To accuse an innocent person who was trying to help in a life and death situation of harming Ray instead."

"Phyllis is right," Bill said. "That can't be what happened. I don't believe it."

"I don't believe it, either," I said. "And our son-in-law, Mark, has his doubts, too."

"Thank goodness Mark's on the case instead of that nitwit detective Paul, whoever. He'll get to the bottom of this. Nancy has nothing to worry about." Phyllis shook her head to emphasize her point, and I ignored the sprinkles of water that landed on my arm.

"I hope you're right," I said. "Claire, Mary Alice, and I were also at the restaurant, but we were seated too far back to see what actually happened. If it's not too upsetting for you both, could you tell me exactly what you saw?"

"Phyllis was sitting on the same side of the table as Ray was, and I was opposite them," Bill said. "I saw everything. As a matter of fact, I had nightmares about it last night."

"Yes, you were very restless," Phyllis corroborated. "I hardly closed my eyes all night."

"We'd just been served a large basket of warm rolls," Bill continued. "People were helping themselves and then passing the basket to the person beside them. When the basket got to

Ray, he grabbed a roll and stuffed it in his mouth. It was like he hadn't eaten for a week."

"Disgusting," Phyllis commented. "No manners at all."

"Anyway," Bill said, shooting his wife a look, "the roll was too large for Ray to swallow without chewing it more than he did, and he started to cough. He coughed harder and harder, and we realized he was choking. Nancy was sitting next to him. She grabbed a glass of water from the table and tried to help him drink it.

"Ray was a wild man by then. He tried to push the glass away. His face was all red and, well, I'll skip that part."

"Thank you," Phyllis said. "I'm glad I didn't see it from your angle. In the end, it was a good thing that my seat was changed. Although I have no idea why we had to be separated."

I wondered if Bill had requested it but banished that thought immediately.

"The next thing we knew, Ray fell to the floor," Bill said. "Your friend Mary Alice tried to do that Heineken maneuver, but it was too late."

"Heimlich," Phyllis corrected.

"That's what I said, Phyllis."

"Did you tell the police all this yesterday, Bill?"

"I tried to, but Paul Wheeler cut me right off. He took my name and address, asked where I was seated, and told me he'd be in touch if he needed more information. I'm not holding my breath waiting to hear from him."

It was time for me to leave and allow Phyllis and Bill to get back to whatever they'd been doing. I didn't even want to think about that.

"Thank you for sharing so many details with me, Bill. I now understand better what happened."

"I hope what I told you will help Nancy," Bill said.

"I hope so, too, with all my heart."

"At least we've confirmed that Nancy's not the only person who touched the water glass," Phyllis put in, not one to be silent in any conversation for very long.

I must have looked puzzled because she clarified. "Ray touched it, too, while he was struggling to breathe. That may be important."

I didn't see how that could possibly help Nancy since Mark had already mentioned that and indicated her actions could make her look guilty of a crime. Rather than point that out to Phyllis, I nodded my head to agree with her.

"Thanks for being gracious about my stopping in without calling first. I promise I won't do it again."

And I got the heck out of there.

Chapter 47

I know we're good friends when I don't feel I have to clean up before you come over.

I scurried across Old Fairport Turnpike to the sanctuary of my own house. Bill had painted such a realistic picture of Ray's death throes that I felt sick to my stomach. Granted, I didn't like the guy. But nobody should have to suffer and die that way.

Don't dwell on it for now, Carol. Do something you enjoy. You're bound to come up with one of your brilliant ideas and save the day for Nancy.

Under normal circumstances—whatever they might be in my life—I'd call my friends and make a shopping or lunch date to cheer myself up. Not this time. Maybe, not for a long time. Or ever, after yesterday's debacle.

I sat on my bed and considered other options, none of which were appealing. I decided to turn to my two canine counselors for suggestions. But first, I had to find them. They weren't in either of their favorite spots—on our bed or snoozing under the kitchen table.

I panicked. I was sure I'd brought the dogs inside before

I crossed the street, but what if I hadn't completely closed the gate? What if the dogs had gotten outside and were now wandering around Fairport? Or had been hit by a car?

It was too terrible to think about.

Be calm, and check the house first. Maybe they snuck upstairs while you were out.

I heard a thud outside like a ball hitting our screened-in porch. And there they were, the little rascals, running around the yard, chasing a green tennis ball. Phew. At least they were safe.

"Lucy, Ethel," I called, shaking a box of Milk Bones to get their attention. "Time to come inside now."

Three blue roan English cocker spaniels came racing toward me.

Deciding I must be seeing things (I never was good at arithmetic), I closed my eyes, then opened them again. Three dogs were prancing around my feet, begging for a treat.

I heard Elizabeth's voice. "Annie, come. Right now. I mean it. Don't bother Carol."

It wasn't that long ago that I would have considered this scenario positive proof that I was losing my grip on reality. But since the unexpected appearance of Elizabeth Porter, I now understood that reality can be flexible. If I had a ghost living in my house (or I was living in her house, depending on your point of view), and I had English cocker spaniels, it made perfect sense that she'd have one, too. Anything was possible.

"Sorry to interrupt your game, but we need to talk," I said. As an extra bonus, I was thrilled I wouldn't have to search for Elizabeth, especially since I had no idea where to look.

I opened the side door and three dogs hurried into the kitchen, followed by Elizabeth. "Phew," she said, "that was some workout."

I decided to put the surprise appearance of a third dog in my house aside and concentrate on what was *really* important.

Was Elizabeth at yesterday's tasting? If yes, why did she disappear?

"I'll warm up the coffee," I said, giving myself time to collect my thoughts. I filled two mugs and nuked them in the microwave while my imagination entered ping-pong mode.

Maybe Elizabeth was the one who poisoned Ray. After all, she killed her husband two centuries before.

But that was in self-defense.

That's what she told you, Carol. What if that's not what really happened?

This whirlpool of doubt only served to confuse me more. I had to trust her, at least, for now.

Willing my face not to betray what I was thinking, I put the mugs on the table. "Careful," I warned. "They're very hot."

"I didn't do it, Carol. But go ahead and ask me if that'll make you feel better. I have nothing to hide from you."

I kept forgetting that Elizabeth could read my thoughts—time to regroup. "I'm not accusing you of anything," I said, hoping she believed me. "I'm only trying to understand what happened yesterday, and I was hoping you could help. Can we take the events step by step?"

Not waiting for her to answer, I plowed on. "Were you at the tasting yesterday or not? When I walked in with Claire and Mary Alice, I saw you sitting next to Jim at the table. Correct? I mean, you were actually there. I didn't imagine it."

"I was really there. Initially, I was next to Jim because that's where my place card was. Each name was printed on both sides of the card. At first, I thought that was odd. Then I realized that Carla Grimaldi's assistant had done them that way, so she'd know who each person was, even if she was sitting opposite them.

"As the front of the restaurant became more crowded, people ignored the place cards and started to sit down anywhere they wanted. The young man from Carla's office was going crazy. I got up to use the restroom." Elizabeth made a face. "A minor inconvenience of my appearing in human form.

"While there, I lost my human form and became my spirit body. It happened suddenly, and I was surprised. I've always had control of which form I take, but not at that time. I was told I should observe the tasting without anyone knowing I was there, and I was lucky nobody was in the restroom when the transformation happened.

"I went back to the restaurant as a ghost and walked in front of each person, per my instructions. As I walked toward Ray, he started choking. I saw Nancy reach for a glass of water and hand it to him.

"Ray took a small sip and refused to drink it. Mind you, he was still choking. Nancy held the glass to his lips, insisting Ray take another drink. He began to fight her like a wild man. He even hit her a few times and then tried to grab the glass again. Nancy wouldn't let it go, even though Ray tried to spill the water on the table."

"I'd heard there was a struggle, but I didn't know Ray deliberately hit Nancy," I said, reeling from this new knowledge.

"Ray collapsed," Elizabeth continued. "Mary Alice tried the Heimlich maneuver to revive him, but it was too late. That's it."

"Why did you have to return to the tasting as a ghost after everyone there had already seen you? It makes no sense. If you'd been in human form, do you think you could have saved him?"

"I don't know. I can only assume everything was supposed to work out precisely how it did. I was only there to witness Ray's death, not interfere and save him.

"I know you don't understand, and I don't, either. I'm just glad I was able to tell you."

I could have skipped the gory details, but I didn't tell

Elizabeth that.

I felt a wet doggy nose nuzzling my hand. "And who's this? We haven't been introduced yet."

Elizabeth snapped her fingers, and the dog trotted over to her side. "The name on her tag was Annie. She was crossing over to the other world while I was. We've become good friends. I've been bringing her to play with your dogs when you and Jim aren't home. I really wanted her with me today. I hope you don't mind."

"Not at all. Dogs are the best stress-relievers in the whole world."

"I knew you'd understand."

"Is Annie a ghost, too?"

"What do you think, Carol?" Elizabeth asked as she and Annie faded from sight.

Chapter 48

One minute, you're 21, staying up all night drinking beer, eating pizza, and doing crazy things. Then, in the blink of an eye, you're drinking water and eating salad, and you can't do any crazy stuff because you pulled a muscle putting on your socks.

For the next two hours, I channeled my excess energy into tackling household tasks I usually avoid like the plague. The more critical ones among you (yes, I see you) have already decided that all this unusual dedication to household drudgery was merely a ploy to avoid another task—checking in on my best friend to see how she was doing after her harrowing experience yesterday.

The more charitable among you will realize I was still on a massive caffeine/sugar overload, which had provided me with an unusual burst of energy I felt compelled to put to good use at home. I'd like to think more of you fall into this category than the previous one.

For anyone who is still suspicious of my motivation, as I vacuumed cobwebs away, my cell phone was always with me as a constant connection to the outside world. And, yes, the ringer was on.

Satisfied and exhausted after my strenuous cleaning activity, I surveyed my now pristine house and metaphorically patted myself on the back for a job well done. I promised my vacuum cleaner another fun date at the same time next year, and it settled back in the hall closet for a well-deserved rest.

My phone pinged with a text.

Claire: Hear anything from Nancy?

Me: No. You?

Claire: No. Mary Alice hasn't either. I'm worried. I drove by Nancy's house just now, and a strange car was in the driveway.

Me: Did you ring the bell?

Claire: No. I was afraid to do that.

Me: I'll go over now. I'll let you know if I find out anything.

Ordering myself not to panic, first I called Nancy's real estate office voice mail and left a message. Then I called the main office number to see if anyone there had heard from her and was told that she'd called in sick.

Okay. Don't panic.

I sent her a series of texts, each more urgent than the last. Nothing. Nada. Nancy always answered her texts.

Okay, now it's time to panic.

I took a quick shower, and even though my body was clean, the hot water and soap did nothing to relieve the guilt I now felt. After sending off quick texts to Jenny (who might have heard something from Mark) and Jim (so he wouldn't panic if he couldn't find me), I fed and exercised the two dogs, then drove the three miles to Nancy's in record time.

The strange car Claire had mentioned, a tan Toyota Corolla sedan of uncertain vintage, was still in Nancy's driveway. I doubted it belonged to the Fairport police, which I found encouraging.

I rang the bell several times, then yelled, "Nancy, it's me. Carol." No answer.

Claire, Nancy, Mary Alice, and I all have keys to each other's front doors, so I let myself inside. "Nancy! Where are you? Are you okay?"

"I'm in the living room. Enter at your own risk."

"If you're trying to scare me, you're doing a great job," I said. "And if you're kidding, I'll never forgive you. My heart's beating so fast I may have a heart attack right here in the hall."

"Please don't do that. I already have enough things to worry about."

"Why is it so dark in here?" I asked as I walked into the living room. "All the drapes are drawn."

"Go ahead, open the drapes," Nancy said. "Turn on all the lights, too, so the whole neighborhood can see me in all my glory."

"Why are you being so dramatic? What the heck is wrong with…oh, my goodness. You look like you were in a fight and lost." The right side of Nancy's face and her chin were severely bruised from her struggle with Ray Thompson yesterday.

"Remind me next time not to be so heroic. I'm lucky I didn't lose any teeth."

"It's really not that bad," I lied. "I just wasn't expecting it. But now that I look at you carefully," I continued, turning her face more toward the window, "I'm sure some makeup will cover it all up while you're healing. Nobody will even notice it."

"You always were a terrible liar," Nancy said. "That's why you were the one who always got caught in school. Sister Rose could always tell."

"And I still can," the Good Sister said, making her way into the living room, balancing a tray filled with leftovers from yesterday's lunch. "There was no sense letting all this excess food go to waste, so the restaurant was kind enough to pack it up for me."

"I'm not that hungry," Nancy insisted as she eyed the

bounty of food. I could see she was weakening, so I hopped up and said, "Maybe you're not, but I am. I'll get some plates and silverware."

Right after I text Claire and Mary Alice that Nancy is okay.

"I would have brought those things, too," Sister Rose said, "but I didn't know where you kept them. I didn't want to open all the drawers and cupboards and invade your privacy."

"No one would accuse you of that, Sister," I chimed in from the kitchen.

I could hear Nancy laughing, and I knew she was remembering all the times in high school when Sister Rose went through our lockers looking for contraband like makeup and cigarettes. Need I tell you whose locker she always found the forbidden items in? No, I didn't think so.

"What did I miss?" I asked as I rejoined the others. "These paper plates are all I could find, Nancy. It's time for you to run the dishwasher."

Nancy scowled. "I asked Bob to do that before he left for work this morning. I guess he forgot."

"More likely, he didn't hear you," I said. "Jim never does." I was happy to hear that Nancy's sometime husband was back in residence and being supportive.

Their marriage is frequently on shaky ground due to Bob's wandering eye, so they don't always live together. However, they do date each other regularly, which Nancy claims is much more fun.

Sister Rose rolled her eyes. "Thank heavens I don't have to deal with that."

"Hang out with us a little more, and we'll share even more marital tidbits," I said. "We've got lots of them, haven't we, Nancy?" I immediately realized from the look on Sister Rose's face that I'd gone just a teeny bit too far. I filled a plate and concentrated on the food, so I wouldn't say something else stupid.

"This is nice," Nancy said. I wasn't sure if she meant the food or the company, but she soon clarified. "I'm glad you're both here. I thought I wanted to be alone, but I was wrong."

"You've been involved in a traumatic event, dear. It will take some time, but believe me, things will get better."

"I can't believe I said all those terrible things about Ray," Nancy said. "He wasn't that bad a person."

"I'm sure he had many redeeming qualities," Sister Rose said. "He must have been one of those people who hid them from others. That reminds me—I must reach out to his wife and express my condolences." Sister Rose made a note on her phone.

"His wife?" Nancy and I chorused. "He was married?"

"I should have called her his ex-wife. Leandra divorced him many years ago."

"Leandra?" Nancy and I spoke together once again. This was getting ridiculous. I zipped my lips shut and motioned for her to pick up the conversation.

"Leandra's a very unusual name," Nancy said. "The only person I can think of with that first name is Leandra Price, the famous fashion designer. I'm sure you don't mean her." She closed her eyes. "The pain pill I took a little while ago is starting to work." In a few seconds, she was fast asleep.

"They were married when they were both very young," Sister Rose said softly, which I interpreted as, "Yes, I do mean her," without actually saying it.

Most mystery books I read suggest the best way to solve a murder is to find out all you can about the victim. They also stress that no one knows more about the victim and is willing to talk about him than an ex-spouse. Therefore, I had to figure out a way to meet Leandra Price and find out anything I could about her relationship with Ray.

If you don't recognize the name, Leandra Price is one of Fairport's few claims to fame. Born and raised here, in the early 1980s here she bought a one-way ticket on Metro North to the bright lights of Seventh Avenue's garment district in Manhattan and never looked back. After a two-year apprenticeship at CK Designs, in 1983, she branched out on her own at New York's Fashion Week with a splashy, daring collection of colorful women's sportswear that belied her preppy roots in suburban Connecticut. Her timing was perfect, and she was suddenly a household name and a superstar in the cutthroat, competitive New York designer fashion industry.

To tell you the truth, I completely zoned out for the next several minutes. How could I get into Leandra's showroom… to talk about her marriage to Ray, of course. If she happened to offer me a sample from her latest collection because we'd hit it off so well, I'd refuse, of course. But then, to avoid being rude, I'd gratefully accept.

"Tomorrow morning at nine-thirty." My eyes snapped open. Who was this rude person interrupting me when I was trying to come up with a plan?

"We're seeing her tomorrow at nine-thirty," Sister Rose said in a low voice so she wouldn't wake Nancy.

"We?"

"I've mentioned your name to Leandra in the past, so she's aware that we know each other. I just reached out to her about Ray's sudden death and asked if I could bring you with me tomorrow as the representative from the reenactment committee to express your condolences, and she agreed."

As thrilled as I was about the opportunity to meet Leandra Price, a small part of me felt uncomfortable about the whole business, even if it was Sister Rose's idea.

"Sister, to clarify, I am not on the committee. Jim is."

"I am well aware of that," Sister Rose said. "However, knowing your talent for assisting the local police in certain circumstances, I felt it could be helpful to all concerned if you accompanied me tomorrow. I'm sure you'll be better than I will at asking Leandra discreet questions about her marriage to Ray. I'm not sure how open she'll be, but she could be very helpful if the police choose to concoct some ridiculous theory about how Ray died." She bent her head toward Nancy, and I got the message. Sister Rose was worried, too.

"Leandra Price is also one of the biggest donors to Sally's Place. She's a very private person, and I want to protect her privacy. I do not want any members of the committee or the police to connect her to Ray Thompson. Not even Jim is to know unless she gives her permission."

"Of course. I appreciate your faith in me."

"That's exactly what we need right now."

"Sorry, I don't understand."

"We need faith that together we will find out exactly how and why Ray Thompson died. As soon as possible." Sister Rose sniffed. "As if any of my girls would be capable of committing such a heinous crime. It's ridiculous."

Chapter 49

Does running late count as exercise?

As soon as I turned the corner onto Old Fairport Turnpike and caught the first glimpse of my house, I knew something was wrong. I saw Jim's car in the driveway, parked in front of the garage at a weird angle. Jim always parks toward the right side of the house, closer to the kitchen door. Plus, the picket fence gates were wide open. Jim and I always keep the gates closed in case Lucy and Ethel try to sneak out of the house without permission.

You may think I'm overreacting, but when you've been married to the same person for as long as I have, any deviation in established behavior patterns is a cause for alarm.

After closing and carefully bolting the gates, I walked up the driveway and peeked in the kitchen window. There was no sign of Jim at the kitchen table, his favorite pouting place. But the yardstick he sometimes uses for marching practice was on the table, broken in two.

Oh, boy. Jim was home, all right, and clearly not in a good mood.

I took a deep breath and whispered, "Onward."

I heard the sound of water running and realized Jim was taking a shower. Okay. Maybe I'd overreacted. Perhaps he had big plans to surprise me with a fancy dinner out at some fabulous restaurant and was sprucing up before he told me.

Maybe pigs really do fly, too.

As I walked into the bedroom, I could hear my husband singing at the top of his lungs. I stopped dead. Was that "I'm Gonna Wash That Man Right Out of My Hair," a song from *South Pacific*, that I heard him warbling?

Impossible, I told myself. Jim hates Broadway musicals and only goes to them when forced. And he'd never know the lyrics to any show tunes.

As I listened closer, however, I realized that Jim had changed the lyrics of the song to, "I'm gonna wash that gang right out of my hair." Hmm. Interesting. And then, I got it. (I hope you did, too.)

The water was turned off, and Jim opened the shower door. If he was surprised to see me standing there, handing him a bath towel, he didn't show it. Instead, he gave me a wet kiss, said, "Thanks, honey," and began to towel off while continuing his singing.

"What a nice singing voice you have," I said, following him into the bedroom and hoping he wouldn't drip on the hardwood floor. "You should serenade me more often."

"I'd forgotten how cathartic a hot shower can be," he said. "I hadn't planned on singing anything, but all of a sudden, that song popped into my head. I switched the lyrics around to fit the current situation, and now, I'm a new man." Jim gave me another smooch.

"And now, dear wife, I will say something I should say more often. You were right." He turned and began rummaging in his dresser for some undies. (In case you were picturing a different scene, he still had a towel wrapped around him.)

I sat on the bed, dislodging the two dogs. I knew they'd

forgive me, though. It was almost their dinner time.

"Would you care to repeat that?" I asked, cupping my ear. "I don't think I heard what you said."

"Don't push it, Carol. You heard exactly what I said. I'm surprised that, by now, you aren't on your phone texting all your girlfriends and gloating about it."

"I would never do that," I protested, especially because I'd probably left my phone in the kitchen.

I waited a beat, then probed a little more. "Pray tell, what was I right about?"

Jim turned and faced me. "The reenactment, of course. You've been complaining that it's the stupidest thing I've ever gotten involved in, and you were right." He slammed the drawer for emphasis. "I'm out. I quit today. I'm sick of the whole thing."

Tread carefully, Carol. You know Jim doesn't mean what he's saying. He's just upset.

"I'm sure Ray's death was on everyone's mind at today's meeting," I said. "It must have been very sad."

"I've never been to anything like it," Jim exploded, following me into the kitchen. "It wasn't a meeting at all. It was a series of ultimatums on how the reenactment will be done."

"I'm surprised Carla Grimaldi was so pushy. She's only been in office a short time."

I poured each of us a glass of lemon-lime seltzer, our new favorite non-alcoholic drink, and gestured for Jim to sit at the table. "Drink this. The bubbles always cheer you up."

"The ultimatums weren't from her," Jim clarified. "They were from Ray."

"Ray?" Unfortunately, I reacted to Jim's announcement by spilling the glass of seltzer all over his lap.

"I'm sorry, honey. My hand slipped." I jumped up to get a dry dish towel to clean up the mess I'd made.

"You've never done that before," Jim said, scowling. "I'm all wet. Now, I have to change my clothes again. I may as well take another shower, too."

"It was an accident," I said. "I'm very sorry it happened."

"Not as sorry as I am," Jim said as he stalked out of the room. "What's the matter with you, anyway?"

I wasn't going to let this go—I knew I'd have nightmares tonight. I followed Jim into the bedroom and started scooping up the wet clothes he'd thrown all over the floor.

"When you said the ultimatums came from Ray, you spooked me out, and I spilled the seltzer," I said, defending myself.

So, it's really your fault.

"How could they be from Ray? He's dead."

"We all know that, Carol. He didn't come back and take over the meeting from beyond the grave if that's what you're thinking. That's just silly, like something you'd see on late-night television. Stuff like that never happens in real life."

Oh, boy, do I have a newsflash for you.

All of a sudden, I had a terrible thought. What if Ray had to stick around for some reason and not pass over when he died like Elizabeth.

Don't let this go, Carol. You can't take that chance!

I followed Jim into the bathroom, hoping for a rational answer to calm my irrational thoughts. "Please explain to me exactly what you meant about Ray and the meeting agenda."

"If I do, can I have some privacy to take a hot shower?"

I nodded.

My husband sighed.

"He dropped off agendas for the tasting follow-up meeting at Carla Grimaldi's office yesterday morning. It outlined how he wanted the reenactment to be run from now on. If we'd had the meeting as planned, we could have discussed and hopefully revised his new plan, but that obviously didn't happen. Carla insisted that the best way to honor Ray's memory was to go along with all his suggested changes. I wanted to vote no, but nobody else would do it with me, so we're stuck with a whole new reenactment approach that I hate.

"I'll only tell you more if you let me take another shower first. With no interruptions. I'll do my best to be in a good mood when I'm finished."

"Deal," I said. "While you're doing that, I'll clean up the mess I made in the kitchen."

I also ordered takeout from Seafood Sandy's for supper since there was no way I'd actually *cook* while a small part of me still worried that Ray could come back as a ghost. That kind of multitasking is beyond me.

The food was delivered in record time and smelled yummy. I tossed the takeout boxes into the recycling bin (after rinsing them first), divided the feast into two portions, and called Jim to come and eat.

No response.

Since Jim never misses an opportunity for food, I figured he hadn't heard me. A quick check of the kitchen revealed that Lucy and Ethel were missing, too. That was unusual.

I found the three of them curled up on our bed, fast asleep.

There's an old saying that goes, "If you can't beat them, join them." So, after putting the food in the microwave for reheating later, that's exactly what I did. And then….

I'm not going to tell you about that.

Chapter 50

I've reached the age where my brain goes from, "I probably shouldn't say that" to "What the hell. Let's see what happens."

When I woke up, my cell phone informed me it was 11:30 pm. That meant we'd already slept five hours. My sleep cycle would never be the same.

With a little prodding and poking, I managed to rouse my bedmates. In no time at all, I'd reheated the people food and poured some extra kibble for the dogs.

Jim stumbled into the kitchen, rubbing his eyes. "Is this breakfast?"

"Don't be silly. It's a late, romantic dinner. Eat first, then give me the details from today's meeting."

I didn't have to wait long for Jim to clean his plate. He eyed mine, then said, "Are you going to finish that?"

"Hands off, buster," I said, holding onto my plate with an iron grip. "No more food for you at this hour. You'll get indigestion. Tell me what else happened at the meeting. And don't leave anything out."

I moved my plate as far away from Jim as possible, folded

my arms, and said in the sternest voice I could muster this late at night, "Talk."

"The important thing for you to remember, Carol, is that Ray's agenda was supposed to be just that—something to be discussed and voted on. Now, it's etched in stone. Period. No filming of any part of the reenactment using professional actors, only local people. The reenactment focus has shifted from the Battle of Fairport to highlighting the wonders of Fairport. Only residents can participate, including the march into town and the battle. Do you see the problem with that?"

I searched my brain and shook my head. "Sorry. I don't get it."

"The problem, dear wife, is that the original march on Fairport from the beach was by *British* soldiers, not American patriots. We practiced being the loyal opposition who rose up against them. Without professionals playing the part of the British, there won't be a march at all because everyone on the committee wants to be a patriot. The whole meeting ended in complete chaos. Several members stormed out in protest.

"Plus, when I texted Mack to tell him he had to film using only local people, and nobody wanted to be a British soldier, he quit the project. No reenactment march, filming, gala ball, nothing."

"So, you're saying the whole thing is canceled?"

"As of now, yes, unless Carla Grimaldi and the rest of the committee can agree to a compromise. I told everyone that I quit and walked out." Jim looked so sad; I was afraid he was going to cry.

So, you can finally shave off that awful beard and get a decent haircut?
Not a good idea to suggest that now, Carol.

"There are still a few months left to figure all this out before July," I said. "How about a parade from the beach instead? Everyone loves a parade, and all of you could march in it."

"Thanks for the suggestion, but I don't think the committee

will go along with it. I wasn't the only one who was fed up and quit."

"Too bad Nancy wasn't able to be part of the meeting. She might've been able to talk some sense into the First Selectwoman."

Jim dismissed that idea immediately. "I doubt it. I'm learning that Carla Grimaldi takes advice from no one."

"How is Nancy? Did you see her today?"

"She's still pretty upset. It will take some time for her to get over the shock of yesterday's tragedy since she was such an intimate part of it."

I figured when she found out what happened, or didn't happen, at the committee meeting, she'd either be relieved that the whole event could be canceled, or livid about Carla Grimaldi's decision. Either way, I wouldn't be the person who told her what had gone on.

"If Carla Grimaldi's the savvy politician I think she is, she'll go along with the majority of the committee," I said.

Once the committee gets its act together, which sounded like it would take a while.

"I hope you're right. And I'm still hungry."

I pushed my plate in Jim's direction. "All right. This is all yours but eat it slowly. And you have to clean up the kitchen when you're finished. I'll take care of the dogs."

Call me a cockeyed optimist, but I was sure that things would sort themselves out in the light of a new day.

Chapter 51

Had a bad mix-up at the store today when the cashier said, "Strip down facing me." Apparently, she was referring to my credit card.

I was up, showered, dressed, and even had the coffee ready before Jim shuffled into the kitchen in his favorite ratty bathrobe the next morning.

"What's the occasion? You're never up this early."

I handed him a full mug of coffee. "It may not be as good as yours, but please don't criticize me. I did my best."

Jim took a tentative sip, smiled, and sat. I figured I'd done a pretty good job since he hadn't immediately made a face and dumped the coffee in the kitchen sink.

"I have a date with Sister Rose this morning," I informed my husband. "I don't dare keep her waiting."

"Just you two? What's going on?"

"Sister Rose has someone she wants me to meet. A woman who graduated from Mount Saint Francis a few years after I did. She's just moved back to town and doesn't know too many people. I couldn't refuse."

I'm embarrassed at how quickly I came up with the huge

whopper I just told my husband. I hope you're not judging me too harshly. Sister Rose made it crystal clear that I was not to tell anyone about Ray's ex-wife. Blame her, not me.

"It's nice of you to reach out to someone new in town."

Jim's praise made me feel even guiltier about lying to him. "Don't give me too much credit. It wasn't my idea. Sister Rose is the nice one. She just volunteered me to help her."

"I have to find something else to wear," I said, hopping up and heading for the safety of the bedroom before Jim asked me any more questions.

"Why are you changing your clothes?"

"I decided I don't like this outfit." *Especially if I'm going to meet a famous fashion designer.*

"You look fine the way you are," Jim called after me.

"I don't expect you to understand," I said as I combed through my closet furiously, looking for just the right duds—comfortable, but not too comfortable; stylish, but not too stylish.

Would it surprise you that I ended up wearing the outfit I started with? No, I didn't think so.

I dashed out the door before Jim had a chance to comment on my wardrobe choice. Let him think that, for once, what I decided to wear was because he liked it.

Chapter 52

I accidentally wore a red shirt to Target today, and, long story short, I'm covering for Becca this weekend.

    We had a memorable ride in Sister Rose's Corolla, most of which I spent silently begging St. Frances of Rome, the patron saint of safe drivers, to get us to our destination in one piece.

    As a point of clarification (and to show off my celestial knowledge a little), this is a different saint from St. Francis of Assisi, the patron saint of animals. According to legend, when St. Frances of Rome went out to do good works, an angel always lit her path, and she was promised a safe return. If you've ever been to Rome during rush hour, you'll know why she's the ideal patron saint for the city. She's also the patron saint of widows, but I'm sure that's just a coincidence.

    I was relieved and excited when Sister Rose entered the Fairport Inn and Suites parking garage. Famous designer or not, Ray's ex-wife probably had a dandy motive or two to bump him off. If she was at the hotel the day Ray died, she'd shoot up even higher on my list of potential suspects.

    Sister Rose sailed across the lobby toward the express

elevator, and I followed in her wake. She tapped a key card, and the elevator doors glided open. In no *time* at all, we were at the penthouse floor. The door of Penthouse A opened as if by magic, and we were greeted by a hotel employee wheeling out an empty trolley.

"Come on in, Rose," a woman called out. "I'm in the kitchen pretending I actually made this delicious breakfast. Make yourself comfortable at the dining room table. I'll join you in a moment."

I couldn't wait to meet the famous Leandra Price until I caught a glimpse of myself in a full-length mirror and realized my black slacks and coordinating blazer were now a mass of wrinkles.

"Why are you hanging back, Carol?" Sister Rose said. "I thought you were eager to have this meeting?"

"I am," I said, following Sister Rose into the dining room and sliding onto a chair as quickly as possible. I hoped that if I already had a napkin on my lap, Leandra wouldn't notice the sorry condition of my outfit.

"Here I am. How's my favorite nun? Come here and hug me," Leandra said, embracing Sister Rose like they were long-lost girlfriends. "If I know you, you've had several adventures since I saw you last. I can't wait to get caught up."

Our hostess turned to me. "And you're Carol Andrews. I'm so excited to meet you in person. Sister Rose has told me so much about you that I feel we're already friends."

"I'd like to think I've matured since my high school days," I stammered, wondering what the heck Sister Rose had said about me.

"I only shared positive stories, so don't worry," Sister Rose clarified with a smile. "I thought it was time that two of my favorite people met."

I was one of Sister Rose's favorite people? Oh, *puleeze*. Nancy, Claire, and Mary Alice would never believe it. Too bad I hadn't switched my cell phone to "record."

Leandra Price was nothing like I had been expecting. I'd anticipated a glamorous fashion designer wearing one of her fabulous creations. The woman pouring me a cup of coffee was clad in a gray sweatshirt and baggy pants that could have come from the Jim Andrews at-home fashion collection. The shirt proclaimed, "Short women have more fun." She wore no makeup, and her white hair was tied back in a ponytail.

I tried to mask my shock. Despite her present casual appearance, Leandra was definitely the woman I'd seen checking in yesterday, right before I went into the restaurant for lunch.

You're here to ask questions about her marriage to Ray, not make a new friend. And remember, many murderers in the mysteries you read are likeable on the surface.

After we'd all helped ourselves to the delicious brunch and chatted about inconsequential things like the weather and how nice the Fairport Inn and Suites was, Sister Rose got the conversational ball rolling.

"Leandra, Carol and I came today to offer our condolences on your loss."

For a tiny second, I saw a sad expression on Leandra's face. She was actually grieving for her ex-husband.

Sister Rose took Leandra's hand and held it without saying another word for several minutes. I sat quietly, waiting for Sister Rose to continue.

"He was a part of your life, and now he's gone," she said gently. "Of course you're grieving, no matter why or how your marriage ended. It's nothing to be embarrassed about. We're here to support you; no one will ever know anything shared here. Right, Carol?"

"Absolutely." I looked at Sister Rose for a hint about what to say or do next. Now, she was sitting with her eyes closed. I figured she was praying, so I did the same thing. (In the interests of full disclosure, first, I took a generous bite of a chocolate chip muffin; then, I closed my eyes and prayed.)

After what seemed like an hour, but was probably only a few minutes, I took a chance and opened my eyes. Leandra had huge tears running silently down her face. Wordlessly, I offered her a napkin. She grabbed my hand and held it tight.

"I really hated him," she finally said. "You can't imagine how many times I wished he was dead. And now he is, and I don't know what to do."

"Deep down inside, I'm sure you didn't really wish he was dead," I said. "Sometimes I've been so angry at Jim—my husband—that I felt the same way. But the anger only lasted a short time. I really do love him."

If Leandra grasped my hand any tighter, she'd break every bone. I wriggled my fingers a little bit, and she loosened her grip.

I looked at Sister Rose, and she nodded her head a little. I took that to mean I should keep going. I took a deep breath. This conversation was a lot harder and more emotional than I'd expected.

This situation isn't about you and Jim. It's about Leandra and Ray.

"How long were you and Ray married?" I held my breath, afraid I'd gotten too personal too quickly.

"We were married twelve months and five days. That's three hundred seventy days, right?"

Not waiting for an answer, Leandra continued. "We met in college. I was an art history major, and he majored in chemistry. Two polar opposites, for sure. But we were happy for the first few months. At least, I was. In hindsight, I was kidding myself. It dawned on me later that Ray was even fooling around when we were on our honeymoon. I just didn't catch on then to what he was up to when he left the chambermaid at our hotel such a big tip.

"We had grand plans to settle in San Francisco, but then

Ray's father died suddenly. Ray inherited the toy store, and we ended up living in Fairport. It didn't take long after we moved here for him to start staying late at the store to take inventory and unpack stock, supposedly."

Leandra grimaced. "He was taking inventory, all right, at the sleaziest motels in Fairfield County. The creep."

"That must have been horrible for you. I am so sorry."

Leandra finally let go of my hand, and I resisted massaging my poor fingers to restart the circulation.

"Horrible, yes. And humiliating, too. Whenever I caught him, Ray would tell me he was sorry, and that none of these affairs meant anything to him. They were all just one-night stands. For Ray, the excitement was always in the seduction part. Once the woman gave in, the thrill was gone for him. I often wondered what would happen if anyone said no to him. I bet he got really angry.

"In the long run, though, he did me a huge favor. He showed me that I could stand on my own two feet. That I didn't need a man in my life to be happy or make me feel complete. If it weren't for our bad marriage, I don't think I would ever have had the courage to pursue my dream of becoming a fashion designer. I wanted to tell Ray that, despite all the bad things, I was grateful to him for changing my life. But I never got the chance.

"Don't get me wrong. I still hated him for what he put me through. But I guess a small part of me loved him, too."

Chapter 53

My son asked if a punch bowl is where you keep the names of the people you want to punch. I usually keep them in my head, but keeping them in a decorative crystal bowl sounds much classier.

Sister Rose and I were both silent on the ride back to my house. I had learned deeply intimate things about two people I hardly knew, one of whom was now deceased. It was an emotional roller coaster ride for me because I couldn't help comparing everything that Leandra Price told me with the relative peace and security and…yes…happiness of my own marriage.

Stick to what's important, Carol. Did Leandra tell you anything to keep her on the top of your suspect list?

"Maybe we'll talk later today," Sister Rose said. "I have to process what I just heard." She shook her head. "Such sadness. Such bitterness."

"I'm going inside to hug both dogs. They always cheer me up."

Sister Rose laughed. "Maybe I need a dog, too." She rolled to a stop in front of my house. "Thank you for coming with me this morning. I think you really helped Leandra open up about her feelings."

"But did we learn anything that can help Nancy?" I shook my head in frustration. "I honestly don't know. My head is spinning right now. Her question about love and hate being two sides of the same thing threw me."

I waved goodbye, walked to my kitchen door, and stopped. The door was wide open. Jim's car was gone, and mine was in the garage. There was no other car in my driveway.

Most people would probably be frightened. But since I discovered a 200-year-old ghost had been living in my house, this was my "new normal." To be on the safe side, though, I'd punched 911 on my cell phone and had my trigger finger on "send."

Elizabeth had made herself at home at my kitchen table. She was dressed in the Lilly Pulitzer leggings and matching top I'd gotten on sale last winter and had hidden in my closet so Jim wouldn't see it. The nerve! I hadn't even taken the price tags off them yet.

My two canine companions were sleeping at her feet. Humph.

"I'm glad to see you're dressed comfortably," I said with as much sarcasm as I could muster on short notice. I heard the sound of water running in my bathroom sink. "And you have a guest, too. How nice. Sorry if I've intruded." I gave her a pointed look.

Elizabeth blushed with embarrassment. "Don't be mad at me, Carol. I was walking by Town Hall and saw Nancy in the parking lot. I wanted to see how she was."

Nancy came out of the master bedroom, dabbing her face with one of my white embroidered face towels. "I know this towel is one of the good ones you save for company, Carol, but I figured that after all I've been through, you wouldn't mind."

Of course I minded, but I am not a petty person. I took

the high road instead.

"I'm just glad to see you. How do you feel?"

"I'm a little better today. I think I still look awful, even though Elizabeth says I don't."

"Can I hug you if I'm careful?"

"Sure. Just don't kiss me. My face still hurts."

"What if I give you a baby kiss?"

At Nancy's puzzled look, I clarified, "The kind I give to CJ." I bussed her gently on the non-injured side of her face, then pulled out a chair and gestured for her to sit.

"Why were you in the Town Hall parking lot?"

"Nancy and I just came from Carla Grimaldi's office," Elizabeth explained.

"Let me tell it," Nancy said, looking miffed that Elizabeth had answered the question I had clearly directed at her. "It was my idea, and then you asked to tag along."

Elizabeth rolled her eyes, and I bit my lip, trying not to laugh. Nancy will never, ever allow herself to be upstaged by anyone. Unless she was caught in a youthful indiscretion or two that she wants to wiggle out of. Not that I'm holding a grudge against my very best friend, mind you. Let bygones be bygones, I always say.

"Anyway, when I woke up this morning," Nancy said, settling into her chair and ready to tell me *her* story without any more interruptions, "I felt so much better than I did yesterday. Then Bob said something at breakfast that really made me think."

I didn't want to risk the ire of a wounded woman, but the thought of Bob contributing anything substantial to a conversation stretched my imagination to its limits.

"How interesting," I said. "I didn't realize Bob was so insightful. What did he say?"

"He reminded me that I should be proud of my attempts to save a dying man, especially one I didn't even like. My efforts to save Ray's life should be celebrated. I'm the hero of the newest Battle of Fairport and have the visible wounds to prove it. I should wear them proudly. Nobody, not even an incompetent police officer, should accuse me of anything different. I'm just like a survivor of the original Battle of Fairport, only hundreds of years later."

"Fascinating," I said, not quite sure if that was an appropriate response, but it seemed to satisfy Nancy.

"Then I got a text of yesterday's committee meeting minutes. When I read them, I was furious. Carla Grimaldi was singing Ray's praises and saying we should honor his memory by running the event according to his wishes, which is ridiculous. He didn't even want to do the gala to benefit a local charity."

Nancy paused to catch her breath, then continued. "I decided while my wounds were fresh to march into Carla Grimaldi's office and tell her to her face that she'd made the wrong decision about the reenactment. Because she did."

"I happened to see Nancy in the parking lot of Town Hall when I was out jogging," Elizabeth added. "When she told me what she was planning, I invited myself along."

"We made quite an entrance," Nancy said. "Fortunately, Carla Grimaldi didn't ask us to leave immediately. I was surprised at how nice she was. She even asked us to call her Carla."

Well, that is her name. For heaven's sake, it's not like she's the President of the United States. She's just the First Selectwoman of a small New England town.

"Thanks to Nancy, I'm now officially back on the planning committee," Elizabeth said. "And we convinced Carla that the reenactment should be filmed professionally, using professional actors, so Mack's back on the project."

I wondered if Jim and the rest of the planning committee knew any of this yet.

Nancy interrupted again. "We persuaded Carla to give us a week to come up with an alternate plan to Ray's and get the committee to back it. Isn't that great?"

Good luck with that. You're going to need it.

"We came right over here to tell you about our meeting, but you weren't home," Nancy said. "Your car was in the garage, so I figured you'd be back soon."

"Nancy insisted we wait for you," Elizabeth said. "I hope you don't mind that we let ourselves inside with her key."

I didn't answer. I just smiled.

"You'll help us, won't you, Carol? You're so good at planning things."

A lightbulb went off in my pea brain. Nancy was shifting the responsibility to me, just like she'd been doing since we were kids.

Once again, I didn't answer. I just smiled.

"We really need you," Nancy said, touching her cheek to remind me she was injured, "You're so clever.

"Don't we, Elizabeth? You tell her."

"Elizabeth is the resident expert on reenactments, not me," I said. "I do have one suggestion, though."

"I knew you'd come up with an idea right away," Nancy squealed.

"Don't give me credit for being brilliant. One of you should contact Mack right away and tell him that he and his film crew are back on the reenactment project. I know from experience what a short attention span he has. Mack may already be involved in something else."

"I'll do that," Elizabeth said. "Nancy, you should go home and get more rest. I'll check back with you later."

"She's right. You're looking tired," I echoed. "It's time for you to take care of yourself. You've already accomplished a lot today."

"Come on, Nancy, I'll walk you to your car," Elizabeth

said. She gave me a "What are you up to?" look as I waved goodbye and closed the kitchen door.

"I thought they'd never leave," I said to Lucy and Ethel. "I need time to think."

Even Ethel looked doubtful at that idea, but I ignored her and soldiered on.

"Here's a question for you both to ponder. Why is Carla Grimaldi so insistent on honoring Ray Thompson's memory? They only knew each other a short time."

The more I noodled that question around my brain, the more I wanted to find the answer.

Although Carla Grimaldi was a key player in the reenactment planning, she never attended earlier organizational meetings. Instead, she sent her assistant. What prompted the sudden change in her priorities?

Leandra Price said that Ray's favorite part of his many affairs was seduction. Was he in the process of wooing Carla? Romancing the First Selectwoman would be a big deal. He might have even planned to brag about it. Was it possible that Carla and Ray…?

Call me crazy (only kidding), but while Nancy and Elizabeth were occupied redesigning Celebrate Fairport, I'd be busy finding out everything I could about our new First Selectwoman.

Chapter 54

There are three types of people in this world: those who make things happen, those who watch things happen, and those who wonder what the heck happened.

I can be the world's number one procrastinator. Unless it's a matter of life or death, I often put off things I know I should do but would rather postpone as long as possible—like making dinner.

Not today.

Instead, in a sudden burst of energy, I threw together the ingredients for a turkey meatloaf so Jim wouldn't starve. I set the alarm on my smartwatch for one hour, which was plenty of time for me to make significant progress on my research project before it was time to cook the meatloaf.

Or…even better…I could use this time to text Mike and see if he had time to help me with my research. My darling son is definitely the computer guru in our family. If he's not too busy running Cosmo's—his fabulously successful, chic South Florida bistro—he gets a kick out of lending a hand to his dear old mom when asked the right way (without any nosy preamble from me inquiring about the current state of his romantic life).

I hadn't heard a word from Mike for two weeks and three days, not that I'm keeping count. Promising to behave myself, I decided we were overdue for a cyber chat.

I checked the time again—four p.m. I realized the pre-dinner/happy hour customers must already be swarming in and wanting service—bad timing on my part.

Better to reach out later in the evening after Cosmo's was closed. Unless Mike had a date, of course.

I allowed my imagination to wonder if Mike had a new girlfriend he was madly in love with, and that's why I hadn't heard from him in a while. Maybe Jenny knew what was going on. I know the siblings are in frequent touch—more than Mike is with his parents, not that I'm jealous. No way. I'm glad they're so close. But still, I do like to know what's going on with my children, even though they're both adults now.

Suddenly, Lucy jumped on my lap, which interrupted my musings. She gave me a pointed stare. I got the message. I was wasting valuable time. After dislodging my canine alarm clock, I focused on my research project.

Sister Rose always taught us that research should be done in steps, starting with what you already know. What else do you want to know? What questions need to be answered to achieve that goal? Where are the best sources to find those answers? Finally, do your research to find those answers.

It made sense to me.

I sat at my computer and wondered what exactly I already knew about Carla Grimaldi. According to the sometimes-reliable local gossip mill, she moved to Fairport two years ago and bought one of the new condos on the beach. She'd had an impressive career as a hedge fund genius for the Manhattan firm of LaSalle and Long, so money obviously wasn't a problem for her. (Believe me, those condos don't come cheap.)

According to her official biography on the Town of Fairport web page, "Connecticut native Carla Smith Grimaldi is a graduate of Vassar College with a double major in mathematics and business, as well as the highly respected Women's Campaign School at Yale University." That was it. Short and sweet.

I added a few more to-do notes on my cell phone: *Find out where Carla is from in Connecticut. If Grimaldi is her married name, is/ was there a Mr. Grimaldi? Or is she divorced or widowed? Any children?*

As I continued my search, I suddenly realized the last name "Grimaldi" sounded familiar. Possibly a schoolmate from years gone by? I racked my brain and couldn't come up with anyone. Sister Rose would know. She knows everybody and everything. Her memory and total recall are the stuff of legends. I made a note on my phone to reach out if I needed to pick her brain.

I couldn't get rid of the feeling I knew the last name "Grimaldi" from somewhere, so I finally Googled it. The answer made me laugh so loud that I earned dirty looks from both Lucy and Ethel, who'd been napping nearby. "The House of Grimaldi is the reigning house of the Principality of Monaco. The current head is Prince Albert II, the son and successor of Prince Rainier III and the Princess Consort Grace of Monaco, formerly known as Grace Kelly."

"I think we can rule out any connection between our current First Selectwoman and Prince Albert," I told the dogs. "Just for the heck of it, let's check out the surname 'Smith.'"

Wikipedia told me, "Smith is the most common surname in the English language, with over four million bearers worldwide."

Another dead end, pardon the pun.

Back to Grimaldi. The Fairport one, not the royal one.

I searched for "Carla Grimaldi, Fairport Connecticut First Selectwoman," which led me to an article about her in the

Fairport News: "*Grimaldi Launches Campaign for Board of Selectman.*"

When asked about her relative inexperience in politics and being a newcomer to Fairport, Ms. Grimaldi replied, "I am basing my campaign on a platform of more oversight and fiscal responsibility for our town. I have years of financial experience, making me the only viable candidate in this election. I'm confident voters will agree."

I guess this made sense. It certainly struck a positive chord with the locals. However, I was interested that she had cleverly ignored the problem of being a newcomer to town. Since Carla was one of only two candidates for a seat in the off-year election race, and the other candidate was arrested for murder and running a drug ring during the campaign, she won handily, and Fairport had its first-ever First Selectwoman. But her early life seemed to be shrouded in mystery, at least to me.

I decided to use a different approach. Instead of searching for information about Carla, I'd see what I could find out about Ray Thompson's early life. I figured Leandra Price might be helpful, but I was reluctant to contact her so soon after our emotional visit earlier today.

Just for the heck of it, I searched for "Ray Thompson, Connecticut." After wading through hundreds of hits about different Ray Thompsons, I hit pay dirt just I was starting to get a massive headache from eyestrain. The unlikely source was the January 12, 1969 edition of the *Beach Beacon*, a now-defunct weekly paper from southern Fairfield County.

On the front page of the newspaper, there was a grainy photo of a boy in his early teens, identified as Raymond Thompson of Beacon Falls, holding the hand of a little girl. Raymond was wearing an Eagle Scout uniform, and the little girl, identified as Carla Smith of Green Meadows, was looking up at him and grinning.

"*Local Eagle Scout Saves Drowning Child*"

"Raymond Thompson went skating with his buddies last weekend on White's Pond and became a local hero. The ice in the pond began to crack due to a recent thaw, and the boys were able to get to safety. 'Then I heard someone screaming for help,' Raymond said. 'A little girl was trapped on the ice, and her family couldn't reach her.' With no thought for his own safety, Raymond immediately skated back onto the pond as close to the child as he safely could, lay down on the ice, and was able to grab the little girl's hands to pull her out. He safely carried her back to the pond's edge and reunited her with her family."

"'I just did what any other Eagle Scout would do,' Raymond said about his efforts. 'I'm not a hero.'

"The teen will be honored by Beacon Falls Mayor William Johnson at a ceremony on Saturday at Town Hall. The public is invited to attend."

Chapter 55

Sometimes I think I'm a genius. Then, I realize I've already seen this episode of Jeopardy!

I was so preoccupied with the information I'd found out from Ray's ex-wife that I barely said two words to Jim at dinner that night. Not that he noticed, mind you. My husband was too busy bringing me up to date on the ridiculous ideas the planning committee was considering to honor Ray at the reenactment while still keeping the spirit of the original event alive.

I can practice selective hearing, too.

I didn't even react when Jim announced (proudly, mind you) that they were considering incorporating Ray's funeral procession into the invasion march from the beach. I knew the only reason behind that stupid idea was so the boys could still play dress-up in their soldier uniforms.

"I'm surprised the First Selectwoman approved this idea."

Jim's face reminded me of Mike's when I caught him sneaking an empty box of ice cream sandwiches back in the freezer, so I wouldn't blame him for eating the last one.

Busted!

"Did you run any of these ideas by Carla Grimaldi?" I asked, knowing darn well that they hadn't.

"Not yet," Jim mumbled. "We're still brainstorming."

Was it up to me to tell him that Nancy and Elizabeth had already met with Carla and been given a week to come up with ideas?

Nope, I was not getting involved. I had too many other things on my mind, and they were going round and round in my brain like wet clothes in an overloaded dryer. There was only one person who might be able to un-muddle my brain. Heaven knows she'd had years of practice—Sister Rose.

Here's a question I bet none of you have ever had to ask: What time do nuns go to bed? Was it too late for me to text her? It was only 8:00 p.m., and now that Daylight Savings Time had started, there was even a small glimmer of light still left on the horizon.

Oh, what the heck, Carol. So what if she gets angry at you? Lord knows it wouldn't be the first time. Besides, she said this morning that you're one of her favorite people. Grow up and text her.

I took a deep breath, said a silent prayer to St. Scholastica, the twin sister of St. Benedict and the patron saint of several religious orders, and sent off a quick text.

Me: Hope it's not too late to reach out. I need to talk.

Ping.

SR: Are you all right?

Ping.

Me: I'm confused. I need to talk about Ray.

Ping.

SR: I'm still at the thrift shop. Just finished a quick supper. Want to come here?

Ping.

Me: Thank you! 15 minutes.

Chapter 56

I may not have lost all my marbles yet, but I'm pretty sure there's a small hole in the bag somewhere.

I admit that I was a little nervous when I snuck out the kitchen door on my way to a clandestine meeting with Sister Rose. Jim and both dogs were already snoring away on our bed. If Jim woke up and found me AWOL, I figured he'd just assume I was trolling away on the computer, roll over, and go back to sleep.

No matter what you may have already heard, I am not accustomed to secretly leaving my house, especially at night. Just wanted to set the record straight.

The porch light was on, but it didn't add much to my vision as I tiptoed across the driveway toward my car. My shoes crunching across the gravel were so loud they sounded like a drum solo in a rock-and-roll band. I'd never make a good spy, that was for sure.

Then I heard more footsteps on the driveway from near the garage. I froze. Someone else was out there in my darkened yard. I gripped my keys. They were the only weapons I had.

Fight or flight? How about just standing there like a jerk, not knowing what to do? That's what I did.

I heard a familiar voice. "Carol, don't be afraid. It's me, Elizabeth."

"Good lord," I said, willing my hammering heart to be calm before I keeled over on the driveway. "You scared me to death. Why are you outside prowling around at this hour?"

Stupid question, Carol. Elizabeth is a ghost, remember. Prowling around at all hours of the day and night is what ghosts do.

She moved toward me, stepping into the moonlight so she was completely visible. "I'm leaving now, and I'm not sure when or if I'll be back. I wanted to let you know."

"You're wearing the blue dress!"

"I hope you don't mind me going into your closet one more time," Elizabeth said. "I could tell you were angry with me this morning because I was wearing your brand-new Lilly Pulitzer outfit before you did.

"Don't worry. I won't do it again."

"Right now, I'm more concerned about you leaving so suddenly than about you borrowing my clothes. You're starting to freak me out. Where are you going?"

"Back to my so-called anniversary party, the original masquerade ball."

"Are you crazy? You know how horrible that night was. Why would you put yourself through all that violence and misery again? I don't understand."

"Let's just say that I have no choice. You have to trust me. I'm doing what I have to do. If I'm lucky, I'll be back by the time you wake up in the morning. If I don't return, please remember that I've loved being a part of your life."

She kissed me on the cheek. "Don't cry, Carol. Think good thoughts for me."

And she disappeared.

There was no way I could drive to the thrift shop now. I

was a nervous wreck. I snuck back into the house and fired off a quick text to Sister Rose, apologizing for being a no-show and saying I'd be in touch with her in the morning. I grabbed a blanket from the linen closet to keep me warm and settled back in Jim's recliner to wait for Elizabeth to come back. As I snuggled under the blanket, I realized I hadn't pulled an all-night vigil in more than a decade.

And now I was waiting-up for a ghost.

Chapter 57

I might wake up early and go running. I also might wake up and find out I'd lost ten pounds overnight and had naturally curly blonde hair. The odds are about the same.

When Jim roused me from a restless sleep the following morning, I did my best to sit up. Don't get any wrong ideas. I wasn't trying to do an *exercise* sit-up. All I wanted to do was uncurl my body from its sleeping position and sit up straight in the recliner. Every bone and muscle in my body told me that was a horrible idea.

My hero husband reached down to help, which increased my level of pain from hurting to excruciating.

"I'll be all right," I panted. "Just give me a minute." *Or an hour. Or the rest of my life.*

"What were you thinking, Carol? Why didn't you come to bed when you started to feel sleepy?"

I could tell that Jim would continue cross-examining and berating me until he got a satisfactory answer, and since telling him the truth was out, I had to wing it.

"I was worried about Nancy, and I couldn't sleep. I came

out here so I wouldn't disturb you. I was being thoughtful and considerate. And I guess I finally fell asleep. And now, I'm in pain." And I gave him a pitiful look.

"Oh, honey, you shouldn't ever worry about waking me. I was concerned when I woke up, and you were gone. Stupid, I guess."

"At our age," I said, moving carefully and slowly enough that I could finally stand, "we have to be very careful of ourselves and each other. I'm better now. You don't have to help me."

I reached in my pocket for my phone to check the time and realized I'd missed three texts and two phone calls from Jenny in the last half hour. I panicked.

"Have you heard from Jenny this morning?"

"No, Carol. Why would I? The sun is hardly up."

"She's been trying to reach me. I'm sure something horrible has happened."

"If something horrible had happened, don't you think our daughter would try to reach both of us?" my reasonable husband asked. "She probably wants you to babysit today."

There is no way she'd text me this early, and this often, for a babysitting gig, no matter what Jim thinks.

But there was no point in both of us hitting the panic button until I found out what was going on, so I replied rationally and calmly rather than screaming hysterically.

"I'm sure you're right. I'll text Jenny as soon as I brush my teeth."

I walked slowly toward our bathroom, and when I was safely inside, I locked the door so Jim wouldn't bother me. I knew in my gut that something terrible had happened.

I said good morning to the old hag in the bathroom mirror, then texted Jenny.

Me: I just got up. What's the emergency? Do you need me to babysit today? I can be there in about an hour.

Ping.

Jenny: Mom, I want you to be very calm when I tell you what's happened. Promise me.

Ping.

Me: Oh, dear God. Is CJ all right? Mark?

Ping.

Jenny: We're all fine. It's Nancy.

Ping.

Me: For Pete's sake, just tell me!

Ping.

Jenny: The police have a witness who swears he heard Nancy threaten to kill Ray Thompson. He signed a statement and is willing to testify against her in court. She's being brought in for questioning today and may be arrested.

Chapter 58

Nothing spoils a good story like the arrival of an eyewitness.

I ran out of the bathroom so fast that I almost tripped on my own big feet and dropped my phone.

"Jim! Jim! Are you still here?"

The kitchen was empty. Even worse, his car was gone, and there was a scribbled note on the counter, which I couldn't read, even with my glasses on.

Aargh! I muttered a few choice words that I never say in front of Lucy and Ethel.

Then I had one of my truly brilliant ideas—I'd snap a picture of Jim's note with my phone, then enlarge it slowly to read the darn thing! After ten minutes of total frustration, I was able to decipher Jim's chicken-scratch handwriting.

Larry called. He just heard from Nancy. She's in real trouble now, and he's on his way over to talk to her. I'm going out to see if I can find out more. Don't worry! Will keep in touch.

You may have met Larry McGee before, but I don't blame you if you don't remember him. Claire's been married to him for years, and we frequently socialize as couples. Not to be critical, and please don't repeat this, but Larry is one of the most boring human beings on the face of the earth. I'm not the only one who thinks that. Even Mary Alice, the soul of kindness, has been known to stifle yawns and roll her eyes when she sits next to him at a dinner party. But he was a crackerjack attorney, and even though he's retired now, I was confident that Larry would figure out a way to get Nancy out of this jam.

I immediately drafted a group text to muster my own personal posse: Claire, Mary Alice, Sister Rose, Maria Lesco, and Deanna, all of whom had been involved with me in previous sleuthing activities at various times. Before I could press "send," I was interrupted by someone banging on my kitchen door, then a familiar voice.

"Carol! Carol! Are you here? Open the door and let me in."

"It's unlocked," I yelled. "Come in before you break it down."

Claire stormed into the kitchen like a general in the middle of a war. "Don't you know what's going on? We have to leave right now, and you're not even dressed yet." She gave me a critical look.

"Hi, Claire. Thanks for stopping by." I hoped my voice was dripping with enough sarcasm that Claire couldn't miss it. "I spent an extremely uncomfortable night sleeping in the recliner. Jenny told me about Nancy. I'm on my way to take a quick shower and get to Nancy's, even though I haven't even had coffee yet. I hope you'll forgive me if I'm not all bright-eye and bushy-tailed yet. I'm working on it, but it'll take a while."

"I don't think Nancy knows yet," Claire said, stopping me dead in my tracks.

"How could she not know?"

"She knows she's going to be questioned again today. But I don't think she realizes how bad things are starting to look for her because of this surprise witness."

"Thank God for Larry," I said. And I meant it.

"Yes. After Nancy's call, he rushed to her house to calm her down. He's trying to find out who the witness is. He wants to be present when the police question her today, but he doesn't know how Nancy will react if he suggests it. She's vacillating between anger and hysteria. You know how emotional she can be. Bob will definitely be with her if he's allowed to be. I'm glad they're officially a married couple again."

"Will she have to go to the station, or will the questioning be at home?"

"As of now, it's at her house, which should make it less frightening. I suppose that could also change, but I doubt it. Your son-in-law is doing his best to go easy on her. But his partner is a real pain in the you-know-what."

"What should we do?"

"*You* should take a shower. I'll sit here and send out a few texts to see if I can find out anything new."

"Works for me."

I usually take my time getting ready for the day (even if I'm not going anywhere), but not today. I skipped my daily shampoo ritual, took the fastest shower ever, and was back in the kitchen in record time wearing a mostly presentable outfit of chino slacks and a navy cotton sweater. It was not up to my usual sartorial standards, but this was an emergency.

Claire was looking down at her phone and frowning, which was not a good sign. I ignored her. If something else was wrong, I was facing it with a strong dose of caffeine from the carafe Jim had thoughtfully provided.

I took a sip. Then another. Heaven. Emboldened by the caffeine rush, I was ready for whatever bad news Claire had to share.

"Okay, what's up? I haven't been gone that long. Nancy hasn't been arrested already, has she?" I was joking but praying it wasn't true at the same time.

"No, thank goodness. Larry just checked in to say they're on the way to the police station so she can sign an official statement. He didn't mention anything about the witness."

"It doesn't sound too ominous."

"I might as well go home and clean the house to keep busy while I wait for more news from Larry."

"Do you really want to do that?"

Claire made a sour face. "What do you think?"

"I have a better way for us to spend the morning. Let's go shopping."

"Oh, Carol, honestly. That is so like you. One of our best friends is in serious trouble, and you want to waste time going shopping!"

"I have an ulterior motive. When you hear what it is, I'm betting you'll want to tag along with me."

"Fat chance," Claire said, digging in her purse for her car keys.

"I think it's important to find out all we can about Ray Thompson. Don't you? All the mysteries I read tell me that."

"*Okayyyy*," Claire said slowly, sitting down again. "So…."

"So, let's go buy CJ a present at Thompson's Toys and snoop around while we're there. While getting dressed, I had this brilliant idea: I called the store and spoke to a lovely woman named Lois, the manager. They'll be open until five o'clock."

"You are brilliant," Claire said.

"Sometimes, not often," I said, which made Claire laugh.

"By the way, Lois didn't sound at all broken up about her boss's tragic death. I thought that was very interesting."

Chapter 59

How to parallel park: Park somewhere else.

After a frustrating twenty minutes circling for parking on Fairport Turnpike, I finally found a spot a few blocks from Thompson's Toys. The knot in my neck and back from spending the night sleeping in a recliner had now spread to my entire body.

"Honestly, Claire, if we'd just walked to the toy store from my house instead of driving, we would have been here much quicker."

"That's because you insisted on finding a spot you could drive straight into. There were tons of others that you just drove right by."

Humph. In the spirit of friendship and knowing she was right, I let that crack go. I hope you're all proud of me because I could have added her remark to the "Honey Don't" list.

"We're half a block away from the toy store now, so let's go over our strategy," Claire said, oblivious to how close she had just come to vacuuming and dusting my entire house, including the rooms we never use. "You take the lead as the grandmother shopping for her grandson. I'll add how sad

Ray's death is when I find an opportunity. We'll see how Lois responds."

"I'm betting we'll have better luck if we just wing it," I grumbled. "But okay. Here we go."

The bell over the door tinkled a friendly hello as we walked inside the most adorable shop I'd ever seen. There were toys everywhere but grouped cleverly according to a child's age. I was drooling over all the goodies I knew CJ would love and scurried to the infant and toddler section.

I didn't get very far before Claire grabbed me. "No serious shopping until we meet Lois," she reminded me. "Remember, we're here for information, not toys."

"Spoil sport," I said. "I can do both at the same time." I was attempting to replace the cuddly brown teddy bear in his designated place when a woman's voice interrupted me.

"Good morning. Welcome to Thompson's Toys. I see you and Charlie are getting acquainted."

"Charlie?" I looked at the bear I still seemed to be holding, then grinned. "We haven't been properly introduced yet."

"Hi, Charlie. I'm Carol. It's nice to meet you. And this is my friend, Claire. She's a little sad today. I'm trying to cheer her up." I didn't dare look at Claire. I just hoped that, for once in her life, she'd forget she was the wife of a lawyer and go with the flow.

"There's nothing like hugging a cuddly bear to make anyone feel better at any age," the woman agreed. "I'm Lois, the store manager. Charlie and I are very close friends."

"I believe we spoke on the phone a little while ago," I said, handing Charlie to Claire to hold. "I came in to buy some toys for my grandson, CJ. I can tell already that CJ and Charlie will be great pals. I'd like to buy him."

"Oh, yes, I remember. You called to be sure we were open for business after the owner's recent death." She gestured around the store, where several women of a certain age were whipping out credit cards so fast that the young woman behind the counter was having trouble keeping up.

"As you can see, business is good. As a matter of fact, this is the busiest we've been in a long time. It's been like that since the news of Ray's death was announced. Customers I haven't seen here in a long time have come in."

I temporarily filed that comment away, hoping to get Lois to expand on it without making her wonder why I was being so nosy.

"I haven't been here since my children were little," Claire said. "As CJ's honorary grandmother, Carol invited me to tag along while she went shopping. I'm thrilled I did." She picked up another bear, identical to Charlie. "I'll take this."

"CJ doesn't need two bears," I said, laughing.

"No, but I believe in planning ahead. And in the meantime, my husband can hug it. Maybe it'll lighten him up a little."

"I haven't been here for years, either," I said. "I had a terrible experience with the late owner and vowed I'd never shop here again."

Lois's eyes widened. "Let's go into the office where we can talk privately." She led us to a small room at the back of the store. The plaque on the door read, "Private! If Door Is Locked, Do Not Disturb!"

When Lois opened the door, we were greeted by a disgusting stench that made me gag.

"My lord, what's that smell?" Claire asked, always one to get right to the point. "It's horrible."

"I'm so sorry," Lois said. "I forgot to open the window when I came to work this morning. Customers used to bring Ray antique toys to buy. He'd refurbish them with a unique cleaning solution he concocted, then sell them on the Internet for a huge profit. For example, you'd be surprised what some collectors will pay for a Luke Skywalker action figure. One made in 1978 just sold for $28,000.

"I don't know what he used to clean them. He was working on something the night before the tasting at the hotel and never bothered to clean up after himself. As usual, Ray left that to me."

"How did he stand the smell while he was working on the toys?" Claire asked.

"Whatever Ray concocted was odorless in its liquid form. The odor comes out while the product is drying. But it goes away rapidly."

Lois rolled a chair out from behind the cluttered desk for herself and gestured for Claire and me to make ourselves comfortable on the sofa. "After a while, I'm sure you won't even notice it."

I had my doubts about that. This would be a test of how long I could hold my breath and still talk.

"Being in here gives me the creeps," Lois said. "One of the first things I'm going to do is get rid of that sofa. And the sign on the door."

In addition to dealing with the smell, the sofa was so soft that Claire and I sank into it. "I hope you'll help me get out of this thing," Claire said, fidgeting. (She outweighs me by several pounds, not that I'm being critical.) "I won't be able to do it on my own."

"That was the whole idea," Lois said. She turned to me. "So, how long ago did Ray seduce you?"

Chapter 60

The more I get to know people, the more I realize why Noah only let animals on the ark.

It was a good thing I was sitting down when Lois asked me her question. Claire grabbed my hand and squeezed it. "Carol, I never suspected that. I knew you vowed never to shop here again, but I never knew why. You poor thing."

"No, no, no," I protested. "That's not what happened at all. Ray accused Mike of shoplifting when he was ten years old. I found the toy he'd been accused of stealing on the floor behind a display case. I was livid."

"You're an attractive woman, so naturally, I just assumed...."

"Well, thank you. But you were wrong."

"I'm sorry. I didn't mean to offend you."

"You didn't offend me. But you sure as heck shocked me."

"Do you mean Ray seduced customers in the store? That's disgusting," Claire said. She shifted her weight. "Oh, my lord, is this his seduction couch? No wonder it's so hard to get out of."

Lois leaned forward in her chair. "I probably shouldn't tell you this." She stopped talking. I was sure she was waiting for one of us to encourage her to continue. I shot Claire a look, and she nodded. Neither one of us said a word.

Finally, Lois said, "His behavior was bad enough with the customers, but he also put the moves on any pretty employees we hired. Do you understand what I mean?"

"We get it," Claire said.

"That's not all," Lois said, obviously thrilled to have an audience to share her late boss's dirty secrets with.

"I'm not sure I want to know anymore. I have a headache now," I said.

"He kept score of his successes and rated them." Lois stood up from the chair, walked back to the desk, opened a drawer, and held up a black notebook. "They're all in here."

"That is truly disgusting," Claire said. "I think I've heard enough. I want to go home and take another shower."

"If you knew what was happening, why didn't you quit? How could you work for a man like that?"

"I couldn't afford to quit. I needed the job. And I get such joy helping people find toys for their children and grandchildren. Sometimes, customers bring the children in to say thank you. That's the best part of all. I never had any children of my own."

It took every ounce of self-control for me to resist grabbing the black book out of Lois's hand and running out of the office. If the names of Ray's victims were in there, one of them could be the murderer. Then Nancy would be off the hook, once and for all.

"I hope you don't mind me talking about Ray," Lois said. "I don't know you at all."

"We don't mind, do we, Claire?"

"No, now that the initial shock has worn off."

"I've never had anyone to share this with," Lois said. "I know your son-in-law is a detective for the Fairport Police,

Carol. So, I feel I can trust you."

I tried to mask my shock. "You know who I am?"

"I knew who you were as soon as you called this morning. If you hadn't reached out to me, I was planning on contacting you. Do you think I should share what I know with the police?"

"I think you should definitely give Ray's black book to the police," Claire said.

Lois looked uncertain. "I don't want to sully anyone's reputation. I've been worrying myself sick about that."

"I'm sure my son-in-law will keep it confidential. Do you want me to contact Mark for you first?"

"Oh! I'd be so grateful if you did that, Carol. Thank you." Lois paused and took a deep breath before she said, "There's one more thing I have to tell you before you go."

Claire fanned herself. "I don't think I can take any more."

"It's about your friend Nancy."

"Nancy?" I repeated.

"Yes. Nancy Green. Ray had been after her for a long time."

My heart stopped. No kidding, it really did. I didn't know what to say.

"What do you mean he'd been *after her*?" Claire asked. "Are you suggesting Ray was stalking her?"

"No, nothing like that. At least, not that I know of. I watched him come on to her for years, and Nancy always turned him down. In the beginning, his flirting didn't seem serious. It was as if he was kidding around. Ray would wiggle his finger at her and say, 'Someday, Nancy Green, you will be mine.' She always gave him a smarty pants refusal. I don't think she ever thought he really meant it."

"Do you think he did?" I had my fingers crossed that Lois would say no. But she didn't.

"Lately, every time Ray returned to the store after a reenactment committee meeting, he was in a foul mood. I once heard him mumble, 'She thinks she's so special. I'll show her who's in charge.' They were always fighting about how to run the event."

Claire coughed, then gave me a look. I knew what she was thinking because I was thinking the same thing.

Whether she meant to or not, Lois had just given Nancy a dandy motive for murdering Ray.

Chapter 61

I wonder why we're so obsessed with finding intelligent life on other planets. We can't even find intelligent life on this one.

"Don't even think it."

"I'm not!" Claire insisted. She waited a beat, then asked, "Are you?"

"Of course not. For heaven's sake, we've known Nancy since grammar school. There's no way she could commit murder."

"Even if she was desperate? What if he threatened her? Or attacked her?"

"They were sitting side by side in public at a luncheon. Nobody was being attacked. You're being ridiculous."

Claire sighed, and I knew she was giving me a disgusted look. "I don't mean *during* the luncheon, Carol. But what if he'd attacked her before?"

"Nancy wouldn't harm anyone," I insisted.

"I agree. But…."

"But what?" I asked, losing patience with this conversation. We were getting nowhere. We needed to *do* something.

"You're going to hate me," Claire said, "but I have to tell Larry what we learned about Nancy and Ray. And you should tell Mark about Ray's black book. Who knows if Lois will actually go to the police on her own?"

My eyes spilled over. "I don't want to. It could just make everything worse for Nancy."

"I think you're wrong about that. I bet there are a lot of new suspects in that black book that the police don't know about."

"Maybe."

We sat in my car in silence for another few minutes, and then I (of course) had a brilliant idea.

"Let's talk to Nancy first and get her side of the story about Ray before you mention anything to Larry, or I talk to Mark. We owe that to her. Maybe Lois was exaggerating. For all we know, she was madly in love with Ray, and he brushed her off. So, she came up with this ridiculous story about Nancy out of jealousy."

"That's fine with me," Claire agreed. "I'll text her to be sure she's home."

I turned the ignition key. "Tell her we're on our way and bringing ice cream. After all, it's almost lunchtime, and I'm hungry."

That got a laugh out of Claire. "I like the way you think. Who wants a sandwich when we can skip right to dessert?"

"Don't forget to text Mary Alice. She'd be hurt if we didn't include her. She's always a calming influence on the rest of us. And text Sister Rose, too."

I also thought about reaching out to Elizabeth, but I immediately dismissed that idea. Claire would demand to know why I wanted to include her, and I wouldn't be able to tell her. I made a mental note (I can sense you all snickering) to remember to check in with her later today.

Claire stopped typing mid-text. "Sister Rose? Are you

sure?"

"Positive," I said as I inched my car into Fairport Turnpike traffic. "The more brains, the better. Although, she may not be able to come on such short notice. I can text her when we get to Nancy's. We just need to buy enough ice cream to go around."

"I know, Carol. Because you're an only child and don't share well."

In the interest of peace, harmony, and a clean house, I let Claire's zinger pass without one of my usual snappy retorts.

Chapter 62

I burn about 2,000 calories when I put on fitted sheets by myself.

"It looks like Mary Alice beat us here," I said as I nudged my car beside a sporty navy-blue convertible.

"Be careful, Carol," Claire said. "Mary Alice won't be so sweet and nice if you're the first person to put a ding on her brand-new car."

"I am being careful," I snapped back, holding my breath, and praying. Sometimes, Claire makes me so nervous that I lose all my confidence. I know. That's stupid.

"Next time, you can drive. Or, better yet, we can take two cars."

"Fine with me." Claire opened her door cautiously, then hopped out of my car with plenty of room to spare. And that's saying something because sometimes Claire needs a little more room to maneuver than the rest of us do. Not that I'm criticizing. We all put on a few extra pounds as we age.

We each grabbed a thermal bag from Tantalizing Treats, Fairport's gourmet ice cream shop, and started up the stone steps to Nancy's house. The front door flew open before either of us could knock, revealing Nancy holding an ice pack on her face and her hair covered with so many bands of aluminum foil she could have contacted the International Space Station without a problem.

"Come in before the ice cream melts," she ordered. "Ice cream for lunch is such a great idea. And you got it from Tantalizing Treats!"

"We decided to splurge," I said as Claire grabbed the bag I was holding and turned toward the kitchen.

"I'll put these in the freezer for a little while. Then you can catch us up on what happened this morning."

"What's up with your hair?" I asked, unable to contain my curiosity any longer. "Did you do this yourself?"

"Of course not, silly. Deanna did. She'll be back in half an hour to finish my color. I wanted highlights in my hair to cheer me up, and I wasn't comfortable coming to the salon. She's making a house call, just this once."

We heard several kitchen cabinets and drawers being opened and closed; then, Claire appeared in the doorway. "Nancy, where the heck are the bowls? Did you move them?"

"Excuse me for a minute," Nancy said, laughing. "I need to find the dishes for the ice cream before Claire wreaks havoc in my kitchen.

"Mary Alice is in the living room. Make yourself comfortable. I'll join you soon."

For someone who had a possible murder charge hanging over her foiled head, Nancy was in a remarkably good mood. The last time I saw her so upbeat in a crisis was the night of our high school senior prom. Her date had canceled the night before, but rather than stay home, she insisted it would be fun to go solo to the dance. She proved it by dancing the night away with everybody else's dates. On the way home with me and my date (not Jim), she finally crashed and sobbed her eyes out. We couldn't get her out of the car. It was a terrible night.

I made eye contact with Mary Alice, then leaned down to hug her. "I have no idea what's going on," she said softly, moving over on the coach so I could sit next to her. "I thought Nancy would be upset, but she's just the opposite. I decided to play along for a little while to see what would happen.

"Shh. She's coming."

"Here we are," Nancy trilled, carrying a tray laden with napkins, six bowls, and spoons. Claire followed with the ice cream.

"We decided not to wait for the others," Nancy announced. "Although we'll save them some ice cream. Help yourselves to bowls and spoons, and let's dig right in."

"Why don't you serve yourself first, Nancy?" I suggested, shooting Claire and Mary Alice questioning looks. "And tell us who else you're expecting."

"Why, Deanna, of course. It would be rude not to offer her some ice cream after what she's doing for me today. And Sister Rose. It's important for her to be here."

Nancy took a large spoonful of coffee praline ice cream and savored it. "This is so yummy. Thank you for bringing it."

She carefully placed the spoon in the ice cream dish, then stood and faced the three of us. Her expression was so severe that she scared me.

"When Sister Rose and Deanna get here, Deanna will finish doing my hair. It shouldn't take her long. Looking my best will give me some extra courage to tell you what I finally told Bob this morning. He was shocked but said he'd support me no matter what. I'm fortunate to have such a wonderful husband. It took me years to appreciate him.

"I'm going to tell you all what actually happened between me and Ray Thompson."

Chapter 63

I'm so glad I was young and stupid before there were camera phones.

What will I do if Nancy confesses to committing murder?

I scrambled around in my brain for the appropriate saint to call on for help. The only one I could come up with was my pal, St. Jude. Our situation certainly fit his criteria, although I knew I'd appealed to him a lot over the past few weeks. I sure hoped he was paying attention right now.

Nancy chose to ignore our silence. "Eat up, everyone," she said. "Don't let this scrumptious ice cream go to waste. I'm trying the chocolate fudge next. I hear it's decadent."

The doorbell rang, and I figured St. Jude was already on the job. What? You don't believe me? Haven't you ever heard the expression, "Saved by the bell"?

It was Deanna, laden with the tools of her trade, including an industrial-sized hair dryer. "I wouldn't do this for anybody else, so don't get any ideas," she told the rest of us. "Come on, Nancy, let's go to your bedroom. I don't have much extra time." Nancy obediently followed her down the hall, leaving the rest of us in shock.

"Even ice cream can't fix this situation," I finally said. "And that's a first."

"Let's not jump to conclusions until we hear what she has to say," Mary Alice said. "Maybe it's not as bad as we think."

"A man is dead, and the police seem to think Nancy's responsible. That's pretty bad," I said.

"We don't know that, Carol," Claire interjected. "Having Larry with Nancy at the police interrogation this morning could have changed the track of the investigation. He's a darn good lawyer."

"I hope he's a miracle worker because after talking to Lois this morning, that's what we need."

"Who's Lois?" Mary Alice asked.

Oops. Me and my big mouth.

"She works at the toy store," I said. "She didn't have much good to say about her late boss."

"I'm not surprised," Mary Alice said. "Ray Thompson was a terrible person. I'm not sorry he's dead. I'm sure that his employees aren't either."

I almost fell off the sofa. I'd never heard such harsh words coming from her.

The doorbell rang again. Mary Alice jumped up to answer it, leaving Claire and me to gape at each other like two lunatics.

"What the heck was that all about?"

"I wish I knew," I said. "Mary Alice has never spoken out against Ray before. Or anybody else, for that matter."

"Except for the reckless driver who killed Brian," Claire reminded me. "I'm not sure she's ever gotten beyond that tragedy."

I started to comment but realized in time that Mary Alice was back with Sister Rose. Being the take-charge person we've all known (and feared) for years, the Good Sister got right to the point.

"Why are we here? When I couldn't find a volunteer to

cover the thrift shop on such short notice, I posted a Closed sign on the door and came right over."

"We're all eating ice cream for lunch," Claire said. "Have some. It'll lower your stress level."

"Ice cream? For lunch?" Sister Rose sniffed her disapproval. "My stress level will be lower when Nancy is completely exonerated."

"Nobody wants that more than me," Nancy said, joining us and looking like a million bucks with her new hairdo. The bruise on her cheek looked a little better, and I figured Deanna had worked some magic there, too. She gestured to Deanna. "I hope you can stay for a little while. I want you to hear what I have to say."

"Before you bring us up to date on what happened today, Nancy," Mary Alice interjected, "let me talk." She looked around the living room and made eye contact with each of us. "I trust all of you, and…." She started to cry, then composed herself.

"I told Carol and Claire a little while ago that I wasn't sorry Ray Thompson was dead. The reason I feel that way is because, right after Brian died, Ray took advantage of my grief. He took advantage of me! Physically. The man was a sexual predator, and I was one of his victims." And she started sobbing.

Chapter 64

Everyone was thinking it. I just said it out loud.

Suddenly, all the delicious ice cream I'd enjoyed threatened to reappear uninvited. I took deep breaths to quell the nausea I was feeling, but they didn't help. "After hearing that, I feel sick. And so sad for you."

"What a horrible person," Sister Rose said. "How brave of you to tell us."

"I never talked about it before because I wondered if it was my fault, like I'd encouraged him somehow, and he misunderstood. I felt guilty and disgusted at the same time. I hated myself. Then I got angry. I finally went to therapy to get over it. And I have. Mostly."

"Believe me, Mary Alice, there is no reason you should feel guilty. You were a victim," Sister Rose said.

"You definitely were a victim," Deanna said emphatically. "And you're not the only one here Ray forced himself on. He used to come into Crimpers a few times around closing for a quick trim. Ray told me how pretty I was, and the way he looked at me made me uncomfortable. One night, he grabbed me and tried to kiss me. I threw him out and locked the door.

Ray banged on it for several minutes, screaming at me and calling me terrible names, but I didn't open the door. He never came back again."

"Thank goodness," Sister Rose said, crossing herself. "You were very lucky."

"I know. I tried never to be alone in the salon again just in case, he came back." Deanna flexed her hand in the form of a fist. "I've got a pretty good right hook, too. That's what happens when you grow up with four brothers who were always picking on their little sister. I learned to defend myself when I was pretty young."

"Ray never tried anything like that with me," I said. "But he did accuse Mike of shoplifting when he was just a little kid. I was livid. Mike was innocent, of course, and I proved it. Ray never apologized."

"So that's why you never went to his store," Mary Alice said. "I always wondered if you'd had an experience similar to mine, but I didn't want to ask you."

"I wonder how many other women Ray victimized," Claire said, her face crimson with rage.

I looked at the remains of the ice cream melting in my bowl. It held no appeal for me now. Maybe ice cream never would again.

"I have something I'd like to add to this discussion, if I may," Sister Rose said softly.

"Please don't tell me he came on to you, too. You're a nun!" Claire blurted out. "I never heard of anything so despicable."

"Calm down, Claire. That's not at all what I meant." Sister cleared her throat like she used to do in high school when she wanted our complete attention. She needn't have bothered. Everyone was holding their breath, waiting to hear what she had to say, although I had a sneaking suspicion I already knew.

"I've talked with Ray's ex-wife. I have her permission to share what she told me about her marriage, but not her name.

If the police want to talk to her, then I will tell them."

"I can't believe anybody would marry that man," Nancy blurted out. She was now shredding a paper napkin, her favorite stress reliever. "She must have terrible taste."

Under different circumstances, Nancy's remark would have made me laugh. I wondered how she'd feel if she knew that Ray's ex-wife was one of the top fashion designers in the country.

"It was a long time ago," Sister Rose continued, "and he began seeing other women soon after the wedding. When she found out what was going on, she divorced him."

"Before we came here," Claire added, "Carol and I did a little undercover work at the toy store."

"We wanted to see what Ray's employees thought of him," I added. I refrained from adding that checking out the store employees was my idea and that I came up with the clever cover story of shopping for CJ. Let Claire take some of the credit. It was fine with me.

"We were amazed at how many customers were in the shop," Claire said. "The cashier could hardly keep up with the sales."

"We also talked to Lois, the store manager. She said business had really picked up since Ray's death. I'm sure a lot of women stopped shopping there because of his behavior. She also showed us a black book Ray used for his list of conquests."

"I wish I had spoken up when it happened to me," Mary Alice said softly. "At least, I should have told all of you. I should have trusted that you'd know I was a victim. Maybe if I had, Ray could have been stopped before he damaged other women's lives. But I was afraid to. I didn't know how you'd react."

"Oh, sweetie," I said, jumping up from the sofa to hug Mary Alice. "We love you. We're here for you. Always. No judgments in this group, right, Sister?

"Maybe you're finally ready to forgive Nancy and me for smoking in the bathroom sophomore year."

My stupid remark diffused the tension a little. Even Sister Rose laughed. "I can't remember that far back," she said. "And I never carry a grudge."

But Ray did.

Chapter 65

If you're not called crazy when you start something new, you're not thinking big enough.

The most outrageous scenario my wild imagination ever came up with had just blasted into my brain. I was so intent on figuring out how it could have been done that I didn't even realize Nancy had started talking until Mary Alice nudged me.

I closed my eyes and sent up a silent prayer to the Lord that, just this once, I'd remember what I was thinking without having to write it down.

"Sorry to zone out. My tummy is a little upset."

Claire handed me a glass of water, and I took a dainty sip. "Thank you."

We all sat there, looking at Nancy and waiting for her to say something.

"Nancy, dear," Sister Rose finally said, "having ice cream for lunch was a treat, but it's not why we're all here."

"I know, Sister. I was trying to think of what I want to say."

"That's never been a problem for you before," I said. "Being your best friend gives me the right to remind you of that, right?"

Nancy burst out laughing. "I can always count on you to give me extra prodding when needed. Okay, here goes.

"Giving another statement at police headquarters this morning wasn't nearly as bad as I expected. Having Larry with me was a blessing, and Mark was kind. Fortunately, his partner wasn't present, so I didn't get rattled by him shooting me dirty looks.

"Ray's autopsy results haven't come back yet, and until they do, the cause of death can't be determined," she continued. "So far, the police haven't ruled it a homicide. To accuse me or anyone else of murder, they also have to come up with a motive that will stand up in court. Larry said I'm in the clear since I had no motive." The napkin in her hands now resembled confetti, and she reached for another one, which she quickly demolished.

"The problem is that I did have a motive," Nancy said. "You've probably figured out I was one of Ray's victims, too. There were lots of times when I wished he was dead. But at lunch, when he started to choke, my instinct was to save him, not kill him. After hearing how he made all of you suffer, I'm not sorry he's dead. I'm not a hypocrite."

Nancy grabbed a third napkin.

"He started coming on to me years ago when our kids were young. At first, it seemed harmless, like he was joking around. After a while, his conversations got more and more personal, and he made me uncomfortable. I started shopping at the mall rather than going into his store. But that didn't stop him.

"There were times that I would run into him outside some of my favorite places, like the gym or Maria's Trattoria. I'd always walk the other way if he tried to talk to me, and I thought I had the situation under control. I convinced myself I was overreacting, so I didn't say anything.

"Things got even worse after I got my real estate license. I had to deal with him about a property he wanted to sell.

Ray knew that Bob and I were living apart at times, and he told me he was available to fill any needs I might have. He leered at me to be sure I got his message. I told him I wasn't interested. I thought that was finally the end of it.

"When the reenactment planning started, I was forced to work with him again. I hated it. I should have resigned from the committee, but I was embarrassed to tell my boss why I wanted to leave.

"I wish with all my heart I'd told you what was going on a lot earlier. We could have been such a support to each other if we'd shared our experiences."

"We'll never know how many others he preyed on," Claire said. "If I had to guess, maybe hundreds over the years. The manager at his toy store said business has really picked up since his death."

"Nancy, he singled you out and harassed you for years. Perhaps he was more blatant with you. But it's obvious you're only one of many people who aren't sad he's gone," Deanna said. "His death reminds me of *Murder on the Orient Express*, by Agatha Christie. If I were writing a book about Ray's murder, I'd have lots of suspects, each with an excellent motive. They would commit the crime together. That way, it couldn't be pinned on any one person."

"That's surprising coming from you, Deanna. It sounds more like something Carol would say."

"I'll take that as a compliment," I said. "I don't know about the rest of you, but all this emotional sharing has worn me out. It's time for me to go home. But before I leave…" I stood and beckoned everyone to join in a group hug.

Even Sister Rose.

Chapter 66

I don't let my age define me, but the side effects are getting harder to ignore.

Mary Alice volunteered to drive Claire home, thank goodness. My brain was now so overloaded I thought it would explode in my car. I only had a small window of time and needed to make the most of it without any negative input from Claire.

Onward.

My first stop was Thompson's Toy Shop. Lois was flipping the "Open" sign to "Closed" when I knocked and begged her to let me inside.

She scowled at me through the glass, and I mouthed, "It's Carol Andrews, Lois. Remember me? I need your help." I held up five fingers and mouthed, "I promise I'll only be five minutes."

Lois nodded and unlocked the door. Phew. Now I had to spin one of my world-famous Carol Andrews' tall tales—the kind I only resort to when I'm desperate. My secret is to talk very fast and hope for the best. That strategy hasn't failed me yet.

"Lois, you are a lifesaver," I said. "My husband came home this afternoon with an old train set he found at a thrift shop. He wants to clean it up and give it to our grandson for his birthday, which is this weekend. The trains are in terrible shape and need to be cleaned before he can give them to CJ, but of course, my dear husband didn't think that far ahead."

I stopped for a second to take a breath and rolled my eyes. "You know how clueless men can be."

Lois laughed like I hoped she would. Female solidarity can be a wonderful thing.

Now, to go in for the kill, figuratively speaking.

"After I read him the riot act, I remembered you mentioned a special cleaning solution Ray used to restore antique toys. I'd like to buy some from you, to see if it will help Jim—that's my husband—clean up the trains. If it doesn't work, I'm going to order him to either take them back to the shop where he bought them and demand his money back or throw them away."

"I'm glad to help you, Carol," Lois said, once more leading me to Ray's office at the back of the store. "As far as I'm concerned, you can have it all. I'm sure it'll never be used again." She opened a cabinet and handed me a small mayonnaise jar. "Here's Ray's special super-duper cleaning solution. Take it, and good riddance. I'm happy to be rid of the disgusting stuff."

"I really appreciate this," I said. "Would I be pressing my luck if I asked you for a bag to put it in?"

"Of course. No problem. I'll give you a plastic one, just in case. Although I know the lid is on tight, you wouldn't want it to leak or spill."

"Thank you again," I said as I grabbed the bag from her. "You don't know what this means to me."

"I'm glad I could help," Lois said as she ushered me to the door. "And happy birthday to your grandson."

"I'll tell him," I said, clutching the bag to my chest like a life preserver. Which, oddly, is exactly what it was.

Chapter 67

The older you get, the tougher it is to lose weight because, by that time, your body and your fat have gotten to be really good friends.

I was pretty proud of myself when I drove into our driveway and parked next to Jim's car. I knew there were more pieces to put into place, and then I had to convince Mark that my outrageous theory was actually what happened at the tasting. Still, I was confident I was on the right path.

Just between us, I was in such a good mood that on the way home, I decided to cook Jim a real dinner tonight. From scratch!

The mouth-watering odors that greeted me when I opened the door saved me from such rash behavior. A pot was simmering on the stove, and Jim was sitting at the table checking his email on his phone.

"Whatever that is, it smells yummy," I said, kissing Jim on the top of his head. "Where did you get it? If you tell me you made it yourself, I'll faint."

"Don't faint," Jim said. "I had some help. Elizabeth was here about half an hour ago. She'd been in Manhattan for the day and stopped by one of her favorite caterers on the way back to Fairport. She had too much food for just her, so she wanted to share it with us. I thanked her and told her it wouldn't go to waste."

"I hope I see her soon so I can thank her."

Like, tonight.

I felt a slight breeze on my neck and knew my message had been received.

I lifted the pot lid and sniffed. "Smells heavenly. What is it?"

"Some French chicken dish that I can't pronounce," Jim said. "Cocky vain, or something like that. And look what else was in the bag." He pulled out a bag of Pepperidge Farm Goldfish crackers. "Elizabeth bought the crackers at Grand Central to eat on the train, but she fell asleep instead. She offered the bag to me, and of course, I accepted. You know how much I love them."

"I read somewhere that these crackers are a great appetizer," I said, opening the bag and grabbing a handful. "I hope they mix with ice cream. That's all I had for lunch at Nancy's today."

"Speaking of Nancy, Claire texted Larry an update on her schedule today, and I figured you were with Nancy, too," Jim said. His face was set in the critical expression that had been directed at me too many times over the years. "I didn't know how long you'd be, so I came home extra early to feed the dogs."

Cue hidden subtext: You didn't bother to tell me yourself what you were doing today. I had to find out from one of your friends' husbands.

Jim had me there, and we both knew it. But rather than admit my guilt or defend myself, I chose to focus on his positive reaction to my being AWOL.

"You're the best husband I ever had," I said. "Thank you."

Heavy sigh from me for extra effect.

"Poor Nancy. She needs me now more than ever. I promised her I'd be there for her, and she could reach out to me any time, day or night if she wanted to talk. I hope that's okay with you."

Jim's expression turned from angry to understanding in an instant. "Of course it is, Carol. She's lucky to have such a caring friend. I'm sorry I was so hard on you.

"Can we eat now? I'm starved."

Dinner went well, as it usually does in our house when there's lots of it. Then I asked Jim what was going on with the reenactment—big mistake.

"It's chaos," Jim said, waving his fork at me for emphasis. "It's been like that ever since Carla Grimaldi took over all the planning. I don't know why the committee still bothers to have meetings since the rest of us don't have any input in the planning anymore. The good news is that she seems to be backing away from doing the reenactment using Ray's last agenda as The Way. Instead, she's delegated Nancy and Elizabeth to figure out the details. I wish them good luck. They'll need it."

I changed the subject to a less volatile one by giving Jim a carefully edited version of my day, mentioning that before Claire and I went to Nancy's, we stopped in at Thompson's Toys. I stressed the fact that I'd bought CJ an adorable teddy bear that I knew he'd love.

"Claire loved the bear so much that she bought one for herself, too. We had to wait quite a while to pay for our purchases. The store was jammed with customers. What do you make of that?"

"Ray told me recently that the toy shop was in trouble, and he was trying to sell it," Jim answered. "It's too bad business has picked up so much now when he's not around to see it."

My husband had missed my point completely, and since I couldn't explain why the shop was so busy now, I turned my attention to the delicious coq au vin instead.

"The property was on the market for a long time," Jim continued. "Nancy was his real estate agent."

"Come to think of it," Jim put his fork down (amazing) and gave me a strange look, "Ray told me that Nancy had already brought him several purchase offers for the business. A few of them were even over the asking price. He refused them all. Wouldn't you think he would have accepted one if he was so anxious to sell? I couldn't figure that out."

Jim turned his attention back to his dinner. Not me. I'd lost my appetite for the second time today.

It would be ironic if all this stress helped me finally lose some weight.

Chapter 68

Wi-fi went down for five minutes, so I had to talk to my family. They seem like nice people.

Jim and Ethel were curled up together on the family room couch. I could tell from the steady rhythm of their breathing that they were both sound asleep. It was a perfect time for a chat with my favorite ghost.

I'd already been in trouble for being AWOL earlier today, so sneaking out of the house now wasn't an option. Knowing my dear husband would never remember what I said if I woke him up now, I shot him a quick text that I was taking Lucy for a walk.

Lucy wasn't as enthusiastic as I'd hoped when I told her the plan. I dangled the leash in front of her face, but Her Highness wouldn't budge.

"Have it your way," I told her. "I'm going to meet your pal Elizabeth; maybe she'll bring Annie with her. You two could run around the yard while Elizabeth and I chat. Too bad. You could have had a fun time."

Lucy rose majestically and gave me a look, telegraphing that she was doing me a huge favor, and she expected me to be grateful. It's humiliating to be bossed around by a dog.

As soon as we hit the back steps, Elizabeth and Annie appeared. Lucy and Annie touched noses as a greeting, then ran off into the yard. I started to go after them, but Elizabeth stopped me.

"I made sure the gate was closed," she said, reading my thoughts as usual. "The dogs will be fine, and I have so much to tell you."

"I notice you're no longer wearing the blue dress."

"It's back in your closet. I don't need it anymore."

I took a closer look at Elizabeth. "You seem different. You even *look* different."

"I'm happy," Elizabeth said. "That's what's different. I'm happy for the first time in more than two hundred years. I'm almost giddy! I never thought I'd feel this way again." She stretched out her hands, and two lawn chairs magically appeared.

"How the heck did you do that?"

"Trade secret." She laughed and gestured toward the chairs. "Sit down, and I'll tell you what happened to me."

"I can't wait to hear." I settled myself as best as I could, then peered into the dark backyard. "Are you sure the dogs are safe? I don't hear anything."

"Don't worry, Carol. Annie is on a mission, and Lucy is helping her."

"In my yard?"

"Yes. While we wait for them, I'll explain.

"It was tough for me to return to the Battle of Fairport again. This time, however, I was an observer of the battle, not an active participant. It was like watching myself in a violent play. I cried when I saw myself rescuing my children, and then, when I saw what happened between John and me… it was horrible. I still can't believe what I did that night. I'll never forget it."

"Why did you go back? You already knew what you'd see."

"I wanted to find someone important to me. My maid, Molly. She was the one who helped me save my children. I had to know what happened to her after the battle. I prayed she was safe and had lived a long and happy life. She deserved it. It took some time, but I did find her. We had such a glorious reunion."

Elizabeth stopped talking, and I could tell she was holding back tears. I kept quiet and let her continue at her own pace.

"Molly told me something about that night that I never knew. It's quite a story." Elizabeth gestured toward the backyard. "I'm hoping the dogs will give it a happy ending."

"You're driving me crazy with these riddles, and you already know I am not a patient person," I said. "Explain, please."

"John was planning to give me a very expensive diamond necklace as an anniversary present at the party. I wouldn't have been allowed to keep it, of course. He only bought the necklace to show it off to his friends and prove what a loving and generous husband he was. Just as he brought out the necklace for everyone to admire, British soldiers invaded the house. I knew nothing about this until I read Bill Stevens' family notes. The legend of a hidden treasure that disappeared after the Battle of Fairport was passed down in his family for generations. I was flabbergasted. I had to find out if it was true, and the only person I could think of who might know was Molly. That's why I went back."

"What a story. Do you know what happened to the necklace?"

"The night of the battle, Molly told me she took the necklace during the chaos and hid it in an apple orchard. She covered it with leaves and brush, hoping the British soldiers wouldn't find it. From her directions, I realized a priceless necklace could be buried under years of compost in your backyard."

Chapter 69

Did you ever notice when you put the words "The" and "IRS" together, it spells "Theirs"?

"Wow, that's fantastic!" I said, wondering what in my current wardrobe I had that I could wear with such a fabulous piece of jewelry. Or, even better, I'd have to go shopping for something more appropriate to show it off. Jim couldn't object to that, could he?

Reality intruded, and my fantasy vanished before I had could really enjoy it. I hate it when that happens.

"The people we bought this house from gave us several old pictures of the property, and there's no apple orchard in any of them," I said.

"There was an apple orchard here over two hundred years ago," Elizabeth said. "Our family loved it. Unfortunately, the orchard was neglected over time, and the few remaining trees were cut down. Everything became overgrown with weeds, and another owner started using it as a compost heap. It's where Jim dumps the lawn clippings after he's mowed the grass."

"Even if the dogs find the necklace, it may be in terrible

shape after being buried for more than two hundred years," I said, refusing to get my hopes up.

"True. It would also have to be authenticated by an expert in jewelry of that period. I have someone who will do that already lined up."

Of course you do.

"It must be wonderful to have friends in such high places," I quipped. "While we're waiting for the dogs to finish treasure hunting, let me tell you what I've been up to and my theory about how Ray died."

I gave Elizabeth a more detailed accounting of my activities than I gave Jim. (I bet you're not surprised.) I finished by telling her that Ray's store manager had given me the remaining cleaning solution he used in his shop, which I planned to turn over to the police for testing. I was confident (okay, hopeful) that it was the same solution in the fatal glass of water.

"You've done an impressive job," Elizabeth said. "I hope you're right. It all fits together, except for one important detail—how the actual poisoning happened."

"I know. The only way I can figure that out is to find out where everyone was originally seated before they started moving around the room. I need the original seating chart from Carla Grimaldi's office."

"We also have to determine when the water was first poured into the glasses by the hotel server and who was originally sitting at that place," Elizabeth added.

I nodded. "The original seating chart should tell us who was sitting near enough to add a pinch of poison to the glass when no one was looking."

"You think it was Ray himself," Elizabeth said.

"I'm sure it was him. He went to that luncheon meeting armed with his unique cleaning concoction to commit a murder. Nobody else there knew about the cleaning solution or had access to it. Because of all the seating confusion, Ray ended up sitting at the place he'd designated for his victim. That's why he tried so hard not to drink from the glass when he was choking. He realized there was poison in it because he'd put it there.

"If a piece of roll hadn't gotten lodged in Ray's throat, he'd be alive today."

"I must admit this weirdly makes sense," Elizabeth said. "Who was his intended victim?"

"Nancy. She'd rebuffed his advances for years, and he wanted to punish her."

Chapter 70

The police officer asked, "You drinking?" I answered, "You buying?" We laughed and laughed...I need bail money.

Proving my theory to my son-in-law turned out to be more difficult than I'd anticipated. It took every amount of my persuasive powers to convince Mark even to *test* Ray's cleaning solution to see if it matched the poison that was in the water glass.

I finally promised Mark that if I was wrong, I'd never get involved in solving another crime, no matter what. I even put it in writing, signed it, and had it notarized. He finally agreed to have the test done. Thank goodness I was right! The alternative would have been horrible.

Elizabeth was able to get the original seating plan from Carla Grimaldi's office. Ray was supposed to sit to the immediate left of the First Selectwoman, where he ended up in all the chaos. My theory was that he added the poison to that glass as soon as he arrived and replaced his place card with Nancy's.

Abbey, the hotel waitress, signed a statement saying she saw

Ray switching place cards as soon as he arrived so he could sit directly opposite Nancy. Ugh. He wanted a prime spot to watch her suffer and die. It creeps me out to think of what a close call my best friend had.

Abbey also took some photos of the lunch starting right at the beginning, which she turned over to the police. I couldn't figure out why a server would do that until Elizabeth told me Abbey was actually her oldest daughter, Abigail, who'd assumed human form to keep a close eye on the committee at the tasting. How 'bout that?

By the way, it was Sister Rose's last-minute addition to the guest list that threw the seating plan off, started all the confusion, and ultimately saved Nancy's life.

The so-called witness who was prepared to testify that he heard Nancy threaten to kill Ray turned out to be one of Nancy's co-workers at the real estate agency. Nancy had stormed into the office one afternoon after another fight with Ray about the masquerade ball. Without thinking, she began complaining about what a terrible person Ray was, how he was making her life miserable, and that she'd kill him if he didn't back off.

The things people say in the heat of anger but don't really mean can easily be misconstrued and get anyone into deep trouble. I think Nancy's learned a valuable lesson about controlling her temper and her mouth. I know I have.

With a bit of prodding from me, Lois turned over Ray's black book to the police. She swore that she'd never read it, and I hope she was telling the truth.

Ray's death wasn't murder, and it wasn't suicide. It was a crazy accident that prevented a murder. How weird is that?

Elizabeth had no trouble finding an expert in the other world to clean and authenticate the diamond necklace. His last name is De Beers, a name unfamiliar to me. I plan to check him out on the internet when I have the time.

The current value of the necklace had so many zeros that it blew me away. We agreed that Bill (and Phyllis) Stevens were its rightful heirs, so Elizabeth hid the necklace under a tarp in the Stevens tool shed, where Bill originally hid the black duffel bag. If Bill doesn't find it right away, Elizabeth plans to drop some "out-of-this-world" hints in his ear. She also has a local diamond expert (a living one) from Fairport Center Jewelers ready to give Bill the good news that he's suddenly become a millionaire.

The negative part of this plan is that when the necklace is finally found, Phyllis will become more insufferable than ever now that she's an heiress (by marriage). That's just something I'll have to live with. I think I deserve extra credit for being a good sport.

I'm hopeful that Phyllis's unexpected rise in status will cut down on her frequent trips around the neighborhood, checking for garbage pails left outside too long and other unforgivable infractions.

The July 7 reenactment plan was completely revised. Instead of British soldiers marching into town and pretending to terrorize people, the committee decided to make July 7 Celebrate Fairport Day. Fairport has always had a big annual Memorial Day celebration, so the date was switched to July 7. It went off so well this year that I've heard the plan is to make the celebration an annual event.

The event started with a parade from the beach, the way the British invasion had in 1779, continued through the historic district and ended up at the Porter Mansion, where there was food and fun for everyone that lasted well into the night. Jim and his buddies were an important part of the parade, in uniform and carrying their "muskets." Phyllis and Bill were the honorary grand marshals.

The best part of the celebration was that our son Mike was one of the patriots marching in the parade. He and Jim had planned the surprise months ago, and when I saw him, I disrupted the parade (briefly) by running out and giving him a huge hug. As far as I'm concerned, that's a mother's prerogative, and I have no intention of apologizing for my behavior. So there.

It's now July 8, Mike is asleep upstairs, and Jim still has his beard and long hair. Although part of me hopes Jim will go to a barber soon, I've gotten used to how he now looks. But please don't tell him I said that.

Elizabeth hasn't told me if she ever found the love of her life in the afterworld. I decided it was none of my business, so I didn't ask her. Even ghosts deserve a certain amount of privacy.

A few days after the reenactment, Elizabeth announced she'd answered another ad in the *Ghost Gazette*. She now has a new event to keep tabs on, so we said our goodbyes.

I'll miss her.

Chapter 71

Courage is knowing it might hurt and doing it, anyway. Stupidity is the same thing. And that's why life is hard.

I saved the best for last.

Remember the Honey Don't List conversation Claire and I had several chapters ago? Those of you who have been paying attention will know without a doubt that Claire continued the behavior she was supposed to refrain from—i.e., criticizing me (and I only wrote down a few of her infractions). The person who did *not* refrain from the agreed-upon behavior for one week had to clean the other's house.

She never told me what I wasn't supposed to do, so I merely went on with my life as usual, solved a crime, and saved my best friend from a murder charge—just a typical week in the life of Carol Andrews.

However, there's a twist to this story that I bet none of you saw coming.

The Monday morning after the reenactment, Claire texted and asked what time she should come to clean my house.

You'll never guess what I answered.

Oh, heck, I'll just tell you.

I let her off the hook. That's right. Even though I was entitled to a free house cleaning, I told her it wasn't necessary. She was pathetically grateful and promised to treat me to an expensive lunch at the restaurant of my choosing as a thank you.

However, before you all start sending me emails applauding my unselfish behavior, I have a confession to make. The real reason I was so magnanimous was that I suddenly remembered how the night before our regular cleaning service arrived—back in the good old days before Jim retired and cut my allowance—I went crazy making the house as neat as a pin so the cleaners wouldn't think I was a sloppy housekeeper. I left the dust alone, but other than that, my pre-cleaner cleaning frenzy almost made their visit unnecessary.

If I did all that pre-cleaning before strangers came, I'd have to do even more before Claire showed up. No way was I going through a pre-cleaning ritual again.

And now you all know. But please, don't tell Claire.

Addendum

This is the part of the book where Carol Andrews pretends she likes to cook and shares a recipe or two. Or, if she's being honest, she shares a recipe from Maria's Trattoria, or another Fairport restaurant she and Jim visit on a regular basis.

Much of this book's plot is centered around the 1779 Battle of Fairport and the masquerade ball at the Porter mansion. So instead of putting pressure on Carol, I had the bright idea of including a recipe from that event (before the British soldiers became the biggest party poopers of all time). I reached out to Elizabeth Porter for help, but she (rather snippily, I thought) reminded me that since she was locked in her bedroom while the party was being planned and ended up running for her life when the above-mentioned party poopers crashed the event, she had no clue, nor did she care, what food or drink was served. She was, however, willing to put an ad in the *Ghostly Gazette* and ask if any other ghost (not Julia Child) could help me.

Imagine how thrilled I was when the 18th century's number one "hostess with the mostess," Martha Washington, graciously allowed her legendary punch recipe to be used in this book. Since her husband, George, was known to sleep around between battles, it's entirely possible that the Father of our Country shared Martha's punch recipe with John Porter during an overnight stay at the Porter mansion in Fairport.

Martha Washington's Revolutionary Rum Punch
Ingredients:
    3 oz. White Rum
    3 oz. Dark Rum
    3 oz. Orange Curacao
    4 oz. simple syrup
    4 oz. lemon juice
    4 oz. fresh orange juice
    3 lemons, quartered
    1 orange, quartered
    ½ Tsp. grated nutmeg
    3 cinnamon sticks (broken)
    6 cloves
    12. oz boiling water

Directions:

To make the punch, mash the oranges, lemons, cinnamon sticks, cloves and nutmeg in a large container. Add the syrup, lemon and orange juice. Pour the boiling water over the mixture. Let cool for a few minutes to allow the spices to open. Once the mixture is cool, add the white rum, dark rum, and orange curacao. Strain well into a pitcher or punch bowl (to remove all the spice marinade). Serve over ice in glass goblets and garnish with wheels of lemon and orange. Serves 8-10.

Enjoy responsibly. Martha cautioned that this punch recipe packs quite a…punch!

A Note From the Author

Dear readers,

The plot for this full-length mystery began in the middle of the pandemic as a short story for the *Suspense Magazine* anthology **Infinity**. This collection of stories written by respected mystery authors (and me) was edited by Catherine Coulter and had a single theme—a number. I had limitless possibilities to choose from—a house number, a street number, a license plate, a birth date, a death date, a character's height or weight—I'm sure you get the idea.

I decided to use a calendar date for my story and created a Revolutionary War battle based on one that actually happened in Connecticut in July 1779.

I'd been thinking of including a ghost in one of my books, just for a little extra fun. My protagonists, Carol and Jim Andrews live in an antique house in a fictitious Connecticut shoreline town. Suppose their house had a ghost living with them, and they didn't know it. A Revolutionary War battle was a perfect way to introduce my ghost. This was going to be fun.

What if only Carol could see the ghost? Even better!

Infinity was published in March 2023 and has received terrific reviews for its wide range of stories, all centered around a number.

After I completed the story, I realized there was more to tell in the adventures of Carol and the ghost. And in order to figure out what that was, I had to write it. Hence, this full-length novel.

I hope you enjoyed reading **Masquerades Can Be Murder** as much as I enjoyed writing it. For the original short story, check out *Infinity* for yourself at htttps://amzn.to/4bVJgSN.

Happy reading.

Susan

Milestones
Can Be Murder

Every Wife Has A Story

A Carol and Jim Andrews Baby Boomer
Mystery
(Book 1 and 2)

Tenth Anniversary Boxed Set

Susan Santangelo

SUSPENSE PUBLISHING

Chapter 1

The hardest years of a marriage are the ones following the wedding.

Here's an amazing weight-loss tip for all the women in America: an out-of-body experience makes you look thinner. Forget about vertical vs. horizontal stripes. I'm telling you, an out-of-body occurrence does the trick. Plus, it can be quite a pleasant sensation to look down and see a movie starring… you. What's not to like?

Of course, there's a downside to my weight-loss tip. Out-of-body experiences are triggered by a traumatic event, like the panicky phone call I'd just gotten from my husband, Jim, telling me he'd found his retirement coach, Davis Rhodes, dead at his kitchen table.

That was bad enough. But when Jim said that the police were grilling him like he was a prime suspect in a crime, rather than an innocent person who happened to be at the wrong place at the wrong time, I could feel my mind and body separate. This was immediately followed by an overwhelming sense of guilt. Because the whole rotten mess Jim found himself in was my fault.

Don't get me wrong. I didn't murder Rhodes, although I will admit I'd often harbored dark thoughts about the guy because of the havoc he'd recently caused in our lives. But I have to confess that I was responsible for introducing Jim to Davis Rhodes. In fact, if I'm being honest, I manipulated Jim into consulting Rhodes about his impending retirement. The thought of having my dear husband around the house 24/7, with little to do except sit in his recliner with the television remote clutched in his fist, appealed to me as much as a root canal without Novocain. On second thought, I'd definitely take the root canal.

I made the decision to stall Jim's retirement as long as I could. By whatever means I could come up with. I admit I was pretty desperate, but I told myself I was doing it for his own good. Jim was too young to retire and have his mind turn to mush from lack of use. Any other well-meaning, loving, slightly devious wife would do the same thing. Right?

How was I to know that the chain of events I'd innocently set in motion a few weeks ago would end up this way?

Four Weeks Earlier

"I'm really getting worried about Jim."

There was no response from my luncheon buddies, who also happened to be my three best friends.

I figured they hadn't heard me, so I raised my voice above the lunchtime din. The patrons at Maria's Trattoria were extra loud today.

"I said—"

Before I had a chance to finish my sentence, Mary Alice

interrupted me. "I don't know why we came here for lunch. It's always so noisy. You can't even carry on a decent conversation. And the food is so high in cholesterol and calories, it can't be good for us."

I rolled my eyes at Claire and Nancy, silently telegraphing, "There she goes again." Mary Alice, being a nurse, often went into graphic detail about high cholesterol, osteoporosis, cancer risk, high blood pressure, hot flashes, menopause, the benefits and risks of soy, and other assorted topics that are part of the natural aging process we're all going through. Guaranteed to kill the appetite, although I doubt that was her intention.

"Why don't you pick the place for next month then, Mary Alice?" snapped Claire. "You always complain when I pick it. And you know we like to come to Maria's because she taught all our children before she retired from teaching and opened this restaurant." She rummaged in her purse for her glasses so she could read the menu. "Damn it. I always leave the reading ones at home." She held the menu out as far as her arm could reach and squinted. "Are there any specials today?"

"Oh, for heaven's sake." My very best friend Nancy waved her perfectly manicured hand to get the attention of a passing waitress, who ignored her. "You know we're all going to get salads anyway. We always get salads. I think I'll have the Caesar this time.

"Did you hear about the new facelift technique?" Nancy continued, changing the subject as usual. "It's called a contour thread lift. It's supposed to be the ideal procedure for forty-to-fifty-five-year olds with premature sagging of the upper neck and jowl area."

She checked her face in a small mirrored compact that cost as much as one week's worth of groceries for the average family. "It's being touted as a way to look younger without the risk and recovery period of traditional facelifts. And it can be adjusted when the face starts to sag, so the results are constant. I'm thinking of going for a consultation. Anybody want to come with me?"

"Can we forget about facelifts for just a second?" I pleaded. "I'm really worried about Jim, and you're the only ones I can talk to about it. I need help. I think he's losing his mind."

"You're always complaining about Jim," Claire said. "Every time we get together, you have something new to add to his ongoing list of sins. What's he doing now? Still getting up at five in the morning to watch The Weather Channel and obsess about when the next major storm will disrupt his commute to the city?"

"Let me guess," said Mary Alice. "I bet he's into his manic coupon-clipping phase again. What was it you called it, Carol? Obsessive Coupon Disorder?"

"Very funny." I was getting more and more aggravated. "This time, it's more serious. Jim's behavior is becoming weirder and weirder. He's impossible to deal with." I paused, then raised my voice again to be sure they heard me. "He's driving me nuts. I think he needs to see a shrink."

Unfortunately, when the word "shrink" popped out of my mouth, it was at one of those quiet times that can happen in very noisy places. Now, everyone in the restaurant was staring at our table.

"Don't look now," said Nancy, "but Linda Burns just walked in the door."

Great. The one person in town who loved to lord it over everyone about her perfect life, her perfect family and her perfect career as a college professor.

"Oh, God, do you think she heard what I said about Jim? That's all I need."

"Well, she's seen us all sitting here so we have to be nice," Nancy said. She gave Linda a friendly wave, and the rest of us pasted false smiles on our faces. "I haven't seen you in ages, Linda. Can you join us for lunch?"

Claire's mouth dropped open in shock.

"Thanks, but I can't. I have just enough time to pick up a takeout meal in between classes. Plus, I have office hours this afternoon. So many students depend on me for advice, even some who don't take my classes." Linda checked her watch. "I have to get back to campus. Enjoy your leisurely lunch. You're fortunate to have so much spare time."

"She is such a pain in the you-know-what," Claire said, once Linda was mercifully gone. " 'Enjoy your leisurely lunch!' She just couldn't resist a chance to stick it to us. Nancy, don't you ever invite her to have lunch with us again."

"You know," Mary Alice said, "the only time Linda was even remotely human was when her cocker spaniel was sick a few years ago. She and Bruce nursed that dog for months before they had to have it put down. It was like the dog was their child."

"That's because they had that nutty idea about starting a new dog breed," Nancy reminded us. "They were going to breed their cocker spaniel to a poodle, and call it a 'cockerdoodle.' Then Bruce found out there already was a cocker spaniel/poodle mix, the cockapoo, so they gave up on that idea. You know it's all about money with them. Money and status."

"I heard a rumor that Linda's going to be named chairman of the college history department this fall," added Claire. "I hate to say it, but if we think she's obnoxious now, she'll be even more unbearable then."

"Look," I said desperately, "can we get back to Jim, please? Nobody else but people our age can understand what I'm going through."

"Actually," teased Nancy, "I believe I'm almost a year younger than you are, Carol."

It's true that Nancy is nine months younger than I am, but because of the arbitrary cutoff dates which determined when a child was eligible to start school back in the 50s, we'd ended up in the same class. I had other things on my mind today, however, so I let her comment pass.

"Well, you certainly have our attention now," said Nancy with a laugh. "Anytime I remind you that I'm younger than you are, you never let me get away with it. So, talk. What's going on?"

"Okay," I whispered. "Come a little closer to me. I don't want to have to say this too loud and have everybody in the restaurant staring at us again.

"Jim's obsessed about retirement. He talks about it all the time. He even bought himself a retirement countdown clock. He's figured out the earliest date he can retire, and programmed the clock to keep track of the time remaining until his big day. It's on our nightstand, ticking away like a time bomb.

"I guess what I'm looking for from all of you is a reality check," I continued. "Have your husbands ever been as consumed as Jim is with retirement? Do they obsess about it, even during those intimate moments we all have? Oh, God, I'm sorry, Mary Alice." My friend Mary Alice had been a widow for more than fifteen years. "I didn't mean to offend you."

"You didn't offend me, Carol," Mary Alice said. "I'm actually starting to think about taking early retirement myself."

"You're kidding!" said Nancy. "What would you do if you stopped nursing? Wouldn't you be bored?"

In response to the "empty nest" syndrome Nancy went through after her daughter left for college, she'd begun a career as a local Realtor. I think her success in business surprised even her. I know it surprised the rest of us.

"Well, I'd still need to make some money," admitted Mary Alice. "I couldn't completely retire. But the everyday hospital stress is really beginning to get to me. And the hours are so long. I went into nursing years ago because I wanted to help people. Nowadays, I seem to spend most of my time doing mounds of paperwork. The time I get to spend with patients is very limited. It's so frustrating. I was thinking I could sign on with a nurses' registry and maybe do some private duty cases."

"That's a great idea, Mary Alice," I said supportively. "But could we get back to Jim for a second?"

"Hi, I'm Sally. I'll be your waitress for today. May I take your order?" Our waitress had finally arrived, and the lunchtime crowd was starting to thin out. "Sorry it took me so long to get to you."

"I'll order for everybody," I said, not giving anyone else a chance to speak. "We'll all have the Caesar salad with chicken, no anchovies, dressing on the side. And iced tea with extra lemon. Be sure the lemons are cut in wedges, not slices. Okay with everybody? Fine. Now, can we get back to Jim?"

"Carol, you really do have our undivided attention now, and thanks for placing the order. Does that mean you're picking up the check, too?"

"Very funny, Nancy. All right. Claire, you're our role model in this," I said. "When Larry was first thinking about retirement, did he get, well…nutty about the idea? It's been three years for you guys, right?"

"Larry is so easy-going," said Claire with a smile. "He doesn't stress about anything. We've always been pretty much in sync with one another. Not that we haven't had our share of arguments over the years. But when it comes to the really important stuff, we usually agree. I don't remember him getting worried about retirement. But I left my teaching job a year before he started thinking about retiring himself. I sometimes kid him that he retired because he saw how much fun I was having. And he still has a license to practice law, so he keeps busy by taking on a few cases every now and then."

Just between you and me, Larry McGee is one of the

most boring men I've ever known. But Claire loves him, and I guess their marriage works, so who am I to criticize? And I am the least critical person you'll ever meet. Just thought I should clarify that.

"You know, Carol, this restaurant is a perfect example of someone who re-invented her life when she retired," Nancy said. "Remember when Maria was 'Miss Lesco', and she taught all our kids in sixth grade? When she retired from teaching, she re-did her kitchen and started offering take-out meals from her home. We all thought that she'd never make a go of it. But one thing led to another and she eventually opened this restaurant. It's been a huge success for her. Retirement doesn't have to mean you stop being productive. Maybe it means you finally get to do the things you always wanted to do. It turned out that way for Maria."

"Yeah, Carol," added Claire. "Remember all those back-to-school nights and parent-teacher conferences we went to over the years? I used to be petrified of Maria back then. She seemed so demanding and cold. Never tried to coddle the kids, that's for sure. But she was a damn good teacher. Who could know that underneath that starched exterior was an artistic soul yearning to express itself through food?"

She turned in her chair and managed to catch Maria's eye. As usual, Maria was front and center in her open kitchen, a huge area which had been expanded during the restaurant's renovations a few years ago so guests could watch the food being prepared and cooked. Food prep is a major source of entertainment these days, and Maria, smart enough to sense the trend, positioned her work area so she is the visible star of her own show.

"So what exactly are you worried about, Carol?" asked Mary Alice, returning to what was, I felt, the main subject of our luncheon conversation.

"You all know how Jim's hated his job at the agency

ever since the new boss was brought in, right?" Jim was a senior account executive at Gibson Gillespie Public Relations Agency in New York City, an easy train ride from our home in Fairport, Connecticut. The agency founder had died last year and his widow, Cherie, who had inherited ownership of the agency along with everything else in the estate, had brought in a 36-year-old whiz kid, Mack Whitman, to run the operation.

"Every night Jim comes home with more complaints about Mack," I continued. "How he conducts staff meetings and does yoga exercises at the same time. Or how he has no real vision for the agency. Jim says that all Mack's doing is pumping up his personal expense account while the agency is floundering. I think what really scares him, though, is that everybody who's been hired since Mack came on board is under thirty-five. Jim's beginning to feel like an old man, and he talks about leaving his job all the time. But then I ask him what he'd do if he left, and he has no answer. You know that his whole life has been that job. He has no hobbies or interests at all. What's he going to do if he retires, stay home all day and drive me crazy?"

"Bingo," said Nancy, aiming an imaginary gun at my head. "That's the real problem. You've got this nice little life here in Fairport, with a home office setup you can use to do occasional freelance work whenever you're in the mood. Your kids are grown and out of the house, and you have a few volunteer activities to make you feel worthwhile. You get to go out to lunch with friends, and go shopping whenever you feel like it. Between seven a.m. when Jim leaves for New York and seven p.m. when he comes home, you're free as a bird to do whatever you want. Your only real responsibility is to be sure to let the dogs out a couple of times a day. You don't want Jim underfoot rocking your boat."

I sat back in my chair, stunned and hurt that Nancy could be so harsh.

"Did anybody read the Sunday *Times Magazine* last weekend?" asked Mary Alice. "It had a huge feature on retirement, because so many baby boomers are retiring now. There's a whole new industry to deal with it. Not the financial stuff; the lifestyle change stuff. Retirement coaching, I think it's called. It was really interesting."

"Hey, Carol," Nancy said. "Maybe that's what you and Jim need. A retirement coach."

"Don't be ridiculous," I said, still smarting from Nancy's comments. "You know Jim would never go to see someone like that."

"Oh, come on," Claire said. "Get real. You know you can get Jim to do anything you want. All you have to do is make him think it was his idea. Remember how you wanted to take that trip to Europe, and you knew Jim would never go for it because he wouldn't want to spend the money? You never directly brought the subject up with him. You called me and told me all about it, knowing full well that he was in the next room and would overhear our conversation. Next thing you know, he was starting to think about it, too. Why don't you go home after lunch, go online, and see what you can find about retirement coaches? It's worth a shot.

"Oh, great, here's our food at last. I'm starving."

I don't remember what else we talked about at lunch. I was itching to get home, turn on my computer and Google 'retirement coaches.'

Books by Susan Santangelo

Retirement Can Be Murder
Moving Can Be Murder
Marriage Can Be Murder
Class Reunions Can Be Murder
Funerals Can Be Murder
Second Honeymoons Can Be Murder
Dieting Can Be Murder
In-Laws Can Be Murder
Politics Can Be Murder
Mistletoe Can Be Murder

Milestones Can Be Murder
(A *Baby Boomer Mystery* Box Set: Books 1 & 2)
Infinity
(A *Suspense Magazine* Anthology)

babyboomermysteries.com